Elementals: Discovery

Dionne Witt

This is a work of fiction. Names, characters, places, and incidents either are the product of the author's imagination or are used fictitiously. Any resemblance to actual events or persons, living or dead, is entirely coincidental.

Published by Sweetpea Publications

Text copyright (c) 2014 Dionne Witt

ISBN: 0615978835

ISBN-13: 978-0615978833

Cover design by Vikki

Author Photo by Deanna Harris

Acknowledgements

So many people were involved with the creation of this book, and I must thank them all!

To Bryson, for following me on this road to publication, from leaving my full-time job to helping to set up my website, and for constantly asking the question, "Have you written lately?" There were many times I wanted to fib just to get you to go away so I could waste time on the Internet, but instead I shut down Pinterest and wrote a few lines. Thanks for that.

To my early readers, Marcia, Jess, and Alison. It means a lot to me that you all read it and gave me honest feedback. And also to Jess, for letting me steal Gus's name.

To my two best friends, Jessie and Sarah, for those crocodile-tear-inducing Christmas gifts, proving that you really believe in me. Sniffle.

To my parents, for never saying no to books, and for watching Olivia one day a week, allowing me to do nothing but write.

To my sister, Deanna, for helping me with my hair and makeup, because let's be real, if it were up to me, I'd look pretty boring.

And to my daughter, Olivia, for being such a fantastic and fun child, and reminding me that popcorn is the perfect brain food.

Chapter One

My father disappeared on a Wednesday evening in April.

The story made headlines all across the country. It was one of the items scrolling across the bottom of the screen on CNN, over and over again. Wendell Benton, a one-time Academy Award winning actor turned media king, had vanished at the age of forty-two, leaving behind a devastated teenaged daughter and an empire that consisted of several newspapers, magazines, television and movie productions worth millions.

His disappearance wasn't particularly dramatic. It wasn't one of those incidents where his private plane went down in bad weather and fell off the radar, or he'd gone missing during a natural disaster, or he'd been forcibly taken from his home. No, he just vanished after spending a wonderful evening with me at the theater to celebrate my eighteenth birthday. My birthday wasn't until July, but he had a confirmed trip out of the country at that time, and he didn't want to miss this milestone in my life.

He'd given me my gift, a gorgeous silver and diamond pendant in the shape of a snowflake, on a silver chain. The winter season was my favorite, and he knew I loved a good snowstorm. He told me the pendant was one of a kind, just like a true snowflake. I put it on immediately and hadn't taken it off since. I didn't want to think it would be the last thing he ever gave me.

There were no signs of foul play, no signs of forced entry into our apartment or his office, and none of his personal possessions had been taken. There had been no activity on his credit cards, and surveillance footage throughout the city was being examined. All of his employees were interviewed, and I was interviewed incessantly, just in case I remembered something that could be of importance. The police had followed every lead they had, hitting dead ends with each of them. We kept waiting for a ransom demand that never came. It was as though he'd simply walked away.

I went to stay with my grandfather, packing only enough clothing for a few days. I could have stayed at our apartment by myself, but it seemed too empty, too quiet and too eerie without my dad there, especially after it had been searched by the police. Things had been moved, and it bothered me that strangers had been in our home. Grandpa had given the household staff a paid leave, "Just until we figure out what to do next," he told them, but I saw the glances pass between them all. They didn't think Dad was coming back.

He was considered by many to be an A-List celebrity, so for someone not to recognize him was unlikely. The paparazzi were following me around, digging for their own clues, and I had received several notes of condolence and support from various people in the entertainment industry. School was hell, as the students, and even a lot of the teachers, wanted to know all of the details. I had none to give, and that was disappointing to them.

People kept telling me, "Oh, he'll turn up somewhere," and that bothered me. Did they mean his body would wash up in the Hudson? Or that he'd be spotted sitting in Central Park enjoying a cup of coffee? He wasn't a misplaced piece of clothing, or a toy that had been left behind by a child somewhere. He was my father, the one person I had always counted on to be there for me, no matter what.

Two weeks after he went missing, a body was found.

My grandfather took the call, his features twisting into a sad grimace, and I felt my stomach flip. He nodded, said he'd be there as soon as possible, and hung up. Before he turned to face me, he squared his shoulders and took a deep breath.

"Dad?" I asked, and he could only nod.

"Aubrey, sweetheart," he said. "They want someone to come down to identify the body. I told them I'd come alone."

I paused for a moment, fighting with myself over whether I should stay behind or go, finally deciding I should go. My grandfather opened his mouth to protest, then agreed. I went to grab my purse from the guest room, moving as though on auto-pilot, taking my cell phone off the nightstand and stepping into a pair of shoes.

I made my way to the foyer of my grandfather's apartment. He was slipping into a suit jacket and hadn't noticed me yet. I could see the tired line of his shoulders, and I knew this was as hard for him as it was for me. Dad was his only child, and my grandmother had passed away years ago.

The ride to the coroner's office was silent. All I could think about was what would happen if this really was my father. What would I do without him?

Two police detectives who had been working my father's case met us at the door, and we were ushered down a long hallway to a small room. The entire place smelled of antiseptic and something else that I didn't dare try to name. I walked with my arms wrapped tightly around myself, wanting nothing more than for all of this to be a bad dream. We were told the body had been pulled from the river, and I gasped at the thought. My grandfather stood behind me and gripped my shoulders, to support me or to support himself, I wasn't sure. The body rested on a metal examining table, a white sheet draped over top. One of the detectives gave a solemn nod to the medical examiner, and the sheet was pulled back, just to the neck.

I steeled myself for the worst, sucking in my breath and suppressing the shiver that curled its way up my back. I let out a cry and shook my head, squeezing my eyes shut and taking several hasty steps backward before slamming into a tray of medical equipment.

"It's not him," I heard my grandfather say, the sound of relief evident in his voice.

We left the room and stopped in the hallway. I gulped in mouthfuls of air, my tears threatening to choke me.

"It's not him," Grandpa said, repeating it again and again as he hugged me.

While I was overjoyed at the fact that the man in there wasn't my dad, it still pained me that someone else wasn't going to be so lucky. Grandpa spoke with the detectives for a bit before we headed for the exit. As we stepped outside, bright flashes went off in front of my face, and someone was yelling at us, asking if my dad was dead. I recoiled at the harsh words.

The detectives helped us over to our car, doing their best to shield us from the reporters and the cameras. I wasn't surprised that they were there, just angry that we couldn't even have had this moment to ourselves.

"Why won't they just go away?" I asked, glaring at them as we passed them. They were still taking photos. "I wish I could hide from them for a while."

My grandfather reached out and patted my knee. "I may have just the solution for that," he said.

"Oh? Are we going somewhere? Not too far though, in case Dad comes back," I said.

"Well, I need to stay here and keep the business going. It's important that we don't let that fall by the wayside."

Grandpa had stepped back into his former role as CEO, and he was handling the everyday tasks that my dad had taken care of. I knew it was hard work, and I kept waiting for him to tell me that I needed to start learning about it for myself.

"How does St. Louis sound?" he asked. "Or at least the suburbs?"

I frowned at him. "St. Louis? Missouri?"

He nodded and gave me a small smile, and the realization sank into the pit of my stomach.

"You want me to go live with my mom?" I asked, and my voice shook.

"Not permanently. Just until we know what to do next," Grandpa said. "She's very eager to see you."

"What about school? I still have two weeks of finals."

"It would be after the school year is finished. We both think that spending the summer away from here would be good for you. And with her, you'd have a more stable home life."

"I've been fine staying with you," I said, crossing my arms over my chest and turning to the window. "Why does that have to change?"

"I'm so busy now, Aubrey. I don't want you spending all your time alone."

"I have friends."

Grandpa gave a polite cough, and I felt my face burn. He knew as well as I did that my friends at school were nothing more than casual acquaintances. Most of them were only interested in me because of Dad, something I had learned very early in my academic career. Because of Dad's fame, I had a hard time making true friendships last. Everyone always wanted something from me.

"She'll be here tomorrow to go over the final details," Grandpa was saying, and I jerked my head around to look at him again.

"What? You mean it's already decided? I don't get a say in this?" I asked.

My grandfather's expression changed then. His lips went into a thin line, and his eyes narrowed slightly.

"Aubrey, please. Your mother loves you very much, and she wants to help. Once you're finished with finals, you'll join her and her family for the summer, and most likely the following school year."

My mouth dropped open. "I have to start at a new school? For my senior year?"

"It's been decided," Grandpa said, and from his tone I knew there would no further arguing with him. "I know it's not ideal, but what you need to understand is that this was not my idea, or your mother's. These are your father's express wishes in his absence."

That silenced me.

My parents had married young and divorced after five years together. My memories of my mother, Maddie, as my father called her, before the divorce were a little foggy, but I did remember leisurely walks through Central Park, play dates with other children, and learning to bake with her. She had been working as a print model when she met my dad, and she continued doing that after they were married. She took me along to a few of her photo shoots, and I remember thinking she was the most beautiful woman in the world.

Somewhere along the way, the glitz and the glam of their successful lives had overshadowed their marriage, and they decided to go their separate ways. The problem was what to do with me. Dad wanted me to stay with him, but my mother wanted me to go with her. She had made the decision to move back to where her family was, somewhere near St. Louis.

My parents went through several months of custody discussions, and eventually my mother ended them. She reasoned that it would be better for me to be raised in a world of wealth and opportunity. Not long after she moved away, she met a new man, a scientist of some kind, and remarried. Several years later, I had a younger half-sister named Alyssa. They all came to visit a couple of times in New York City, but I didn't see them for very long. If I were completely honest, it was my fault. A part of me resented my mother for leaving me with such ease, and so I wanted little to do with her. I didn't know much about her husband or my sister, and I fooled myself into thinking I was okay with that because I had Dad, and he wasn't going anywhere.

I could understand that she wanted me to have luxuries that she couldn't provide for me on her own, but I often thought she hadn't given herself a chance. I always felt a twinge of regret that maybe I hadn't given her a chance either.

When she arrived the next afternoon, it was with a single suitcase and a tentative smile. I hadn't seen her in almost a year, and then it was just for a brief and uncomfortable lunch with her and Dad to celebrate my last birthday. She stood in the gallery, one hand fiddling with the strap of her purse, the other gripping the handle of her suitcase.

"Hello, Aubrey," she said.

"Hi," I said. She hugged me, a quick barely touching hug, and I took her suitcase and allowed her inside. My grandfather came to the door then, and I made my escape.

She stayed for a week, spending most of her time with Grandpa as they made plans for me to move. I stayed in my room, studying for finals, emerging for dinner because Grandpa insisted that we eat together. We made polite conversation whenever we saw each other, but anyone could see that things were awkward between us.

Before I could leave New York and join her in Missouri, Mom and her family were thoroughly checked out, just in case they had anything to do with Dad's disappearance. Her parents had passed away a few years earlier, and like Dad, she had been an only child. The background check didn't take long, and she was cleared by the local authorities and the FBI. I never even considered the possibility that she could be involved. It was just too ridiculous a thought.

The night before she left, I found her standing alone on the balcony. She was leaning on the railing, her arms crossed at the wrists, looking out over the city. I held back, just watching her, surprised at how sad she seemed, and I realized that she did still have feelings for my dad. Whatever had happened in their marriage didn't mean that she stopped caring about him.

I joined her on the balcony, and she smiled and beckoned me closer. I took up a similar pose beside her.

"I'm...sorry," I said, chewing on my lower lip.

"For what, sweetheart?" she asked.

"For not being around much this week."

"Oh, that's all right. I knew you were busy with your tests."

"Yeah, but I've been avoiding you too."

She reached out and patted my hand. "I know. It's all right though. We have some work to do to repair our relationship, and I'm willing to try if you are."

I nodded and said, "I'm actually okay with leaving the city. I'm so tired of all the reporters hanging around and following me everywhere I go. A bit of normalcy will be good for me."

"I agree."

She hugged me the next day before she boarded her flight back to Missouri, and this time it was a warm embrace. I finished the last week of my junior year at Radcliffe Academy, then I packed up the things I wanted to take with me and said goodbye to everyone. Mom and I had talked about waiting until later in the summer to move, perhaps Dad would return, but then I decided that I wanted and needed to get away from the craziness of the constant media attention. I also reasoned that I would have the whole summer to become adjusted before school started. I would keep our penthouse apartment, at least for a while. It was the only home I'd ever known, and I couldn't bear the thought of getting rid of it just yet. What if Dad came back? He'd go home first, and I wanted it to be there for him.

I boarded an early afternoon flight out of LaGuardia International Airport after a goodbye brunch with my grandfather. He promised to keep in constant contact with me. He had a team of private investigators looking for Dad, and he had also made plans for me to join him next summer after I graduated high school, to start attending meetings with him and learning the business. Even though he left his sentence unfinished, I knew he was thinking, "If your father hasn't been found by then."

Chapter Two

It was supposed to have been a straight flight to St. Louis, but there had been some sort of mix up with my reservation, so I was transferring in Chicago. This delayed my arrival by a few hours. I sent my mother a text message letting her know of the change.

There was no one seated beside me for the first leg of my journey, and for that I was grateful, since I didn't feel like talking with anyone. I wasn't so lucky on my connecting flight from Chicago to St. Louis. My seat mate introduced herself as Monica Orson, and she was headed home for the summer break from college. She was cheerful and sunny, and she had wanted to chat about everything from the weather to movies to favorite colors, and all I had wanted to do was ignore her and everyone around me. Monica had gotten the hint and left me to listen to my music and sulk in peace for the remainder of the short flight.

A gentle tap on my shoulder jolted me out of my reverie, and I jerked upright in my seat. A uniformed flight attendant was looking at me expectantly. I blinked and pulled my earbuds from my ears.

"The announcement has been made to turn off and stow all electronic devices. We'll be descending into St. Louis soon," she said.

"Oh, sure, thanks," I said. I turned off my iPod and reached down to shove it into my purse under the seat in front of me.

Monica stared out the small window, her face close to the glass. "There's the Arch," she said. "Isn't it beautiful?"

"Uh huh," I replied without looking. Instead, I checked my seatbelt and smoothed my skirt over my legs, noticing how sweaty my palms were.

"Is your family meeting you at the airport?" she asked, turning to face me.

The word sounded funny when she said it. *Family.* I nodded in response.

"Are you excited to see them?"

I shrugged and swallowed hard. I wasn't sure how to respond to that question. Monica tipped her head and gave a little smile. "I'm sure they're excited to see you," she said, trying to sound encouraging.

The plane landed smoothly and began its journey toward the gate, or in my mind, a journey toward an unknown chapter of my life. As I stared straight ahead, I thought about how unbelievable the entire situation was, like I was watching a movie.

The seatbelt light went off, and the cabin came alive as everyone stood up to stretch, turn on their cell phones and open up the overhead bins to grab their belongings. I picked up my purse and checked my own cell phone out of habit, expecting to see a missed call or text message from my father as I always did when I traveled. I threw the phone back into my purse and slung it over my shoulder as I got to my feet.

"Well, Aubrey, I hope things work out for you," Monica said. "If you ever need a friend, give me a call sometime." She passed me a slip of paper with her name and phone number written on it.

"Yeah, sure," I said, forcing a smile and putting it into my wallet. I got my carry-on suitcase from the overhead bin and exited the plane into the terminal.

There were signs along the walls, welcoming me to St. Louis and displaying bright pictures of all the local attractions. I sighed and followed everyone to the baggage claim area, walking at a brisk pace to get away from

Monica in case she wanted to talk some more. As I rode the escalator down to the ground level, I spotted my mother standing at the bottom with a large but timid smile on her face. Upon making eye-contact with me, she raised her hand to wave. I swallowed the lump in my throat and waved back.

Once I reached the bottom, she pulled me into a hug, and I could feel her trembling.

"It's so good to see you, Aubrey," she said. Her voice was soft and nervous. "How was your flight?"

"It was fine. Where are Eric and Alyssa?" I asked, pulling away. I glanced around for her husband and my younger sister. I hadn't seen them in a while, aside from random pictures sent here and there. I wasn't even sure what Alyssa looked like anymore.

"Eric's bringing the car around, and Alyssa's at home with a babysitter. She doesn't do well with crowds." She took a step back too. "Let's get your luggage, shall we?"

I nodded and we walked over to the luggage carousel. Her arm was still around my waist, and it felt nice to be near her again, although it was still difficult for me to see her as "Mom". Aside from her infrequent visits, and a few phone calls and birthday cards over the years, we hadn't communicated much before Dad went missing.

We stood side by side for a few minutes, not saying anything as we waited for the carousel to start moving. Across from us, I spotted Monica, busily chatting with another passenger from our flight.

"How's your grandfather doing?" Mom asked, breaking the silence.

"Oh, he's okay. Working all the time."

"Were you still staying with him?"

I nodded and said, "Yeah. I couldn't bring myself to go home yet."

Mom tucked a stray strand of hair behind her ear, a nervous habit she had, and one that I had inherited, I thought, as I did the same. Where her hair was a gorgeous natural blonde, mine was a dull, dark brown. Sometimes, when I was feeling nostalgic, I would sneak into Dad's office and pull out the old magazines that she'd been featured in during her time as a model, and wish to look more like her. Feminine and soft, rather than so rugged like my dad.

The luggage carousel buzzed and began to move. People crowded closer to pull their overstuffed suitcases from the belt without hurting themselves.

"What do yours look like?" Mom asked.

"They're brown, monogrammed Louis Vuitton."

She smiled. "Very nice."

"A birthday present from Dad," I said, my voice dropping a little.

We spotted my suitcases, and we each went after one, meeting near the door.

"Did the rest of my stuff make it okay?" I asked as we stepped outside.

"It's all in your new room. But don't worry, I didn't unpack any of it. Your room is like a blank canvas. I didn't want to decorate it without you." Her words came out rushed, revealing again how anxious she was.

"Oh, that's great," I said. "Really thoughtful of you."

She smiled and wrapped an arm around my shoulders. "We can go shopping tomorrow, how does that sound?"

"Yeah, we can do that."

A horn beeped and a black SUV pulled up to the curb.

My step-father, Eric Vaughn jumped from the vehicle and hugged me. "Aubrey! How are you, sweetheart? How was your flight?"

I resisted the urge to roll my eyes. I knew he was just being polite, but if everyone asked me that same question, I was going to scream.

"Fine. How are you, Eric?"

"Never better, glad to finally have you here. Your mom has been a wreck waiting for you to get here."

"Eric, stop," she said, shaking her head. "Let's get going. Alyssa's waiting."

"And she's so excited to see her big sister again," Eric said while loading my luggage into the back of the SUV. He held the door open for me as I climbed in.

I buckled my seatbelt and checked my phone again out of habit, mentally kicking myself for forgetting that there would be no message. My mother twisted in her seat to face me and saw my disappointed expression.

"How did your school year end?" she asked.

"Great," I said. "All A's." I turned my attention to the passing cars. I didn't want to talk about school and everything else I'd left behind. "So where are we going again?"

"Hamilton Green," Eric said. "It's a lot smaller than New York City, but still nice. You'll love it. It's a close community, and the high school is one of the best in the country."

Eric continued to talk about the history of Hamilton Green, and I tuned out. I knew it was rude, and it wasn't even Eric that I was annoyed with. No, Eric was great. He was always courteous to me and showed me nothing but decency and affection whenever we were together, and it was so obvious he loved my mother. I just couldn't get a grasp on the fact that a few hours earlier I was saying goodbye to my comfortable existence in the big city. I knew that my mother had grown up here, and that was why she'd moved back, and she'd never been happier. I just didn't know if I could be happy here without my dad.

"Aubrey?"

"Huh?"

"We're home," Mom said, her voice hesitant as she spoke the words.

I hadn't even noticed that we'd left the highway and made it to Hamilton Green. As we pulled into the driveway, I looked out the window at the two-story light gray house with a white porch and colorful potted plants. A small bicycle leaned against the two-car garage, pink tassels on the handlebars. It was like the perfect American dream.

We all got out of the SUV, and Mom guided me inside while Eric handled my luggage. We entered through the back door into a mudroom, and I found myself taking in the jackets and umbrellas hanging on hooks, the rain boots lined up against the wall on the polished wood floor, and thinking how different it was from the entryway to the apartment in New York that consisted of an antique Louis XIV table and a vase of fresh flowers. Through the mudroom was the kitchen, and on the table sat the remains of a child's lunch. There were crumbs from a grilled cheese sandwich, a bowl of applesauce with a few bites left, and a glass of orange juice.

The kitchen opened to a family room with a sliding door that led to the deck. A huge television was mounted to the wall, and Mom informed me they didn't use it much. The formal living room had a fireplace and was set up for entertaining with nice furniture, and built in bookshelves filled with books and framed photographs. We passed a small bathroom and a dining room before stopping at the stairs.

Mom called out for Alyssa. "We're home, honey!"

A thump was heard from upstairs, and then excited footsteps followed by a skidding halt at the landing. I looked up to see my younger sister staring down at me, her green eyes bright and inquisitive, her blonde hair in two braids that fell over her shoulders. I guessed her to be seven or eight, if I remembered correctly. I felt bad that I didn't know for sure.

"Hi," I said.

The little girl took one step at a time, slowly and carefully, as if deciding how far to go. She stopped on the third step from the bottom so she was eye level with me and said, "Hello. Are you happy to be here?"

Mom's laugh was uncomfortable. "Sweetheart, she just got here. Why don't we give her a chance to get settled first, okay?"

"Okay."

"Where's Mrs. Cameron?"

"Cleaning up. She'll be down soon." Alyssa took the last three steps and then walked right past us and out to the kitchen. We could hear her talking with Eric as he brought in my luggage.

"Let's see your room," Mom said to me.

Upstairs, we ran into Mrs. Cameron, a neighbor that sometimes watched Alyssa. She said hello, averting her eyes to the floor, then good-bye and hurried on her way. I wondered if everyone was going to be awkward with me because they knew why I was here after all these years.

Mom pushed open the door to my new bedroom. It was bigger than I'd expected. The hardwood floors had been polished, and the walls were white. It was big enough to hold a queen bed, nightstand, dresser with mirror, a chest of drawers, a desk and chair and a bookcase. The bed had been made up with a deep purple comforter and sheet set. Matching curtains hung from the windows. The closet doors were open, revealing a large open space and empty hangers. One window faced the front street, and I had a nice view of the neighborhood. Boxes were stacked up all around the room.

My entire life is in those boxes, I thought. *How strange.*

"The furniture is new, and you can decorate the room however you want. I wasn't sure what you were into these days," Mom said. "If you don't like the bed set or the curtains, we can exchange them."

"No, everything's great. I'm not sure what I'm into these days either," I said, shrugging.

"Still taking pictures?"

"Yeah. Radcliffe had a great photo club."

Her smile faltered a bit. "Oh, well, Hamilton Green High School has an art club. I'm not sure if photography is part of it though."

"That's okay. I'll figure something out."

"Whoo, these sure are full," Eric said, scooting past us with my suitcases. He set them by the dresser and clapped his hands together. "That's everything. I'm going to start the grill. How do you like your hamburger cooked?"

"Actually, I don't eat red meat anymore," I said, leaning on the desk.

"Really?" Eric said, sounding puzzled. "Huh."

Mom put her hand on his arm. "We have lots of stuff to make salads, and I can cook up some pasta for you instead. Or chicken. We have chicken. Is that all right?"

I nodded. "Chicken sounds good."

"We'll give you some time to get yourself organized then. The bathroom is through that door," Mom said, pointing. "You and Alyssa will share. Her room is on the other side. Let us know if you need anything, okay?"

"Yeah. I'll be down in a few minutes."

Mom nudged her husband out of the room, pulling the door shut with her. Before she closed it completely, she said to me, "I know this is going to be hard at first, but we'll make it work. I promise."

I waited until the door closed with an audible click before I dropped my purse on the bed and lay down beside it. I dug around for my phone and dialed my voicemail, selecting the last one my father left me before he went missing. I listened as he told me he was sorry he was going to be late for dinner, and to go ahead and eat without him. It was so mundane and unexciting, but I must have listened to it a hundred times since his disappearance.

The message ended, and frustrated, I threw the phone to the floor, wincing as it hit with a hard thud and slid under the bed. I curled myself into a ball and hugged a pillow to my chest, breathing in the clean scent and trying to calm down. My mom wanted to try, and I knew and understood that. I just couldn't stop my doubts about how well I would adjust here. I knew I didn't want to stay here forever, in this strange house with people I didn't feel connected to.

Everyone at school was shocked that I had to leave, but I wasn't eighteen yet, not officially an adult to be left on my own. While they promised to keep in touch, I knew better than that because I'd made the same promises to others that had moved away. Radcliffe Academy was an elite prep school whose students prided themselves on their academics and athletics. Forming close personal relationships was not part of the curriculum. I knew that they would move on without me, and that was still upsetting, even though I wouldn't consider any of them a best friend. Who would be my friend here?

"Don't cry, Aubrey. I'll be your friend."

I sat up, startled at the words, and even more startled at who had spoken them. Standing in the doorway to our shared bathroom was Alyssa.

"How did you know what I was thinking?" I asked.

"You're sad, but it will pass," Alyssa said. Then she turned and went to her room, closing the door behind her.

Chapter Three

"When did she stop eating red meat?" Eric asked as he flipped the burgers on the grill and listened to them sizzle.

Mom poured glasses of lemonade. "I don't know. Wendell never told me, and I apparently failed to notice when I was there. There's a lot about her I don't know," she said, sighing. She finished with the lemonade and set the pitcher on the table. "Is this going to work? She resents me, you know. I can see it in her eyes when she looks at me."

Eric set down the spatula and moved to stand beside her, hugging her close. "She doesn't resent you. She needs time to adjust. I think tomorrow will be a good bonding experience. You'll help her decorate her room and get to know her better. We have a lot of summer left before she starts school. By that time, we'll be a real family, and it'll feel like she's always been here."

"I hope so. I just wish she were here under different circumstances. What if Wendell is…" She didn't finish her sentence.

They were quiet for a moment, and I decided to make my presence known then. I'd come downstairs and heard them talking, stopping by the open glass door to the deck so I could hear them better. Just as I was about to step outside, I heard Mom ask, "When should we tell her about Alyssa?"

Eric bristled beside her, and he moved back toward the grill, resuming his flipping of the burgers. "We'll have to wait for the right time."

"I hope she doesn't get scared."

I was pondering what that meant, when Alyssa came up behind me. I whirled around, embarrassed to be caught, and unable to give some sort of explanation. She smiled at me, and then stepped past me out onto the deck. I shook off my confusion and followed her. She sat down at the table and reached for her lemonade. "This is lovely, Mom," she said after taking a sip.

Mom reached over and patted her shoulder. "Thank you, sweetie."

"Did I miss anything?" I asked, taking the seat beside Alyssa. She said nothing about catching me eavesdropping a minute earlier.

"Right on time," Eric said, setting a plate of hamburgers on the table. "Are you sure you don't want to try one? I use a special seasoning, my own recipe."

"No thanks, this is fine," I said, reaching for the platter of grilled chicken.

We all filled our plates and started to eat. The only sounds were the chewing noises and the clanking of utensils from around the table.

"So, where are we going shopping tomorrow?" I asked, looking at Mom.

She seemed grateful that I'd been the one to speak first. "We can drive into the city, hit the malls. Do you have a preference for certain stores?" she asked. "Just remember that we may not have some of the stores you're used to in New York."

"No, that's not a problem. Any mall is fine. I'm sure I'll find something."

"Did you want to paint your room at all?" Eric asked.

"I hadn't thought much about it yet."

"It's your room. You can change it however you want. We want you to be comfortable and happy here."

Alyssa chewed her burger, her expression thoughtful. "She'll be happy here," she said.

I glanced sideways at my younger sister. There was something oddly calming about her that I couldn't figure out. She seemed so mature.

"Are you going with us?" I asked Alyssa.

"Oh, crowds, um," Mom said, shaking her head.

"I'll give it a try," Alyssa said, smiling at me. "As long as you promise to stay with me."

I thought that comment was a little strange, but I nodded, and Alyssa's face lit up. Mom looked apprehensive, and I caught the look that passed between her and Eric. I wondered what that was all about. I didn't have time to question it, as footsteps could be heard coming around the side of the house, and a friendly voice called out hello.

"Maddie, Eric, are you all back here?" A woman peeked up at us, and she lifted a covered plastic bowl. "I brought over some of my ambrosia salad for Aubrey. Is she here yet? Oh my goodness, she's beautiful!"

Mom laughed and stood up to greet the woman. "She is, isn't she? How are you, Camille?"

"Fantastic. This weather is gorgeous, perfect for outdoor activities."

Eric went inside and came back with two more chairs which he set up at the table. "Paul, don't be shy. Come on and sit down. Help yourself to some food, there's plenty left."

I glanced over my shoulder to see a boy my age making his way up the steps of the deck. He was tall and slightly muscular, and his movements were awkward, like he'd recently had a growth spurt and wasn't quite comfortable with his limbs yet. He pushed his hair back from his forehead to reveal piercing blue eyes.

"Hi," he said.

Mom introduced them as Camille Nesca and her son Paul, neighbors from down the street. Camille was the head librarian at Hamilton Green High School, and Paul was going to be a senior in the fall, just like me.

"I'm sure you'll be the best of friends," Camille said with a huge grin.

Paul gave a nervous laugh and busied himself with putting together a burger. He ate quietly, rarely looking up from his plate. I caught him sending shy looks in my direction, and then his gaze would dart away. The next time he did it, I kept eye contact with him and smiled. He smiled back, and his shoulders relaxed.

His mother peppered me with questions about my life in New York, being careful to skirt around the topic of my dad, and I answered as best I could without getting too personal. Alyssa listened intently, propping her elbows on the table and resting her chin in her hands. After dinner, I offered to take care of the dishes, and Paul jumped up to help, carrying in plates and glasses to the kitchen.

"Sorry about my mom," he said. "She gets a little excited sometimes."

"It's okay. I'm probably the best gossip this place has seen in awhile."

"Because of your father?"

I looked at him, and he coughed and focused on the dirty dishes.

"I'm sorry. It's none of my business," he said.

Mom and Eric had a dishwasher, and so had I back in New York, but I always preferred to wash the dishes by hand. As strange as it sounded, I enjoyed it, and it calmed me. I filled the sink with hot, soapy water and placed the dishes in to soak for a few minutes. In the meantime, I wrapped up the leftover food and placed everything in the fridge.

"So what do you do for fun around here?" I asked, changing the subject.

He shrugged and picked up a clean dishtowel. "Depends on what you're into."

"I love photography."

"Really? That's cool. How did you get into that?"

"My mom did some modeling while she was married to my dad, and she used to take me along to some of her fashion shoots. The whole experience fascinated me, and I fell in love with it."

"You must have been young."

I paused, trying to remember. "Probably around four when I realized what was going on. That was around the same time she gave it up too," I said.

The reason she stopped modeling was to try and save her failing marriage. I didn't say that to Paul.

"What do you take pictures of?" he asked.

"Pretty much everything. I'm always seeing the world in terms of color, angle and lighting. It can get kind of annoying to people who don't understand."

"I'll bet your pictures are great."

"Maybe I'll show you sometime," I said, and Paul's cheeks colored a little. "I mean, uh, when I get unpacked and everything." I turned back to the sink and plunged my hands into the water.

"I'll dry," Paul said.

We worked together in silence on the dishes. I washed and rinsed and passed them to Paul, who dried and put them away.

"You know where everything goes," I said, pulling the drain plug and taking the towel he handed me.

"Oh, yeah. Sometimes I watch Alyssa if my mom's not available. She's a cute kid, super smart."

"I've noticed."

We joined everyone back on the deck. Our parents were talking about the weather and the upcoming Fourth of July holiday. Alyssa colored a picture of a farm scene, her crayons lined up in a perfect row beside her paper. She was concentrating on not going outside the lines.

"And the fourth is also Aubrey's birthday," Eric said, motioning to me. "We should do something special to celebrate."

I shook my head quickly and said, "No, it's okay. Not a big deal."

"Of course it is," my mom said. "You'll be eighteen."

I swallowed hard, remembering the early celebration of my birthday that turned into an unsolved mystery. Both my mother and Eric must have realized it at the same time, because they started apologizing and saying that we could talk more about it later, after I was settled in. An uneasy silence fell around us.

"Hey, do you wanna go for a walk or something?" Paul asked me. His voice was low, but everyone heard and turned their gazes to him.

"Yeah, sure," I said, eager to get away.

Paul and I walked around the house and headed up the street.

"Thank you," I said, and he shrugged and smiled. "No, really. I know everyone feels sorry for me, but I don't need the sympathy. I just want some answers. Good or bad, I just want to know what happened."

"I get it," he said, nodding. "So, what is it like living in New York City?" he asked as we walked. "The real scoop, not what you told my mom just to appease her. Will you miss it?"

The sun was starting to dip below the horizon. It was casting everything in an orange glow, and I found it surprisingly peaceful. When Paul asked that last question, it threw off my newfound balance, and I stumbled over a crack in the sidewalk. He reached out and caught me by the elbow, steadying me.

"Whoa, you okay?"

"Fine." I stood up straight and Paul released me, shoving his hands in his pockets. "New York City, yeah, it was great," I said. "I love living in the city. The atmosphere is so alive."

"Oh. We have atmosphere here all the time. It consists of weekend cookouts and school concerts though. Not as cool as the big city, but the Fourth of July festivities are rather well known." He grinned at me, and I couldn't help but smile back.

I noticed he didn't repeat his question about me missing New York, and I was grateful for it. I didn't know how to answer it at that moment.

We continued walking until we reached the end of the block. "This is my house," Paul said, pointing. "You're free to stop by anytime you want to. I mean, *if* you want to."

Paul was very endearing. "Sure thing. It'll be nice to know someone at school."

"Ah, you probably won't want to hang out with me there."

"Why's that?"

"I'm not the most popular kid you'll ever meet."

"Well, I hate to break it to you, but I'm not either."

Paul glanced at me sideways. "Right. Like you expect me to believe that. A girl like you? Not popular?"

It was my turn to eye him strangely. He blushed and ducked his head.

"I mean, well, you're really pretty and you're from New York City, so you're sophisticated and stuff," he mumbled. "You'll end up hanging out with all the cheerleaders and dating the quarterback or captain of the basketball team."

I shook my head. "Trust me, I'm not like that. I prefer to blend into the background if possible."

He grinned and said, "Me too."

We walked up to the front porch of his house and sat on the steps. I noticed Paul's knee continued to bounce up and down, and I figured it was because he was working up the courage to ask me about my father. So I beat him to the punch and started talking.

"We were celebrating my eighteenth birthday the night before he disappeared. My birthday wasn't for a few months, but he knew he was going to be out of the country on business, and he didn't want to miss it. We went to my favorite Italian restaurant for dinner, and then he took me to a Broadway show. I enjoyed every second of it, mainly because I was spending time with him."

Paul was staring at me in silence, allowing me to speak without asking questions, and I felt the words just pouring out of me. This was the first time I'd really talked about it to someone other than the police. It felt good.

I told Paul that my father said he was so proud of me. He said that he didn't get to make his own choices when he was my age. It was just expected of him to take over the family business. He rebelled by going into acting, and even though he'd had success, his father still wanted him to come and work with him, so that's what he did. He was happy that I'd found something I cared about and wanted to pursue. We enjoyed the play, and then we went home. I went to school the next morning without seeing him. That wasn't uncommon, even though the police asked about it. A lot of times he was out the door before I was even awake. I didn't think anything of it. But when I was called to the headmaster's office during my first class, I got this weird feeling in my stomach. Two detectives were there to speak to me about my father. He hadn't shown up for work, and he was unreachable by phone or email.

The police investigation yielded nothing to clue them in to his whereabouts. His business and personal life were checked out, and nothing seemed to be amiss. He was a divorced, single father who ran a huge business, and he was nowhere to be found.

"If he doesn't come back before I turn twenty-five, his estate will be left to me," I said, and Paul's eyes widened in shock. "I'll gain control of the entire business, and the thought of that scares me to death. I never paid attention to any of that stuff while I was growing up."

"Who's handling it all now?"

"My grandfather. He hasn't made me, but I've started checking into business schools and thinking about life in the corporate world, rather than in a photography studio or traveling the globe as a photojournalist."

Paul reached out and patted my hand. "I'm sure everything will work out. Your dad will come back, and you'll still get to follow your dreams."

I hoped so. I nudged Paul with my shoulder and said, "Hey, you're not going to sell my story to the tabloids, are you?"

My tone was joking, but he looked aghast that I'd even asked him. "No, of course not. I'd never do that. I know that the neighborhood is buzzing about you, but I won't sell you out, I promise."

We sat there a while longer, just thinking. I took in the sights of the neighborhood as the streetlights came on, illuminating the homes and the trees and the beautiful flowers everywhere. I suddenly itched for my camera. This place was full of color and shadow and I wanted to capture it.

"Should we head back now?" I asked. "I'll bet our mothers are gossiping about us."

Paul laughed and agreed. We turned around to go back to my house, how strange that felt for me to think of it like that, and continued to talk. Paul told me about the high school and the kids, and the town. He'd lived there all his life, and he liked the community a lot. He also liked the proximity to St. Louis. And I found out that we had something in common in that our parents had divorced, except his had split up within the last year.

"Dad lives in St. Louis now," Paul said. "It's not far, but I don't see him much."

"Does that bother you?" I asked, and instantly regretted the question.

He looked at me then, right at me, and again I was struck by how blue his eyes were. "Yeah, it does," he said, and I could feel the hurt in his words.

We went into the backyard, and everyone was still on the deck. The adults were drinking coffee, and Alyssa was curled up in her chair, her head resting on the arm. She was either asleep or she was faking it well.

"I think she has the right idea," I said. "I'm going to turn in for the night. It was nice meeting you, Mrs. Nesca."

"It was my pleasure, dear. I hope that Paul was a polite gentleman," she said.

"Mom, stop," Paul mumbled.

"He was," I said, smiling at him.

"What time did you want to head out tomorrow?" Mom asked.

"I don't usually sleep in, so how about after breakfast?"

"Sounds good. What would you like for breakfast? Waffles? Pancakes? Do you still eat breakfast?"

I almost laughed at my mother's worried expression. I knew she was trying.

"You don't have to make anything special. Toast is enough for me."

I said goodnight and excused myself. I waved to Paul and he grinned and waved back. I knew my secrets were safe with him. I was halfway up the stairs to my bedroom, when I heard soft footsteps behind me.

"Hey, Alyssa," I said. "Are you going to bed too?"

She stepped toward me and took my hand in hers. Her fingers were cool, which surprised me for some reason. "Can I spend some time with you?"

I nodded, and we went to my room. I picked her up and set her on the bed.

"I can help you unpack," she said. "I know where things go."

I grabbed the first box off the pile and peeled off the packing tape. Inside this box was my iPod docking station and some clothes. I plugged in the docking station and connected my iPod to turn on some music. Alyssa hopped down from the bed and swayed back and forth as the group Lifehouse started to sing.

"I like them," she said.

I was very surprised. "You know who this is?"

"I'm eight, but I listen to all types of music," she said. "Dad has a huge collection."

She spotted something poking out from under the bed and bent to pick up my fallen cell phone, handing it to me without saying anything. It was almost as if she knew it was important to me because of the message it held. Then she dug into the box and started hanging my clothes in the closet.

We opened up a few more boxes, and she helped me fill the dresser and arrange things on the desk and in the bathroom. She even hooked up my laptop computer without any assistance from me, which I thought was pretty amazing. But the strangest thing was that I didn't have to tell her which drawers to put stuff into, or where to place items in the medicine cabinet. She seemed to know where I wanted it all.

We chatted, as much as a seventeen-year-old and an eight-year-old can, and I realized that she was more like me than I could have ever imagined. She loved pictures and art, walks in the park, and fudge brownies. I asked her about school, and she shrugged and climbed back up onto my bed.

"Mom teaches me," she said.

"You don't go to school?"

"I go to school with Mom. She does a fantastic job, and whatever she's not sure about, Dad teaches me."

I sat down beside her. "Is there something about public school that you don't like?"

"I don't know. I've never been."

Just as I was about to ask her more, she slid from the bed and turned to face me and said, "I'm excited to go shopping with you. I think it'll be great fun. Wait here, I have something for you." She reached up and hugged me, and then went to her room. She returned a minute later with a small potted plant and set the pot on the windowsill next to the desk. "It's a blue poppy anemone," she said. "It'll bloom well in the sun. Good night."

I watched her leave, still puzzling about her. I tried to recall if I had been like that when I was her age. All I remembered were piano, swimming, dance, and riding lessons. My father was determined to make me a well-rounded young woman for polite society. Examining the plant closer, I saw that it had barely poked through the surface of the soil. It wouldn't bloom for several days yet.

Without changing into pajamas, I pulled back the blankets on the bed and slid beneath them. Once I was comfortable, I stared at the ceiling, wishing again that things were different. I wanted to get to know my mom and my sister, and I also wanted to be back in New York with my dad, listening to the traffic outside my window and looking forward to another day of photographing the city. So far, I had one friend here, maybe, if Paul didn't find me or my situation too weird. I continued to lay there, thinking about my future and what it might hold for me, until I fell asleep.

Chapter Four

I woke up to sunlight streaming in through my windows. Rubbing away the sleep in my eyes, I sat up, momentarily confused as to where I was. Then I remembered, and my heart felt heavy.

Someone had turned off the light and the music during the night. I could hear Alyssa giggling downstairs. It was eight o'clock, later than I usually slept, and I wondered why no one had come in to wake me up before now.

I grabbed fresh clothes and went into the bathroom. I started the water in the shower and turned to see signs of

Alyssa all over the place. There was a Dora the Explorer toothbrush on the counter, a small pink washcloth draped over the edge of the sink and a step-stool against the wall. I checked the door to Alyssa's room, opening it and peering inside. Her room was like any typical little girl's room, with a twin-sized bed, dresser, pink ruffled curtains and stuffed animals everywhere. There was a small round table with three child-sized chairs in the middle of the room. Coloring books and crayons covered the table, along with a blue and white tea set. She also had stacks of thick books piled on every available surface. I picked one up, expecting it to be a collection of fairytales, surprised to see it was a book on physics. Thumbing through another stack, I found books on biology, chemistry, botany, and zoology. These were far more advanced than anything I had even studied, and I wondered what she was doing with them.

I remembered that Eric was a genetic scientist for some type of lab in St. Louis, but I couldn't understand how Alyssa could comprehend this material. I heard footsteps on the stairs and scooted back into the bathroom, closing the door. I didn't want to get caught snooping, although my curiosity level was quite high about my sister. Even though I hadn't spent much time around young children, I could tell that she was different from others her own age.

I showered and dressed, pulled my hair into a ponytail and went back into my room. I booted up my laptop to connect to the Internet and check my email. As I was waiting for the page to load, I noticed the plant on the windowsill and did a double take. I distinctly remembered it was nothing more than a tiny bud the night before. Now it was in full bloom with beautiful blue-violet petals. Reaching out, I touched one of the petals, not sure what to expect, awed by the fact that this flower was real.

How was that possible?

Ignoring my email, I did a search for the flower, researching its growing habits. The information I found stated the soil needed to be moist, and the flowers would normally bloom in spring. This was early summer, and as I pressed a finger to the soil, I felt it was almost dry.

Grabbing my camera, I took a few pictures to prove to myself that I wasn't imagining this. Then I went downstairs, still marveling at how much the flower had changed in such a short period of time. The kitchen was warm with the smells of food, and Alyssa was busy buttering a slice of toast when I entered the room. Her face lit up when she saw me.

"Good morning," she said. "Did you sleep well?"

"Fine, thank you," I said. I tried not to stare at her as I sat down at the table, and Mom placed a plate of waffles and eggs in front of me.

"I know you said toast would be fine, but it's your first breakfast here. I wanted it to be special," she said.

"This is great," I told her.

She nodded and sat down, sipping from her coffee cup.

"Where's Eric?" I asked.

"He leaves early for work. He should be home a little after six."

"What does he do again?"

"Dad works with genetics at Wilton Labs," Alyssa said around a mouthful of toast. "He creates things."

"Do you like science?" I asked her.

She nodded. "It's very interesting to me."

Mom cleared her throat. "So. Ready to shop?"

"Yeah."

"Did you decide if you wanted to paint your room at all?"

"Maybe, or I could just hang some photographs. I want to get a feel for the room before I do anything drastic."

She nodded and got up to refill her coffee. As she poured, she nodded at Alyssa. "Sweetheart, are you sure you want to go with us? I can get Mrs. Nesca to stay with you otherwise."

Alyssa brushed crumbs from her fingers and wiped her lips with a napkin. "I'll be okay, Mom."

I saw the nervousness creep into my mother's eyes. She caught me watching her and smiled at me. We finished breakfast, cleaned the dishes and piled into Mom's minivan. Alyssa was buckled into the backseat, and I sat up front.

"When school starts, you can either take the bus or I can drive you," Mom said. "Unless we can find you a car. Eric's been checking with some friends at his workplace."

"That's okay, you don't have to," I said. "If the school's not far, I could always walk, or take the bus." I'd never taken the bus in my life, but it felt like the appropriate thing to say.

"Well, we want you to have a vehicle anyway, for emergencies. How did you get to school in New York? You have your driver's license, right?"

"I do, but we had a personal driver who took me places."

"Of course. I forgot. Well, Paul drives to school. Maybe you'd rather ride with him?"

"That would work. I'll ask him."

We settled into silence as we headed into St. Louis. The drive wasn't that long, and we were soon pulling into a parking spot at a huge shopping center. Alyssa hopped out of the van and immediately grabbed my hand, holding it tight. We walked through the main entrance side by side, and I felt her move closer to me. It was a beautiful summer day, and already, the stores were crammed full of people who'd rather be indoors than out enjoying the weather.

We checked out a home furnishings store and I found a nice floor rug to match the comforter set already on my bed. Alyssa helped to pick out a desk lamp, and even found one for herself. I also picked up some new picture frames and a wall clock. As it neared lunchtime, we went to the food court for pizza. We found an empty table and placed our bags beneath it while we ate.

"Is there anywhere else you'd like to go?" Mom asked me, cutting Alyssa's pizza into smaller pieces. Alyssa turned my way and rolled her eyes, but didn't say anything. "Do you need clothes for school or anything like that?"

"I'll need a new backpack," I said. "I don't think the one I have will fit in here."

"What do you have now?"

"It's Prada," I said, avoiding her eyes. "Dad bought it for me."

"Oh."

"I've been thinking, maybe I should just get rid of all that stuff," I said, stabbing my straw into my drink cup. "I don't want to stand out."

"It's nothing to be ashamed of, sweetheart," Mom said. "It's okay to have nice things."

I was about to say something when another family sat down at the table next to us. A little boy around Alyssa's age was with them, and he stared at her with wide eyes. I glanced at her, not seeing anything out of place. She had stopped eating though, and was staring back at the boy. He turned to his mother, pulling at her shirtsleeve to get her attention. When she leaned down to him, he whispered in her ear. The mother looked at Alyssa with a quizzical expression, and a minute later, the family was leaving to go to another table. Alyssa didn't blink as her gaze followed the family. The boy glanced back at her over his shoulder and shuddered before moving closer to his mother.

"What the heck was that about?" I asked softly.

Mom pretended not to notice, but I could see that she had. She appeared pained as she moved to drop a kiss on Alyssa's head. "It's okay, baby," she whispered.

Alyssa turned back to her food and continued to eat.

"Mom?" I asked. "What's going on?"

"It's nothing. Why don't we finish up and head home? We can take a look at your room and move things around if you want."

I wanted to pursue the issue, but decided not to. I'd talk with her later, when Alyssa was out of earshot. I had a lot of questions, such as why Alyssa had all of those science books, why she didn't attend school, and what was the deal with that flower?

We finished our food, dumped our trash and started for the exit. Alyssa held my hand and kept up with me as we walked. Just as we were leaving the food court, two groups of teenagers met up right in front of us. They appeared to be angry with each other, and I knew this was not going to end well. A boy stepped forward from each group, insults were exchanged, and the next thing we knew, there was a full-on brawl going on, with everyone involved.

Mom stepped in front of Alyssa to shield her, and I felt her grip on my hand tighten. "We'll go out the other way," Mom said.

Security guards were making their way to the scene, as food containers and drink cups were being thrown around. I yelped and jumped back when a chair bounced in front of me. I lost my connection with Alyssa, and she whirled to find me. I reached out to her just as a girl with dyed pink hair slammed into Alyssa, knocking her to the floor.

In that moment, the strangest feeling washed over me. It was like a tremor of power had filled the room. I couldn't tell where it was coming from, and it would take me a few seconds to conclude it was emanating from Alyssa. She was on her knees, her features calm, and her eyes were closed, as if she were concentrating. The girl with pink hair rolled away, staring at Alyssa with a mixture of fear and astonishment. There was a nanosecond of silence, and everyone seemed to freeze, and then, just as I took a step toward her, Alyssa opened her eyes, and an enormous gust of wind swept through the area with a loud whoosh! Everyone and everything that wasn't nailed down tipped sideways and fell to the floor.

I pushed my hair from my eyes and staggered to my feet. I couldn't help but gasp at the sight in front of me. It was complete and utter chaos, and something inside me was indicating that Alyssa was the cause of it.

Mom gripped me hard by the shoulder, startling me. "Get your sister. We have to go now," she said. Her tone sent a cold shiver up my back as I took Alyssa's hand, and we hurried out the door to the parking lot. I kept my eyes down until we reached the van, and then I hurried to buckle Alyssa into her seat before jumping into mine. It was then I realized we'd left all of our shopping bags behind.

Mom was pulling out of the parking lot, at the same time dialing Eric's private work number on the van's phone system.

"You need to come home," she said without hesitation.

"What happened?" Eric's voice was tight with worry.

"We'll discuss it when we see you."

"Were any of you hurt?"

"No, no one was hurt."

"I'm on my way," Eric said.

Mom disconnected the call and glanced in her rearview mirror at Alyssa. "Are you okay, baby?"

"I'm fine," she answered back.

I twisted in my seat. She appeared completely unharmed as she stared out the window. The only evidence that she'd fallen was that one of her barrettes was missing from her hair.

"I'm sorry," she said to me. "I lost control."

Mom shook her head. "It wasn't your fault. Those kids scared you, that's all. No one was hurt."

I looked at my mother, then back to my sister in disbelief. "Wait a minute," I said. "What are you saying? Alyssa did that? Knocked everyone over? How?"

"Sweetheart, we'll explain when we get home. I want to talk to Eric first," Mom said.

"No, I want to talk about it now. What's going on? How did she do that?"

"Aubrey, please," my mother begged, and I clamped my lips shut.

My head was spinning, and I couldn't make sense of anything. It was obvious Alyssa was different from other kids. Was it possible that she really had powers of some sort? It sure would explain the flower in my room.

We arrived at home, and I was shocked to see Eric's SUV parked in the driveway already. I had no idea how far away Wilton Labs was, but I had the feeling that he must have sped back here. He was waiting for us in the kitchen, and he leapt up from where he sat at the table to scoop Alyssa into his arms.

"It's already been reported on the news of an incident at the mall. What happened?" he asked, and his voice seemed harsh to me. I reasoned that he was just scared. About what, I wasn't sure yet. He set Alyssa on the counter and began checking her over.

"I'm okay, Daddy," she said, wiggling away from him. "It wasn't a big one this time."

"Are you sure? Did anyone notice you?"

Mom set her purse on the table and ran her hands through her hair. "We left right away."

"Tell me everything, from start to finish," Eric said. He was looking right at me.

I blinked, uncomfortable under his gaze. "We left the house after breakfast, drove to the mall, and we did some shopping," I stammered. "Then we decided to get lunch at the food court."

Eric turned back to Alyssa. "What did you eat, sweetie?"

"Pizza. Thin crust, cheese. And a small Diet Coke with no ice," she said.

"Dessert?"

"Nothing."

Eric focused on me again. "Go on."

"That's all. We were leaving, and these two groups of teenagers started to get rowdy with each other. A girl fell into Alyssa, and then, then…" I trailed off and shrugged. I didn't know how to describe the next part.

"It's okay, honey, just tell us what you saw," Mom said.

I took a deep breath. "It got weird. There was this, this, power in the room. I could feel it in my bones. And then, it was like a big gust of wind came through and everyone was on the floor."

Eric scrutinized me for a full twenty seconds, until Alyssa reached up and placed her hands on either side of his face, forcing him to look at her.

"It's okay, Daddy," she said. "We should tell her."

Eric swallowed. "Are you sure?" he asked.

Alyssa nodded. "She's safe."

I watched my mother exchange glances with Eric, as if they were having a silent conversation. Finally, I couldn't stand it any longer.

"Will someone please just tell me what's going on?" I said. "I'm on the verge of freaking out!"

"Why don't we all just sit down, and we'll discuss it," Mom said. She motioned to the chairs at the kitchen table.

"I'll stand, thanks," I said, crossing my arms over my chest.

Eric lifted Alyssa from the counter and set her down. She climbed into a chair at the table and faced me.

"I'm different," she said. "I can control things."

"What kind of things?" I asked.

"The elements."

I felt the frown crossing my face and tried to stop it. "I don't understand."

Eric took a deep breath. "Aubrey, your sister has the ability to control the major elements. Wind, water, earth, fire, you know them. You learned about them in science class."

"Yeah, but I still don't understand what this means. You're saying that she has super powers or something?"

Mom stepped closer, placing a hand on my shoulder. "Not super powers, just powers. And she hasn't quite learned to fully control them yet, which is why we try and keep her away from crowds. There have been incidents before."

"How did this happen? Is it a genetic thing?" I asked, and then a light clicked on in my head, and I turned accusing eyes to Eric. "Did you experiment on her or something?"

"What? Aubrey, no, not at all. We didn't realize she had these abilities until she exhibited them when she was six months old. She made a sunflower grow in the middle of winter."

"It was pretty," Alyssa said with a smile.

"We took her to the doctor for a checkup, but there was nothing physically different about her," Eric said. "We thought the sunflower was a fluke, a weird coincidence or something. Then she started doing other things, like making little dirt tornadoes in the yard."

"Candles would light themselves," Mom said, "and when a water main broke down the street, we were the only house on the block that still had water because she made it rain over the backyard. All because Alyssa wanted to fill her kiddie pool."

"It was hot that summer," Alyssa said.

"I took her to my lab, ran some tests," Eric said.

"And this was approved?" I asked.

"I'm in a position that gives me special access to certain areas of the lab. I determined that while she's a healthy little girl, she does possess a slightly altered genetic makeup. Because of this, she's able to do special things. She's also very gifted and understands complex subjects. Mentally, she's well beyond her current age. We haven't figured out how this has happened, or why, but we keep a close eye on her and notate any changes."

"What if something changes for the worse?" I asked. "What if something bad happens and people find out about her?"

Something in my mother and Eric's expressions changed then, and I felt that same shiver from earlier.

"Someone has found out about her," I stated matter-of-factly.

"Not quite," Eric said. "But there have been a couple of close calls."

"That's why we're very careful," Mom said. "We've heard there may be other children like her. We haven't been able to make any connections with them, and we've also heard of a group of people searching for them. We can't put Alyssa at risk."

I leaned against the counter, nibbling on my thumbnail. A multitude of thoughts were racing through my mind, and they all focused on the little girl who was staring up at me with expectant eyes.

"I'm really not so different," she said. "I don't know what makes me this way, but it doesn't change anything else about me."

I nodded. "I can understand that."

"We didn't want to scare you," Mom said.

"I'm not scared. I'm just a little confused. Who are these people that you said were searching for kids like Alyssa?"

"There's some kind of research organization that exists. We don't know the name of it, or where it's located," Eric said.

"So how do you even know it exists? How did you hear of it?"

"There was a news story about seven years ago," Mom explained, "about a young boy from Chicago that went missing and was never found. He disappeared in the middle of the night from his home while his parents and older sister were sleeping. They claimed that someone had been following them for several months, and they had even filed a complaint with their local police department. The police investigated and found a car deserted a few miles away from the house. There were signs that the boy had been in it, but it wasn't registered to anyone. The police checked every possible database and came up with nothing."

"How is that possible?" I asked. "I mean, I don't know a lot about cars, but aren't they traced back to someone or somewhere? Maybe it was a brand new car stolen from a dealership?"

"The police checked it all out and hit dead ends. There weren't any fingerprints left behind either, except for the boy's. The family went on the news to plead for help from the general public. That's how we learned about them. They started telling everyone about their son's special abilities."

"Abilities that matched Alyssa's," Eric said. "We decided to try and contact them to find out more, but they disappeared a few weeks after the kidnapping. The people that we did talk to made them out to be a normal, happy family that went a little crazy after their son was gone. They were always talking about some secret lab that wanted to take him and perform tests and experiments on him."

"We keep an eye on any news stories about missing children now, in case any of the families mention unique abilities. We've come across three others with similar situations." Mom's voice trailed off and she glanced toward Alyssa.

"What happened?" I asked. "Did you try to make contact with those families?"

"They all disappeared."

"Like, went missing?"

"More like, they packed up and relocated, or went into hiding," Eric said. "We haven't been able to find any of them."

"Are you sure this secret group, or whatever it is, hasn't found them and, uh," I faltered and looked at Alyssa, "maybe gotten rid of them?"

Eric made a face and said, "That's another possibility."

"One that we'd rather not think about. It's also a reason why we've done so much to keep Alyssa out of the public eye," Mom said. "We don't want to endanger others."

"Does anyone outside of the family know? Did Dad know?"

Mom shook her head. "The people in this room are the only ones that know, and we'd prefer to keep it that way. You have to promise us, Aubrey, that this stays here, just between us. You can't let on that you know anything about your sister's abilities."

I couldn't ignore the fear in her eyes, and I saw that same fear mirrored in Eric's expression. When I faced my sister, I saw nothing but calm. She was even smiling a little, as if she were pleased that I was in on the secret now. I held her gaze for a minute or two. The kitchen was silent as everyone waited for my response.

"Of course," I finally said. "I won't say anything to anyone, I promise."

Mom and Eric breathed heavy sighs of relief.

"But I want to know everything," I added. "I want to know all about her abilities and the tests you've done on her. And I want to try and find this research lab, or whatever it is that's searching for these kids."

"If it does exist, the people who run it stay well beneath the radar to be noticed," Eric said. "I have professional connections all across the country, and there hasn't been any indication that this agency or lab runs in any of the legitimate science circles. I go to conferences several times a year, and I've made inquiries into government run programs and privately operated experiments concerning the elements. I've received no feedback. Of course, it could be a secret government program of some kind."

"Dad was good friends with a private investigator," I said. "We could call him if you'd like. He's excellent at what he does."

"Thank you, Aubrey, but I think we'd rather keep this to ourselves," Mom said, and I could tell she didn't want to talk about it anymore. "Alyssa, why don't you go upstairs and change into your play clothes? I'll make us a snack."

Alyssa said nothing as she walked past me. We listened until her footsteps faded away and her door closed.

"Mom, you need to let me help you," I said, my voice low but firm. "This PI is excellent, and I can vouch for him. He takes his client's privacy very seriously."

I watched as she busied herself washing and cutting up apples and slicing cheese. She put everything onto a plate, arranging it in a circle, every other slice an apple or piece of cheese. She said nothing as she pulled a box of crackers from the pantry and dumped a handful into the center of the plate. I glanced at Eric, and he just shook his head at me.

"Mom?" I pressed.

She set the plate on the table and then went back to the refrigerator and took out the carton of apple juice. Eric and I watched her pour four glasses and set them next to the plate. As she passed us to put the juice away, Eric grabbed her hand. She was shaking, and she swallowed hard and turned away from us. I could see the tears leaking out from the corners of her eyes.

"Honey, maybe we should consider this," Eric said softly. "We've been trying for years to track down these other families and this mystery organization on our own with no success. Wouldn't it be better to know for sure what's going on?"

She collapsed into a chair then, and Eric dropped to his knees in front of her. She placed her head on his shoulder and cried. At that moment, she changed from being just someone I referred to as Mom to actually *being* Mom. She was scared, and she feared for the safety of her child. My mind jumped back almost thirteen years, to the day that she left me with my father.

We were in the foyer of our penthouse, and a doorman was taking a cart full of her luggage down to a car waiting for her outside. I was wearing a red party dress with black patent leather shoes. She had dressed me herself that morning. She knelt down so she was eye level with me, and she told me she loved me and this decision was best for me and my future. I was four years old, and I didn't understand anything about what she was saying. All I knew was that she was leaving, and I wasn't going with her. I remember starting to cry, and she wiped my eyes with a tissue. My vision was blurry because of my tears, but I could see she was crying as well. It made me sad, and I realized that all I wanted to do was to stay with her because she made me feel safe and loved. She was trying so hard to be brave that day, and I could see a repeat of that morning playing out in front of me, this time with a different daughter.

"Mom, it's going to be okay," I said, moving closer to her. "I know you're scared, but we're a family, and we can handle this. We'll keep Alyssa safe."

She wiped at her tears and laughed a little. "I'm being so silly," she said. "I know you would never suggest anything that could put Alyssa in harm's way."

"You're right. If you'd like to wait a little while before I talk to the PI, we can see what I can dig up. Dad showed me how to do a few things on the sly."

She reached over and hugged me, and we shared a laugh.

"Is everyone okay?" Alyssa asked. She came into the kitchen and joined in the group hug.

It was a mushy moment, one that I wouldn't have expected to experience with them so soon. We all sat down at the table and shared the snack Mom had prepared. While we ate, I listened as they told me everything about Alyssa. Eric and Mom showed me all of the news clippings and results of their searches about the other families with children like her. We sat there for nearly two hours, sifting through all of the details. There didn't seem to be any type of connection between the families. They all lived in different parts of the country, all of the parents' professions were different, and the missing children were both males and females. The one thing that could count as a connection was that the children were all under the age of nine when they disappeared.

We winded down, and I gathered up all of the information and shuffled it into a nice, neat pile. Eric checked the time and excused himself to make a call to his office. "I left in kind of a hurry," he said. "I told my assistants it was a family emergency, so they're probably a little worried."

I remembered that we'd left our packages at the mall that morning, and I offered to go back and get them, if someone hadn't taken them.

"Why don't you wait until tomorrow? I'd rather have everyone home for a little while," Mom said. She got up, took the plate to the sink and began tidying up.

I agreed and turned to Alyssa. "Do you want to watch a video with me?" I asked. She nodded and we went together to the family room.

She chose an animated movie and put it into the DVD player. Then she crawled up onto the sofa with me and curled up next to my side. The movie started, and we stayed quiet for a few minutes.

"Mom's bothered about what happened today," she said softly, breaking into my thoughts.

I realized I hadn't even been paying attention to the television, and neither had Alyssa. I reached for the remote and paused it.

"Are you?" I asked.

She shrugged and fiddled with the hem of her shirt. "I didn't mean to make everyone fall down today."

"I know that. It was an accident."

"I've been trying so hard to control it. Dad works with me sometimes."

"How's that?"

"He tries to get me to concentrate on staying calm and focus on using the powers when I need them. We do a lot of outdoor activities, and I read a lot about science, so I understand the elements. But when I get scared, I sometimes lose control."

"Does that happen often?"

"Not really."

"Well, that's good then," I said, trying to sound positive. "Hey, were you responsible for making that flower bloom? The one in my room?"

"I wanted you to have something pretty."

"It's beautiful. I have to admit though, I was very surprised to see it this morning."

Alyssa blushed and ducked her head. "I got excited. It wasn't supposed to bloom quite so much, just a little at a time. It's stuff like that," she said, "that makes Mom and Dad so anxious. Dad is afraid that when I hit puberty we'll be in big trouble."

"Why's that?"

She grinned and giggled. "Because then I'll be a hormonal teenager with special powers. He says he'll feel like Clark Kent's parents. I think he's secretly been watching episodes of *Smallville* to see how they handle it."

I ruffled her hair and hugged her close. "As long as you don't start flying, we're still okay."

"But wouldn't that be super cool?" she asked, laughing.

I hit the play button and we finished the movie.

Chapter Five

The next day was Saturday, and I drove Mom's van back to the mall alone. Mom and Alyssa were staying at home, and Eric went into the office for a few hours to finish up some work. If the packages were gone, I was going to buy the same things again. I also wanted to see if anyone working in the food court was talking about what had happened. There was grainy cell phone video footage being shown on the news. Thankfully, we weren't visible, and it was a mere five seconds long. Mom was still upset about it though, and I knew she wasn't going to let Alyssa out of her sight for a while.

From the outside, the mall didn't look any different. It was another beautiful day, and the parking lot was full. I headed straight into the customer service office and asked about our bags. The woman working the desk was polite and said there had been some items dropped off with them by security, and that I would need to show the receipts in order to take them back. Since Mom had given me all the receipts, it was no problem. There was one item missing, the lamp that Alyssa had picked out, so I bought another one. I took all of the bags back to the van, and then I went back inside.

I took my time, retracing our steps. As far as I could remember, nothing out of the ordinary had occurred in any of the stores we'd been in. We hadn't encountered anyone suspicious, and no one seemed to be following us or hanging around. Of course, I hadn't been looking for anyone either. I reasoned that it was simply the fight that broke out in the food court that had triggered Alyssa's reaction.

I ended up back at the food court, where I stood and stared at the Chik-Fil-A and the Panda Express. Next to that was the pizza place where we'd gotten our food, and then a sub sandwich stand. I used my cell phone to take some pictures of the layout. I replayed the scene in my head, remembering the gust of wind that was so strong it knocked us all to the floor and somehow didn't harm us.

Everything had been cleaned up, and there were no traces that anything strange had happened the day before.

I could still feel a sense of power in the room though. I shivered and turned to head to the exit when I smashed into something solid, or someone, as it turned out to be.

"Oh wow, I'm so sorry."

I blinked and peered into dark green eyes that were warm and focused on me with such intensity that I felt the blood rush to my face. I had turned right into a boy, shoving myself against his chest. His large hands gripped my upper arms, steadying me.

"Are you all right?" he asked.

I nodded, unable to speak, wondering if I'd swallowed my tongue.

"Do you need to sit down for a moment?"

I gulped hard and shook my head. "No, I'm okay. I'm sorry," I managed to squeak out. "I didn't see you."

He smiled and released his hold on me, putting his hands in his pockets. "It's okay. I'm hard to miss sometimes."

I snorted and immediately heard my father's voice in my head, scolding me for being so unladylike.

"I think I saw you here yesterday," he said, motioning toward the tables and chairs.

"You did?"

"Yeah. Weren't you here when everything got knocked over?"

I felt myself tense at the question. "Did you see how it happened?" I asked.

He shook his head. "Nope. I was over by the ice cream stand. Wasted a perfectly good mint chocolate chip cone."

I couldn't help but smile. "Too bad. Mint chocolate chip is my favorite flavor."

He grinned back at me, and I felt a little tremble of excitement go through me. "If you're not in a hurry, would you like to join me for some ice cream? My treat."

I hesitated for a moment and checked my watch. I'd told Mom that I wouldn't be long, but I was intrigued by this boy. "All right, sure."

"I'm Connor Davenport," he said.

"Aubrey Benton," I said.

"Aubrey," he repeated with a half-smile. "Very pretty."

I pressed my lips together to keep from giggling like some air headed school girl with a crush. We walked together to the Baskin Robbins stand, and he ordered two cones. We stood to the side, eating our ice cream, and he told me he had just graduated with his bachelor's degree and was going to be a graduate student at Hamilton University.

"What are you studying?" I asked.

"Legal studies. I guess you could say it runs in the family. What about you? What's your major?"

I felt myself blushing again. I didn't want to tell him I was still in high school, and I knew I couldn't lie either. "I'll be a senior this fall at the high school."

He didn't bat an eyelash. Instead, he said, "Have you thought about college yet?"

"Oh yes. I'm hoping to go into photojournalism."

"So you have an interest in photography. Have you done a show or anything?" he asked.

"No, nothing like that. I had a small display at my previous school, but that's all."

"And where was that?"

"Radcliffe Academy in New York City. It's a private school."

"Like a prep school?"

"Sort of."

Connor finished his cone and wiped his hands with a napkin. "So are you some kind of debutante or something?"

I blushed again, cursing my inability to control it, and focused on my cone. "I guess you could say that."

He touched my arm, and I looked up at him. "Hey, I'm sorry. I didn't mean that in a bad way. I hope I didn't offend you."

"No, no, you didn't. I just…well, it's kind of a difficult situation…"

"And I'm a strange guy you've just met," Connor said. "Say no more. My mother always said my curiosity would get the better of me."

I finished my ice cream and checked my watch. "Your mother sounds like a wise woman. Speaking of mothers, mine's probably wondering where I am. I should get going. It was nice meeting you, Connor, and thanks for the ice cream."

"It was my pleasure." He seemed like he wanted to say more, so I paused before walking away. "Well, I guess I'll see you around then," he said.

"Yeah, maybe."

"Do you hang out here often?"

I tried to ignore the butterflies flapping around my stomach. I didn't have much experience with the opposite sex, so this was all new to me. I couldn't figure out if he was interested or if he was just being polite because I was so awkward.

"I'm kind of new around here, so I haven't got any regular hangouts yet," I said.

"Oh, right. Makes sense."

"But I may be checking out more of the area, to take pictures," I said. "Is the campus pretty at Hamilton University? I love scenery shots."

Connor's expression brightened. "Yeah, it's beautiful. I did my undergrad there. I'm taking a couple of summer classes, so I spend a lot of time in the library."

I nodded and felt myself grinning. "I may have to check it out sometime."

He nodded and laughed a little. "This is turning out badly. If you haven't figured it out yet, I'm trying to ask to see you again."

I felt my heartbeat speed up, and I ducked my head to focus on digging in my purse for a piece of paper and a pen. I opened my wallet, thinking I could grab a receipt or something to write on. A small slip of paper fluttered out, and Connor caught it before it blew away. He glanced at it before handing it back to me.

"Don't want to lose this, it looks important," he said.

It was Monica's information, the girl from the plane ride. "Oh yeah," I said, tucking it back into my wallet. I took another paper out, checking it over. It was a receipt from a magazine stand at the La Guardia airport. Turning it over, I wrote my name and number, then handed it to Connor. His hand was large and warm as he took it from me.

"I need to get going," I said, and he nodded.

"I'll see you later then."

I stifled a giggle and walked away. After about a dozen steps, I dared to look over my shoulder, and Connor was still standing there. He waved at me.

I was back in Hamilton Green before I stopped smiling.

* * *

"You're up early."

I looked up from my bowl of Cheerios to see Mom coming into the kitchen. She was dressed in jeans and a sweatshirt, and she pulled her hair back into a ponytail before she started filling the coffeemaker with water.

"Trouble sleeping?"

"No, I'm usually awake early. I think it's a result of trying to catch Dad before he left for work."

"And how often were you successful?"

"Not too often," I said, laughing a little.

"Don't feel bad. I didn't have much luck with that either."

She finished with the coffeemaker and came over to sit next to me. "How are you doing with that? I mean, your dad. I know there hasn't been any news…"

I swirled my spoon around the bowl, watching the Cheerios chase each other in a circle. "I miss him a lot. I didn't think anything was going on. He didn't talk to me too much about work, but I would have hoped he'd told me if he was in any kind of trouble. It's just such a shock."

She nodded and patted my hand. "Take all the time you need. We're all here for you."

We sat quietly for a few moments, until the coffee started to drip. She got up to pour herself a cup.

"Mom, what do you think I should do about the apartment?" I asked. "And the business? I know I have some time to think about it, but I don't have a clue as to what I would need to do to keep it going. Grandpa said he'd help, but I know he enjoyed being retired, and I don't want to burden him."

"Well, I doubt your grandfather will let you fail. If there's one thing I know about him, he always keeps his word. As for the apartment, your dad may return soon.

And, well, if not," she paused, mulling over her words, "you always wanted to attend college in New York. If you still decide to do that, you can use the apartment, or you can sell it when you're ready. There's no law that says you need to take care of everything at once." She stirred cream and sugar into her coffee and came back to the table. "What I don't want you to do is make any decisions without thinking them through first. You're a smart girl, Aubrey. Keep your options open."

We changed the topic of conversation to school and getting ready for my first day. Paul had no problem with me tagging along with him. I told him that once I had a car, we could switch back and forth.

"So what do you think of Paul?" Mom asked. She sounded casual, but I could hear the hint of motherly curiosity in her voice.

"He's a nice guy," I said.

"Yeah? That's good."

I half-smiled at her. This was new for me. Dad hadn't shown much interest in my love-life, except to tell me to be careful of people who weren't up front and honest about their intentions, and I'd never had a love-life anyway. I knew lots of students at school that were boys, and while I had no trouble talking to them, none of them were interesting enough for me to consider dating.

"Paul's a friend, Mom, and anyway, I don't want to get clingy with the first guy that talks to me here," I said, shrugging. "You never know who else I'll run into."

She studied me then, and her eyes crinkled in the corners as she put the pieces together.

"All right, who is he?" she asked. "Where did you meet him? Somewhere in the neighborhood? The mall?" She gasped and snapped her fingers. "That's it! You met someone at the mall when you went back there."

"It's nothing," I said, getting up and taking my empty cereal bowl to the sink.

"What's his name? Would I know him?"

I rinsed my bowl, trying to drown out my mother's questions. When I turned off the faucet, she was leaning over the breakfast bar, her eyes wide and expectant. I laughed at her expression.

"His name is Connor Davenport. He bought me an ice cream cone, and I gave him my number."

"Has he called yet?"

"Not yet, but it's only been a day. He's taking summer classes at Hamilton University."

"He's a college student?"

"He'll be a first year graduate student."

Her smile faltered a little bit. "He's older then."

I shrugged. "A little. I'm almost eighteen," I reminded her.

"I know, sweetheart, but college boys are different, more experienced."

"I'm not going to sleep with him on the first date," I said, and her cheeks darkened with embarrassment. "He hasn't even called me yet."

"I know you wouldn't," she said. "I just want you to be careful, that's all."

"And not make any decisions without thinking them through first," I said, echoing her statement from earlier.

"You are a smart girl," she said with a smile. "So, what do you have planned for today?"

"I'm going to finish unpacking, do a little room decorating."

"Need any help?"

I shook my head. "Not yet."

Mom nodded and picked up her coffee cup. "Then would you mind keeping an eye on Alyssa for a little while? I have some errands to run, and I need to stop at the grocery store. Is there anything special that you want?"

"Peanut butter," I answered without hesitation. "Extra crunchy."

She smiled at me and nodded. "I should have remembered. You always did love peanut butter."

"Still do."

"I'll be sure to pick up some. Alyssa doesn't eat peanut butter, but she sure loves grape jelly."

I made a face at that. "Yuck, jelly."

"What's wrong with jelly?" Alyssa asked, walking into the kitchen. She rubbed her eyes sleepily and yawned. "I'm hungry."

"Would you like a sandwich?" I asked her. "I'll make one for you."

She nodded and sat down at the table. "Grape. Toasted, please, and no crust."

Mom finished her coffee and prepared to leave. She kissed Alyssa's jelly smeared face and said to me, "Call me if you need anything."

"I'm going to help Aubrey with her room," Alyssa declared proudly.

I grinned. "Sure thing."

Mom's happiness was evident as she left the house. She was glad that her two daughters were getting along, and I had to admit, fitting into this family was happening a lot easier than I'd expected. Aside from the unexplained origins of Alyssa's abilities, everything was pretty normal in Hamilton Green, and for the first time, I felt like I might be okay. The only thing that would make my life even better was if my dad showed up on my doorstep, safe and sound.

Alyssa finished her breakfast, and then she hurried up to her room to get dressed. She met me in my room a few minutes later and asked to play some music. I let her pick what we were going to listen to, surprised when she selected an Irish singing group. Again, I commented on how she knew them.

"Dad listens to everything," she reminded me. "He thinks that music is inspiring."

"I agree."

We continued to unpack my belongings, and I hung up some pictures. Alyssa sat on the bed and flipped through one of my portfolios and stopped at a portrait of a sunset that I had taken while in the desert outside of Las Vegas. It was during one of my trips with Dad.

"This is beautiful," she said in awe. "It's just the way I'd imagine a perfect sunset."

"Thank you," I said. "Would you like it?"

She looked up at me in surprise. "Really?"

"Sure. I can have it matted and framed for you. We could hang it in your room."

"I would like that very much," she said.

The phone rang then, and I reached over to grab it from the desk.

"It's Paul," Alyssa said, her face brightening.

Puzzled, I answered it, only half shocked that it was Paul calling.

"Wanna go for a walk? I could show you some more of the neighborhood."

I glanced over at Alyssa. She was still thumbing through the portfolio, but from the way her head was tilted, I could tell she was listening.

"I'm watching Alyssa," I said. "Mom went out to run some errands."

"Well, bring her along," Paul said. "We can go to the park, climb the jungle gym or swing."

"I haven't been on a swing in years."

"You're missing out then!"

I laughed. Paul's exuberance was contagious. I turned to Alyssa.

"I like the park," she said.

"All right, we'll be outside in ten," I said to Paul.

We rushed to put on our shoes, and I sent Mom a text message, letting her know we were with Paul. I grabbed my camera, and then we stood on the porch and waited for him to arrive. Alyssa spotted him first. He was hurrying along, sprinting a couple of steps, then slowing to a brisk walk, then sprinting again. He was also messing with his hair and straightening the collar of his shirt. It was almost like he was trying not to appear too eager, and I found it cute. He raised his head, saw us watching, and even from the end of the driveway, I could see the blush coloring his cheeks.

"The park isn't far," he said as we joined him on the sidewalk.

Alyssa walked between us, clutching my hand. The sun was shining, and it was just too pretty to stay cooped up inside.

"So did you get everything you needed at the mall? I saw on the news there was some weird gust of wind in the food court. They think it was a faulty vent or something."

I wanted to tell him about what happened with Alyssa. Of course, I couldn't, so instead I told him that I'd gotten some things and was planning to get some pictures developed and framed to decorate my bedroom.

"I'd love to get some new scenery shots," I said, motioning to my camera. I lifted it and aimed it at Paul.

He stopped and ducked behind Alyssa, who giggled and released my hand. I snapped a couple of pictures.

We reached the park and went right to the swings. Alyssa hopped on one, and Paul gave her a push. I kept taking pictures, capturing the pure joy on my sister's face as she closed her eyes and smiled toward the sun. Through the lens of my camera, I caught movement off to the side, and I turned to follow it. A black car was moving slowly along the street. The windows were tinted, so I couldn't see who was inside the car, and there was something about it that didn't sit well with me. I clicked off a couple of pictures, then lowered the camera. The car sped up and disappeared around the corner.

"What's up?" Paul asked, coming up beside me. He was out of breath, and Alyssa was hanging off his back, her arms wrapped around his neck.

I frowned and shook my head. "Nothing. Thought I saw something." I shrugged it off, chastising myself for being so paranoid, and said, "Race you to the slides," and took off running.

We stayed at the park for another hour, and I didn't see the black car again. I kept my eyes open for it as we walked back to our house, wondering if I was worrying for nothing. Mom's van was parked in the driveway, and she was pulling groceries from the back as we approached.

"Hello, Paul," she said. "How are you?"

"Just great, ma'am. Here, let me help you with these."

He grabbed several bags and took them inside, setting them on the counter. Alyssa and I began unpacking everything.

"Would you like to stay for lunch?" I asked, then turned to Mom. "If that's okay."

She nodded. "Of course."

"Spaghetti!" Alyssa said loudly. "Can we have spaghetti?"

"Sure," Mom said. She pulled a large pot from the cupboard and started filling it with water. She spotted my camera sitting on the counter and asked if I'd been taking pictures.

"Some. I kind of stopped for a bit after, well, Dad," I said. "I've started up again though."

"Do you do digital or old school?" Paul asked.

"I can do both, but I've been focusing on digital photos. I have a great computer, printer and software for the digital shots. I just haven't set anything up yet. I'm not sure where I'd put it all anyway. It takes up a lot of space."

Mom put the pot on the stove and turned on the burner. "Eric and I were talking about that just last night. There's a room in the basement that we use for storage, decorations and odds and ends. We thought that if you'd like it, we could clear it out and turn it into a studio for you."

"Wow, that's incredible," I said. "Yes, I would love that! Thank you so much!"

I was so excited at the thought of my own studio, I barely paid attention to the conversation going on around me over lunch. Dad had bought me all of the equipment and said I could convert one of the rooms in our apartment whenever I wanted to. I never got around to it, and besides, I had access to a fantastic studio at Radcliffe.

Paul and I cleaned up the dishes, and then Paul said he should get going. I walked him to the door, then to the end of the driveway. He had his hands in the pockets of his jeans, and he was kicking at pebbles on the cement.

"Aubrey, um, I was wondering, if, um," he said, tripping over his words. He took a deep breath and sighed. "Shoot. Nevermind. I'll see you around."

"I was thinking of heading over to the university tomorrow afternoon," I said, "to take some pictures. Would you want to go with me?"

Paul's face lit up at my invitation. "Sure. I can drive us. What time were you thinking?"

"Around one or so? Mom's working with Alyssa to put together a mural in her room, so I figured I'd do a little exploring."

"Cool. I'll swing by and pick you up. See you, Aubrey."

A part of me felt a little guilty. I could tell that Paul liked me, and I liked him too, just not romantically. He was a terrific guy, but I would be lying to myself if I didn't admit that I was curious about Connor, and I was hoping to run into him again.

Alyssa was waiting for me when I went back inside, standing at the bottom of the stairs, her hands on her hips. She was glaring at me, and I jerked back, startled at her expression.

"Is something wrong?" I asked her.

She gave me a scowl of disapproval. "You need to be careful," she said, and then she turned and stomped up the stairs.

Chapter Six

Alyssa was upset with me the rest of the day, and she didn't speak to me the next morning either. My blue poppy anemone had wilted, a sure sign that I was in deep trouble of some kind. Mom asked me what was up, but I didn't know. I was still trying to figure it out when Paul picked me up at one o'clock.

"What's got you all grumpy today?" he asked, his normal smile replaced by a frown the instant he saw me.

I buckled my seatbelt and put my camera bag between my feet. "Alyssa's mad at me, and I don't know why."

"Did she want to come along?"

I shook my head. "No. She wanted to hang out with Mom today." I shrugged it off. "Let's go. I want to take full advantage of the light."

Paul drove us to the campus of Hamilton University. I had visited colleges before with my dad and my grandfather. There had been speculation since the day I was born about where I would attend college and what I would do with my life. Even though I'd traveled across the country and through Europe and Asia, I still had no idea where I wanted to go for sure. Especially now because I felt like I should take over my father's business. But my heart was still set on someplace with an excellent photography program.

"So tell me about yourself," Paul said.

He'd parked in the visitor lot near the visual arts studio, and we were walking across the large expanse of lush, green lawn. I was busily snapping pictures of the old buildings and thinking about printing some in black and white rather than color.

"That's an odd question," I answered. "Haven't you known me for a few days?"

"That's exactly right. Just a few days."

"What else do you want to know?"

"I'm not sure," Paul said, laughing. "If I said your hopes, dreams and fears, would you think I was corny?"

I nudged him in the side with my elbow. "Not at all." I paused to focus and shoot a picture of some students tossing a football in the quad. "I hope to make it through my senior year without too much trouble. I dream of being a successful photojournalist, and I fear..."

My voice trailed off as I realized what I really feared. I feared that my father was never coming back, and I would never know what had happened to him. I feared that something bad would happen to Alyssa if she were ever found. I could talk to Paul about my father, but not about Alyssa. He wouldn't understand, and I didn't want to freak him out.

"Aubrey!"

Paul and I turned at the sound of someone calling my name, and I felt a flutter in my stomach as I saw Connor jogging toward us. His eyes were bright as he reached us, and he was smiling. Glancing to my left though, I saw that Paul was not.

"What are you doing here?" Connor asked. "I'm sorry I haven't called you. I had a huge paper due." He turned to Paul and nodded. "Hi. I'm Connor."

He extended his hand, and Paul reluctantly shook it. "Paul Nesca. I live down the street from Aubrey." He looked from Connor to me, then back to Conner. "So, uh, you two know each other?"

"We met the other day," Connor said, "at the mall. We shared an ice cream cone."

"I had my own," I explained. "Ice cream, I mean. I had my own cone."

There was tension rising up between the boys, and I didn't want to be a part of it, even though I knew it existed because of me.

"Would you like a tour of the campus?" Connor asked. He was trying to be polite, while sizing up the competition at the same time.

"I was thinking of getting some brochures," I said, nodding. "I'm curious about the undergraduate programs."

"Sure thing. I can take you to the admissions building."

Paul stood up straighter and said, "I know where it is. I can take her." He put his hand on my elbow and started steering me in the opposite direction.

Connor's smile faltered a bit, and he raised a brow. "No problem. I need to get to my next class anyway. I'll see you around, Aubrey."

I could only nod. We watched as Connor walked away, shifting his backpack from one side to the other. He glanced over his shoulder at me, and then continued on his way.

In that moment, I understood why Alyssa was annoyed with me. I hadn't said a word to her about Connor, yet somehow she knew.

"I think I should go home," I said, and my voice sounded meek, even to my own ears.

Paul said nothing. We were halfway back to my house before he spoke.

"I'm sorry, Aubrey. I have no right to be jealous and act stupid."

"I'm sorry too," I said. "I didn't mean to *make* you jealous."

"Do you like him?"

I played with the strap of my camera. "He seems like a nice guy," was all I said.

The rest of the ride was uncomfortable, and I felt horrible. When we arrived at my house, I invited Paul to come in and hang out for a while. He declined, saying his mom wasn't feeling well, and he should get back to check on her.

"I'll call you later," he said.

I dragged myself into the house, not surprised to find Alyssa waiting for me in the living room. She was sitting in one of the armchairs, a book on advanced physics open in her lap. She acknowledged me with a shake of her head when I came inside.

"I warned you," she said, and then went back to reading her book.

I dropped my bag on the sofa and sat down. "How did you know? I never told you I met another boy."

Without lifting her eyes from the book, she said, "I just knew. I like Paul."

"You've never met Connor," I countered.

"True. So it is rather unfair of me to form an opinion of him. However," she said, "he is a stranger."

"Did you kill my poppy?"

She stared at me in horror. "Not on purpose! I just felt kind of sad, and it wilted. Don't worry though, because I can fix it."

For the second time in one day, I felt a stab of guilt, as I realized I'd spoken rather harshly to Alyssa. I needed to remember that even though she was a very intelligent and seemingly mature girl, she was also only eight years old and didn't have much experience with people.

"I'm sorry," I said. "How about we go upstairs and take a look at it?"

She closed her book and placed it on the end table beside the chair. Then she came over to me and grasped my hand. We walked upstairs together, Alyssa running her free hand along the banister and humming under her breath.

"Where's Mom?" I asked.

"She's digging around in the basement, moving Christmas decorations around and sorting through junk."

"Christmas decorations?"

"She's emptying the storage room for your studio."

"Oh, yeah. After we check out the flower, I'll go down and help her."

The flower was still in the pot, drooping sadly over the edge. It was sitting in direct sunlight, which just made it appear sadder. I hung back in the doorway while Alyssa moved toward it, her face serene as she focused on the shrunken petals. Even the color had darkened to an almost inky black. I didn't think there was any way it could possibly recover.

Alyssa ran her fingers over the flower's center, then the petals and stem. She turned the pot a little and stepped back. With her eyes closed, she appeared so small and innocent.

A few seconds passed, and nothing happened. I was about to say something when she opened her eyes, and at that precise moment the flower started to move. Alyssa stared, unblinking, and the flower began to come back to life again. I watched in open-mouthed shock and awe as it regained its color and former beauty. Alyssa half turned and smiled at me, and I exhaled hard.

"That was...amazing," I breathed. "How did you do that?"

"I just stayed calm and concentrated. I pictured how it should look, and I could see all the tiny pieces of soil and the liquid in the pot." She shrugged. "I simply moved them together into the correct formation to reenergize the flower. It should last for a few more days. We can go help Mom now."

I moved aside as she walked out of my room and down the hall. Before I followed her, I had to examine the flower myself. It certainly felt real and alive. I had witnessed Alyssa's power, and it was unbelievable. I set the pot back on the windowsill, moving the curtains aside to allow more light to shine down on it. As I positioned the flower, a black car cruised down the street, and I felt a momentary pang of panic. I froze and ducked down, peering cautiously out the window. The car pulled into a driveway a couple houses away, and I watched four teenage boys get out and start bouncing a basketball in the driveway. I laughed a little at my paranoia, shook my head and went to join Mom and Alyssa.

* * *

The blue poppy ended up lasting until Saturday. Alyssa offered to fix it again, but I declined. Instead, I decided to press it so I could frame it and keep it as a souvenir. Alyssa helped me with the task, carefully layering a piece of cardboard, newspaper and tissue paper to place the flower on, then adding another before placing a heavy biology book on top of the stack. It would take several days before it would be completely dry, and Alyssa was excited to see the result.

I had talked to Paul a couple of times since our trip to the Hamilton University campus, and while he assured me things wouldn't be weird for us, I still felt like I needed to make it up to him. I had also talked Mom and Eric into letting me contact my dad's private investigator friend about others like Alyssa.

They asked that I take it slow, so I offered just a few details. The PI, Mark O'Donnell, was discreet and one of my dad's trusted friends. In addition to this new task, he was also working for me on a separate job. My grandfather had his army of investigators, and I had mine, albeit a lot smaller. Mark was keeping me informed of any new leads or questions that had to do with my dad.

Buried deep in the bottom of my dresser was a thick folder containing copies of all the police reports and interviews conducted after Dad went missing. I had copies of the background checks of all of our household staff, the people who worked at my school, and every single one of Dad's employees. I flipped through the information every few days, hoping to find something that would give me answers, something that I or the authorities had missed before. So far nothing useful had emerged, and Mark promised to keep digging.

Because of his discretion, and his loyalty to my dad, I knew he was perfect for looking into the mystery of the missing children. He didn't ask unnecessary questions, just took the information I had about the family in Chicago whose little boy had disappeared, and promised to get back to me within a couple of days.

I hadn't seen or heard from Connor, and while I was disappointed, I wondered if maybe it wasn't for the better. After all, he was older, and I had a lot to focus on with my family.

Mom and I had bought some supplies to fix up the basement room for my studio, and we were spending Sunday morning painting the walls a cheery lilac color when Eric came down the steps, talking on his cell phone.

He waved at me, then kissed Mom's cheek and continued talking.

"Sure, sure. I'll be over to help this afternoon. Is there anything that you still need?" he asked. "No problem. See you after lunch." He pocketed the phone and stepped back to admire our handiwork. So far, we had two walls down, two to go. "You've been busy," he said. "It looks great."

"Thanks," I said, dipping my paint roller in the pan and wiping off the excess before applying it to the wall.

"Is something wrong?" Mom asked. "Something at the office?" She wiped at her nose, leaving a small trail of paint behind. Eric and I laughed, and I passed her a rag.

"That was Len Morris," Eric said. "The construction of the float is taking longer than they thought it would, so they're asking for more help. I told him I'd throw in a couple extra hours."

"Float?" I asked.

"For the Fourth of July parade," Mom explained. "The neighborhood is entering one, and Len is housing it in his garage."

"Hey, maybe you'd like to join in," Eric said to me. "You could meet some more people."

I nodded. "Sure, sounds like fun. I've never worked on a parade float before."

"Excellent!"

"I think I'll stay here with Alyssa," Mom said. "She wants to make cookies today."

Eric nodded. "That sounds like fun. I'm going to take my jog now, sweetie. Be back soon." He kissed my mom again before going back up to the kitchen. We heard the back door close as he left the house.

"He takes his running very seriously," Mom said, grinning. "He's tried to get me to go with him, but I'm just too darn lazy."

I laughed and said, "Me too."

We finished painting the other two walls, and it felt like our arms were going to fall off. I went upstairs to shower and get ready for the day. On the way to my room, I passed Alyssa's. Her door was partially open, and I peeked inside. Alyssa was still sleeping, and she was curled up on her side, facing the door. The comforter was tucked up around her chin, and she looked so peaceful and angelic. I would never have guessed that she possessed special abilities to control the elements.

She must have sensed me nearby, because she opened her eyes and blinked at me. She smiled and waved for me to come into the room. I sat down on the edge of her bed.

"Good morning," she said. "How are you feeling today?"

"Just fine. How about yourself?"

She stretched and sat up. "I feel like today is going to be a good day. Are Mom and Dad up?"

I nodded, and she threw back the covers. "Then I need to get moving. I like to start my day with them." She went to her dresser and began pulling clothes from the drawers. "May I use the bathroom first?"

"Sure. Take your time."

I went back to my room and closed the door. I decided to call Paul to see if he'd be around this afternoon to work on the parade float. He answered on the first ring.

"I'll probably be able to come over, just not right away," he said, and he sounded kind of down.

"Are you okay?" I asked, hoping it wasn't because of me.

"My dad called."

"Oh. Isn't that a good thing?"

"Not when he makes my mom cry."

"I'm sorry, Paul."

He was quiet for a little while, and I wasn't sure if I should keep talking.

"Anyway, enough about me," he said, forcing himself to be upbeat. "The float is at Len Morris's house, right?"

"Yeah, I'm pretty sure that's what Eric said."

We talked for a few more minutes, but I could tell he was distracted. He said he'd try and make it over to help with the float, if his mom was feeling better.

I felt a little down myself after we hung up. I'd only met his mom once, and she seemed so nice. I hated to think that she was upset over her ex-husband. I dug around in the desk drawer for one of my photo portfolios, searching for a specific one. A couple of summers before, I had taken a month long trip with Dad to Italy. He was there on business, and I tagged along. I studied the art museums and the architecture, and I must have taken at least a couple thousand pictures.

When I got back, I chose one hundred of the best ones for editing. The one that I was looking for was of a seaside cliff. It was a spot that represented hope for the locals and inspired them to always be on the lookout for the upside to things, no matter how bleak the situation. I wanted to enlarge it and frame it for Paul's mother.

"She'll like that," Alyssa said, stepping into my room.

I yelped and jumped, spinning around. "You've got to stop doing that," I gasped.

"Sorry," she said, shrugging. She was wearing her bathrobe, and a pink towel was wrapped around her head.

"How did you know what I was thinking? Can you read minds?"

"Not exactly," she said. "It's more like I can sense things, ideas and feelings. I don't quite know what to make of it yet, and I don't know how to control it." She came over to look at the picture. "That's beautiful, Aubrey."

Then she left my room as quietly as she'd entered.

Chapter Seven

Eric and I said goodbye to Mom and Alyssa. They were elbow deep in baking flour and food coloring, making sugar cookies in the shape of American flags and patriotic stars. We headed out toward Len Morris's house, a few blocks away. As we walked, I realized this was the first time I'd ever been alone with Eric, and I suddenly felt unsure of myself. I'd never thought of him as my step-father. He was always just the guy my mom had married, Alyssa's dad. Just...Eric. I didn't really know him at all.

"So, aside from the incident at the mall and learning some interesting things about your sister, how are you doing here?" he asked me.

"I'm adjusting. It's a nice town, and I'm excited to start school."

We walked another block before Eric spoke again. "You know, under different circumstances, we would have loved to have you visit more often, or even to come live with us. But your mom wanted you to have as normal a life as possible with your dad. She missed you though."

I stared at my feet as we walked. "I know she did. For a long time, I was angry with her for moving so far away. I think I was too stubborn to admit that I missed her. I understand she and my dad weren't compatible, and it might have just been worse if she'd stayed nearby."

"I know that I'll never take his place," Eric said, "and I don't want to. I do want you to know that I'm here for you, with whatever you need."

I looked up at him then, saw the compassion and kindness in his eyes, and I knew that I could trust him with my life. "Thank you," I said, and I meant it. "So…what do you like to do for fun besides jog three miles a day?"

He laughed, and we chatted about hobbies and found out that we did have some things in common. He loved music and books, and he was fascinated with making the world a better place with the help of science. When we arrived at the Morris house, Len hurried out of the garage to greet us. He introduced himself to me and everyone else that was there, and then showed us the float.

"We need 200 more of these stars," he said, holding up a cardboard star covered in aluminum foil.

"How many do we have so far?" Eric asked.

Len grimaced and said, "Twenty."

Eric and I exchanged glances and got to work. After several minutes, and five mangled stars, Eric gave up and went to help paint the wooden sides of the float.

"I can mix samples in a Petri dish with an eye dropper, but I'm all thumbs at arts and crafts," he said with a laugh.

He offered to bring me back some lemonade. Not long after Eric left, I noticed a pretty girl with short black hair and glasses had come over and was standing nervously across the table from me.

"Hi. You're Aubrey, right?"

I nodded and continued wrapping the cardboard stars with aluminum foil.

"I'm Charlotte Taylor. I live a few blocks over from your parents." She fiddled with the streamers in her hands and moved a few steps closer. "I just got back into town a couple of days ago. I was visiting some family in Oregon, cousins and such, so I didn't know you were here already. I didn't think you were coming until later in the summer."

"Oh, well, plans got changed a little," I said.

"Sure, sure. That happens. Ours did too. We were supposed to have gone to Oregon two weeks earlier, but then my mom got sick and we had to postpone."

I looked at this girl and thought about how the kids at Radcliffe would have given her a once over and dismissed her as someone they wouldn't want to associate with. To be honest, I would have as well. Now I was determined to change and not be so judgmental. So far, it was working with Mom, Eric, and Alyssa.

"Your family is really well liked in this town," Charlotte continued. "Your mom and dad are so nice, and they volunteer for every committee there is."

"Well, Eric is my step-dad," I said lightly, and she gasped, dropping the streamers and covering her mouth with both hands.

"I am so sorry, I totally forgot about your dad. Please, I didn't mean to be insensitive."

"Don't worry about it. It's okay. Eric is a great guy."

Charlotte giggled and blushed. "Yeah, he's so nice, and good-looking too."

I paused for a moment when she said that. "I guess I never really thought about him that way."

"Geez, that was stupid of me to say," she said, shaking her head. "I mean, duh, he's your step-dad. Ew, right? But you've got to know that every woman in town thinks he's attractive. Your mom is lucky. Not that she's unattractive or anything. She's so beautiful. Was she really a model in New York City?"

"Yeah, for a little while."

"Why did she quit?" Charlotte asked, then she shook herself and her eyes went wide. "I'm sorry, I don't mean to be so rude. It's none of my business. I'll shut up now." She started cutting the streamers apart to make little tails for the stars.

"It's okay," I said. "Mom wanted to stay home and take care of me. She thought it was more important at the time to be a mother rather than a model."

"That's so cool that she loves you so much."

I nodded then, smiling. "Yeah, very cool."

At three, we ran out of supplies, so Eric and some of the others offered to run out to get more. I asked Charlotte if she'd like to go back to my house to hang out for a little while and get a snack. Her answer was immediate and excited, and I got the impression that she didn't have many friends.

Mom had left a note on the fridge that she and Alyssa were at the park and to help ourselves to the cookies. I poured two glasses of lemonade, and we sat at the kitchen table and chatted some more about the parade, the float, and others in the neighborhood that I might know. She and Paul had grown up together, and she thought he was a great guy.

I liked Charlotte. She was bubbly and talked fast, but she was real. Unlike some of the people I'd known back in New York, she wasn't out to be something she wasn't, and she didn't seem to care what other people thought about her.

"So are you nervous about starting a new school your senior year?" she asked me.

I swallowed my cookie and shrugged. "A little, but I have a couple of friends now, you and Paul, so I'm not totally alone, right?"

She beamed at my calling her a friend and took another cookie. The sound of a car in the driveway caught our attention, and through the kitchen window I saw Eric's SUV.

He spotted us as he came in the side door and smiled as he set several bags on the table. "Thought you'd be here. Hello, Charlotte. How was Oregon? Is your family doing well?"

Charlotte blushed to the roots of her hair and ducked her head, mumbling something unintelligible. I stifled a giggle and took a drink of my lemonade. I had forgotten about her self-proclaimed crush on Eric.

"How's the float coming?" he asked. "I hope I got enough stuff."

"It's looking good," I said. "Did you get some more blue crepe paper?"

Eric dug around in one of the bags, pulled out two rolls and tossed one toward each of us. I caught mine with ease. Charlotte fumbled hers. The crepe paper, along with her cookie, went flying to the floor. I didn't think she could turn any redder as she dropped down to her knees to pick up the crumbs. Eric got the dust pan and broom and swept everything up. Charlotte babbled her apologies and then looked at me like she wanted to die before running toward the bathroom. We heard the door slam shut.

"Is she all right?" Eric asked as he dumped the crumbs into the trash bin.

I grinned and gave him a playful punch on the arm. "She thinks you're hot," I said.

It was Eric's turn to fumble as he dropped the dust pan. It hit the floor with a clang and he hurried to pick it up.

"Uh, what?"

I laughed and went to check on Charlotte.

"I'll just take this stuff back to Len's place," Eric called after me.

I knocked on the door to the bathroom. "Charlotte, are you okay?" I asked.

"I am such a dingbat," she moaned. I waited until she cracked open the door and peered out at me. "You must think I'm such a loser."

"No, I don't think you're a loser," I said, nodding reassuringly at her. "I used to feel the same way about one of my friend's dad, too. I was a real klutz whenever he picked us up from school. Very embarrassing."

She gave me a small smile. "I know you're just saying that to make me feel better. Thank you."

"Wanna head back and work some more on the float? I was going to call Paul and see if he could join us."

Paul said his mom had decided to go out with some friends for the afternoon, so he would meet us at the corner and we could all walk together. He gave Charlotte a friendly hug and asked, "How was your family vacation?"

"Fantastic!" she said, and she began sharing all the details. I listened and laughed along as she told us about the horseback ride she went on that got out of hand when the horse got spooked. As we crossed Burrows Street, I got the unsettling feeling that we were being watched. I did a cursory glance around and spotted two men in dark suits sitting in a parked black luxury sedan with the windows rolled down. It was the same make and model as the one I'd seen at the park that day with Paul and Alyssa. It caught my attention because all of the other cars on the street were family vehicles, and no one was wearing a suit because of the warm summer weather.

I slowed down and turned slightly to get a better look. It was then the car pulled away from the curb. It started toward us, and as it passed, the passenger lowered his shades and his eyes locked with mine. The look sent a chill down my spine, and it flustered me enough that I forgot to check the license plate.

"Hey, are you okay?" Paul asked me, touching my arm.

I jerked away in alarm and swallowed the sudden lump in my throat. "Did you two see that car?"

"What car?" Charlotte asked, looking up and down the street.

"Nevermind," I said. "Let's just go. They're probably waiting for us."

"You're shaking," Paul said. "What's wrong?"

"Nothing," I said, trying to sound convincing. I knew he didn't believe me, but he didn't question me further.

I pulled Eric aside as soon as I saw him and let him know.

"It's not the first time either," I said, keeping my voice low. I saw the fear flash across his face, and his gaze darted around suspiciously as I told him about the park. I was positive it was the same car.

"When is your PI friend supposed to get back to you?"

"Tuesday."

Eric's jaw twitched and he said, "I think you better call him. Today."

Chapter Eight

I was hiding out in my room, curled up in the space between the bed and the wall with my cell phone pressed to my ear. The doors to the bathroom and the hallway were locked, and I'd turned on some music, just loud enough to cover the sound of my voice. I didn't want anyone to hear my conversation. My hands were shaking as I listened to the voicemail message play for Mark O'Donnell. The message stated that he was unavailable at the moment, and that he would call back as soon as he could. When the beep sounded, I babbled something about needing to speak with him right away, regardless of what he'd found out so far.

Before I ended the call, Mark picked up. He sounded tired, but happy to hear from me. He was always pleasant to me, and I knew that Dad had the utmost respect for him. I hadn't seen him since before I'd left New York, and any new information he'd found about Dad had been sent to me via secure email.

"Aubrey, I'm sorry, I don't have much at the moment," he said. "I'm waiting to get some records from the Joliet PD."

"What do you have?" I asked. "I'll take what I can get right now."

"Is something wrong?"

"Not yet," I said, and he left it at that.

"Are you at your computer? I'll email you the file."

I opened what he sent me, browsing through the three pages. Nothing significant jumped out at me. He'd gotten a short family history, educational backgrounds of the parents and the oldest daughter, and an abbreviated copy of the official police report detailing the boy's alleged abduction.

"Will you call me the second you get anything else?"

He promised me he would, and then I clicked off the cell phone. What he had sent me wasn't much more than Mom and Eric were able to discover on their own, but I was confident in his abilities.

The family's surname was Mason, and the parents were Jeffrey and Amelia Mason. Jeffrey was a freelance writer, and Amelia was a stay-at-home mom. Their oldest daughter was Emily, and their son was Travis. The children were thirteen and eight at the time of the disappearance. They had lived in Joliet, just forty miles outside of Chicago, and Jeffrey and Amelia had been lifelong residents. They were high school sweethearts with lots of family connections in the surrounding areas.

Three weeks after Travis went missing, his parents and sister disappeared.

I fought back the fear I felt rising, and I let the frustration through instead. How was it possible for an entire family to go missing without a trace? Could there be a connection between Travis and Alyssa? And was there some kind of group hunting down kids with special abilities?

A gentle knock on my door startled me, and I closed the lid of my laptop with a snap. Eric was in the hallway, and I let him inside the room.

"I talked to your mother," he said. "She's keeping pretty calm."

"Did you tell Alyssa?"

He shook his head. "She already senses something's up."

I watched as Eric circled my room, taking in all of my stuff, and I followed his gaze. A few weeks ago, this had been a spare bedroom. Now it was filled with my books, my clothes, belongings I'd brought with me from New York City, and some new things that I'd gotten here. I was comfortable, and Eric saw that.

"Were you able to get in touch with your PI friend?" he asked.

I nodded and showed him the information Mark had sent. He sat down at my desk and took his time reading through it all.

"Do you think the age has anything to do with it?" he asked.

"What do you mean?"

"The other families that we found with similar situations," he said. "Those children were around the same age as Alyssa, seven or eight."

I sat down on the bed and stared at the ceiling. "I'll see if Mark can find out any info on those other families. Maybe no one has made the connection yet because they're all from different areas."

Eric stood up and stretched. "I think it would be a good idea to keep Alyssa close to home for the next few days," he said. "And your mother and I will speak with the police regarding the car."

"Do you think that'll help?"

"I won't go into detail," Eric explained. "But we should make them aware in case…"

His voice trailed off, and I didn't finish his thought out loud.

* * *

My photo studio was complete, and I was ready to use it. I had taken several hundred pictures since my arrival in Hamilton Green, and I wanted to hang new pictures and also give some to Mom and Alyssa. My poppy was dried and Alyssa helped me to frame it. I hung it proudly above my bed. I'd never had much love for flowers before. Dad used to buy me roses for my birthday and other special occasions, so I just believed that was my favorite flower. The poppy was so vibrant, even dried, and the fact that it came from my sister made it incredibly special to me.

We hadn't seen the black car again, or noticed anything else suspicious. Alyssa shared with me more of her talents, not just in making things grow, but also in her ability to light candles without matches, and cause small rain showers in the neighborhood. Mom and Eric showed me how they worked with Alyssa to control her abilities. As long as she could concentrate fully and without interruption, she was able to keep everything from going too far.

Mark got back to me with some more information a few days later. He'd compiled a list of children who'd gone missing in the past ten years who were under the age of nine, and whose families had also disappeared. He emailed me his reports and faxed me copies of all of the police records from Joliet regarding Travis Mason, including a color photograph. His bright smile reminded me a lot of Alyssa. The little boy disappeared from his bedroom sometime between midnight and 3am on September 20. He was last seen by his mother before she went to bed that evening. His sister, Emily, was the one who noticed he was gone when she woke from a bad dream. She went to check on him, and his bedroom was empty. The police were called immediately, and an investigation ensued. There was no sign of forced entry to the house, and all of the doors and windows were locked except for the one in Travis's room. It was cracked open with the screen removed. There were no reports of any strange activity in the neighborhood that night, and suspicion eventually fell on the parents.

The police investigated the Mason's claims of being followed. Nothing came of it. After the family disappeared, another investigation was launched, and nothing came of that either. Mark wrote in his email that he had a lead in the Miami area, and he was off to track it down. He would keep me updated if he found out anything.

I shared all of this with Eric and Mom as well. The missing children were from across the country, seven total. Their families were all normal, working class, and with clean records. Mark had conducted interviews with friends and extended family members and found they all had the same thing to say: the children had been a little different, yet friendly and very bright. The parents had all seemed overprotective and overcautious. Perhaps they'd had reason to be.

"He works fast," Eric said, impressed.

"I told you he was good," I said.

Connor called, and to say that I was surprised would have been an understatement. I figured that after our uncomfortable encounter at the university campus he wouldn't want anything to do with me, but he proved me wrong. We talked frequently after that, sometimes spending a couple of hours on the phone, chatting about everything and nothing at the same time. I wondered if he was ever going to ask me out; then I wondered if I should just ask him out. Even though it was so easy to talk to him on the phone, the thought of spending time with him in person set my nerves on edge. During one conversation with Connor, Alyssa kept creeping past my open bedroom door, peering inside every few minutes and grinning, so I finally pushed the door shut. It didn't latch, and she shocked me by using a gust of wind to open it again. Then she ran away giggling.

Chapter Nine

"Are you sure about this?" I asked, uncertainty filling my voice.

Paul shielded his eyes with his hand and stared up at the Gateway Arch. It gleamed in the sunlight, casting paths of light and shadow across the park. Tourists crowded near the entrances, preparing to go inside and take the trams to the top, 630 feet above ground. This had seemed like a good idea when Paul suggested it. However, now standing near one of the legs of the Arch, I was having second thoughts.

"Are you afraid of heights?" Paul asked, turning his attention away from the structure and focusing on me.

I shrugged. "I didn't think so. I mean, our apartment in New York is pretty high, and I fly all the time. This just looks...unsafe," I said.

Paul laughed and poked me in the arm. "It's completely safe. There hasn't been an accident for, oh, I'd say at least a couple of days."

I punched him back. "Not funny."

Alyssa, who was standing between us, stared up at the top. "The most notable accident was in 1980," she said, "when a gentleman tried to parachute onto it early in the morning."

"I didn't know that. What happened to him?" Paul asked.

"He died," Alyssa answered matter-of-factly. "Can we go in now?"

We exchanged glances, blinking in surprise at the way she had explained this terrible accident. Paul led the way inside the south leg and purchased three tickets. After a short wait, we were seated inside an egg shaped car that would transport us to the top.

"Excuse me," I asked the attendant, "how long does the ride take?"

"About four minutes," the woman said. She must have noticed I appeared a bit anxious and added, "It's a relatively smooth ride. You'll be there in no time."

Then the little door closed and we were alone inside the car. I took in my close surroundings, trying to ignore the sudden feeling of claustrophobia that was gripping my insides and making my head spin. While Alyssa and Paul stared through the small window at the inside of the Arch's leg as we rose to the top, I kept my eyes closed and tried to remember to breathe.

Paul had stopped by to hang out, looking for something to do. He asked me if I'd ever been to the Arch; I said I hadn't, and then Alyssa expressed her desire to go too. She'd never been either, and Paul thought this was just a travesty. She had to beg my mother to let her go, and finally she relented after a lengthy phone conversation with Eric. Then we loaded into Paul's car and headed out. Mom pulled me aside before we left, telling me to keep a watchful eye on my sister. She explained that the reason they'd never taken her was because of the crowd and the enclosed space. They weren't sure how she would react. I promised to watch her, and I had my cell phone with me in case there was an emergency.

I knew Mom was nervous, but I felt that it was important for Alyssa to go out and experience the same things other kids did. She had special abilities, sure, and those abilities could be the cause for those other children being taken. However, from what Mark had found out, those other children had been very sheltered, kind of like what Mom and Eric were doing with Alyssa. It stood to reason that if she were treated like everyone else, she wouldn't be as noticeable. Mom and Eric didn't like my logic, but they didn't argue against it either.

The tram car slowed to a smooth stop, and the doors opened. We stepped out and walked up several stairs into a narrow area no wider than a hallway with a slightly sloped floor. On either side were sixteen rectangular shaped windows. Alyssa immediately ran to one, standing on tiptoe to see out. Paul lifted her so she could see without hindrance. It was a clear day, and looking out to the West we had a spectacular view of downtown St. Louis. To the East was the Mississippi River. I took a lot of pictures of the scenery, until Paul took my camera and insisted on taking some shots of me with Alyssa.

Laughing, we posed together for serious and silly pictures. I couldn't wait to print them. As Paul was handing me back my camera, another tram had arrived with its passengers. A group of about thirty children and adults spilled into the observation deck, the children running for the windows, screaming and squealing. Alyssa grabbed my hand with both of hers, and I felt her tremble.

"Are you all right?" I asked her.

She inhaled slowly and held it, her eyes large, her lower lip twitching ever so slightly. She exhaled, her breath coming out in a quiet whoosh, and then she nodded.

"Can we go please?"

"Sure thing." I caught Paul's attention and told him Alyssa wasn't feeling well.

We had started toward the elevators when two young boys bolted in front of us, crossing from one side of the observation deck to the other. One of them bumped into Alyssa's shoulder, spinning her, not quite knocking her over. The boy looked at Alyssa and sneered.

"Watch it, weirdo," he said.

"Hey, you watch it," Paul said, his voice deeper than usual. He stooped to check on Alyssa, who was standing stone still, staring at the boy. He jerked back a little when he saw her expression.

I saw it too. Her eyes were open and staring straight ahead, but it didn't appear as though she were seeing anything. She was breathing fast, too fast, I noticed, and I wondered if she was having a panic attack.

"Let's go," I said to Paul.

We took two more steps, each of us holding Alyssa's hands, guiding her away from the people.

"What the heck?" someone behind me exclaimed.

I threw a glance over my shoulder. A couple was staring, openmouthed, through the window in front of them. I turned to my right and did a double take. Just minutes before, the sun had been shining bright, and there wasn't a cloud in the sky. Now, the clouds were rolling in fast, and the sky was turning blacker with each passing second. A streak of lightning flashed, followed by a crack of thunder so loud that several people covered their ears.

"Please remain calm," a park ranger announced. "Lightning strikes the Arch several times a year, and there is no danger."

Wind came next, a howling sound that rose to a fevered pitch. And then, the floor beneath my feet trembled. I thought I had imagined it, until I saw the startled expressions on the faces of everyone else.

"Ladies and gentleman, please remain calm," the park ranger said again. "The Arch will only move about an inch in a fifty mile-per-hour wind. I'm sure this is a just a brief storm front passing through."

As soon as the last words were out of the ranger's mouth, I felt the floor move again, and it was definitely more than an inch. A creaking sound rose up around us, and the structure swayed, throwing everyone's balance off. I planted both feet and braced myself as we moved one way, then the other.

The screams were louder than before, as children latched onto their parents, and adults tried to steady themselves against the walls. I fell to one knee and turned Alyssa toward me, cupping her face in my hands and forcing her eyes to meet mine.

"Alyssa, look at me," I said, my voice low and firm. "Focus on me. Breathe slowly."

Paul watched in amazement, his gaze switching from us to the window, and then back again.

"You're all right," I said soothingly, tucking her hair behind her ear. "You're okay."

A few seconds passed, and we stopped swaying. I wanted to check on the outside conditions, but didn't dare break my eye contact with Alyssa. I listened to the startled and relieved gasps around me, taking that as my cue that the weather had returned to normal. Alyssa blinked and fell against me, sobbing.

The park ranger made his way from person to person, and when he reached us, we assured him we were fine. He patted Alyssa's back and said he could understand how a child would be frightened.

"I've never seen anything like it," he said, shaking his head and walking away.

Alyssa had slowed her tears, but she was shaking. I scooped her into my arms and bolted for the elevator ahead of the crowd. We hurried inside the first tram car. The three minute ride down seemed to take three times as long. Alyssa sat in my lap, and I could feel Paul's eyes on me, asking silent questions.

None of us said a word until we were back in Paul's car. Once all the doors were shut, he said, "I think I need an explanation."

I stared out the passenger side window. There was no hint of the storm that had occurred. No clouds or lightning. Just clear blue sky and sunshine.

"Aubrey," Paul said, putting his hand on my leg. "What just happened up there?"

My mouth was dry, and no words came out.

"We can tell him," Alyssa said from the backseat. "We can trust him."

I knew we could; I just didn't know where to start. My cell phone gave a loud, shrilly ring, and I fumbled for it in my purse. I saw it was Mom, and while I didn't really want to answer this call, I knew if I didn't, she'd just freak out even more than she probably already was.

"Aubrey! What happened?"

"Mom, we're okay."

My phone beeped, indicating I had another call coming in. I checked the screen. "Mom, Eric's calling me too."

"I'm not surprised. Where are you?"

"We're in Paul's car. We'll be home soon."

"How is Alyssa? Is she scared?"

I looked back at my sister. She didn't look scared anymore, just tired. "She's fine," I said. "We'll be back soon. I need to answer Eric before he puts out a missing persons report."

I switched lines, only to hear Eric mumbling to himself.

"Eric?" I asked.

"Aubrey, where are you?"

I resisted the urge to roll my eyes. Parents were so predictable. "We're on our way back home." I motioned to Paul to start the car. He did, while still shooting questionable looks at me. "I already talked to Mom. How did you guys find out?"

"It's all over the news. The freak storm out of nowhere, and the Arch moving. I had hoped it wasn't related to Alyssa. What happened?"

"Everyone's okay, no one was hurt. Just call Mom, will you please?"

Eric sighed and said he would. I tucked my phone back in my purse. We were cruising along the highway now. Paul had his hands on the steering wheel, and I could see his knuckles were white.

"Start talking," he said. "Anytime."

"I don't know if I should."

Alyssa cleared her throat. "I can control the elements," she said.

"Uh huh," Paul said, frowning, sounding unsure. "So that was all you up there? You caused the weather to change?"

"I did. I'm not proud of it, but that boy upset me. He called me a weirdo."

"Uh huh," Paul said again. He was quiet until he pulled into our driveway and turned off the car. Alyssa let herself out and went right inside the house. I started to go after her, pausing when I noticed Paul hadn't moved.

"Are you coming in?" I asked.

"Is this for real?"

"Is what for real?"

He waved a hand. "This. You. Your sister. Did I really witness that, or did I imagine it? Maybe I'm still sleeping." He pinched himself, wincing when he felt the pain. "Guess not."

"It's very real."

"Do you have the same abilities?"

I shook my head. "Nope. I'm totally boring."

He smiled, and together we went inside.

"So it seems as though we've added another to the secret circle," Mom said, hugging Paul. "I'm so sorry to bring you into our issues."

"Don't worry about it, Mrs. Vaughn. I've always thought Alyssa was a little different. Not in a bad way," he said quickly. "Just...different. I never would have expected this though."

Mom sat us down to go over what happened. Eric was staying at the office this time. He didn't want to raise suspicion by rushing out again.

"Well, none of the news stations have any cell phone video from the observation deck yet," Mom said, "but there are the security cameras."

I cringed at that. "I have no idea if anyone noticed us or not."

"Let's just hope they didn't."

I saw the lines around my mother's eyes, and I knew this was taking a toll on her. "I'm sorry, Mom," I said. "I keep insisting that Alyssa go out, and something always happens."

"Please don't blame yourself. It was bound to happen, with or without you. Eric and I have been too scared. It's probably a good thing that you're forcing us to acknowledge that she has these abilities and not ignore them. At least it gives us an idea of what she's capable of."

"I promise to keep your secret," Paul said then. "And I'd like to help in any way that I can."

Mom smiled at him. "Thank you so much."

Alyssa was exhausted and excused herself to lie down. Mom went upstairs with her, and Paul and I moved into the family room to talk more. I elaborated on the disappearances of kids like Alyssa. Paul was fascinated and intrigued, especially about a secret agency being behind the abductions.

"I'll bet they want to test the kids," he said. "Think of the possibilities. A child like Alyssa could manipulate the weather to act however they want. She could do so many things for good."

"Yeah," I said, "and she could be used for bad things too."

"Good point."

We fell into silence, until Paul suddenly sat up.

"What's wrong?" I asked.

"My dad," he said. "My dad used to come home with all sorts of stories he heard on the job. He owns an architectural firm, and a few years ago there was talk of some rich scientist building labs all over the country to do experiments related to the elements." He stood up and began pacing back and forth. "It was at a conference or something, too much alcohol was involved, and some guy started spouting off about all the high-tech requirements for the labs. I wonder if this is the agency your mom and step-dad are talking about."

"That's super creepy, Paul. This scientist could have places set up anywhere for experimenting on children. Can you find out more about it? I have an investigator friend doing some research for me."

"I'll call my dad, see what else he remembers."

I stood up as well. "This is good, really good."

Paul checked the time. "Dad will still be at work. I'm going to go home and see if I can reach him. I'll let you know what I find out."

After he left, I called Mark O'Donnell for an update. He had hit a dead end in Miami and was heading back to New York City in the morning to start over. I was disappointed, and he was getting frustrated.

"I know you don't want to give me too much information," Mark said, "and you must have your reasons, but I'm running into walls here, Aubrey. Is there anything else at all you can tell me?"

I gave him the information from Paul.

"Experiments regarding the elements, and labs," Mark said, and I could hear him scribbling on a notepad. "Do the kids have something to do with the labs?"

I hesitated for a moment, nibbling on my fingernail before answering, "Maybe."

"I'll look into it," he said without hesitation. He hung up with me, and I was grateful he didn't question me further.

I went upstairs to my room to check my email and just think about the day's events. My inbox was pretty empty. I hadn't had much communication with anyone from the city since I'd been in Hamilton Green, and I figured that I wouldn't anymore.

There was one new message waiting for me though, with nothing in the subject line, and I didn't recognize the email address. I clicked to open it, thinking it was just spam, hoping it wasn't a virus. The message was very short and bolded, three words, yet they hit me like a punch to the chest.

Please Be Careful

I forwarded the message to Mark with the request for him to look into it. I shivered and looked out the window, searching for any sign of a black car. Seeing nothing, I read the message again.

If this was a warning, it was very polite, and that threw me off. Why would someone who was out to harm my sister ask me to *please* be careful? No, this had to be another kind of warning. I just didn't know what kind.

Chapter Ten

Mom had been invited to attend a day of shopping in St. Louis with Mrs. Nesca and some of the other neighborhood moms. At first she didn't want to leave us, worried that something would happen with Alyssa. I persuaded her to go and have a good time, promising to keep Alyssa at home, and she agreed that we would be all right. She was even a little excited about having an "adult day" as Alyssa called it.

With Mom out, and Eric at work, Alyssa said that she wanted to make cookies. I started searching the refrigerator for a package of pre-made dough. Seeing that there was none, we decided to be brave and make some from scratch. We found Mom's recipe book and selected an earmarked page for chocolate chip raisin cookies.

Our first batch didn't turn out so well. Smoke rolled out of the oven and flooded the kitchen with a burnt scent. Alyssa covered her mouth and nose with a kitchen towel and hid in the mudroom, peeking around the corner while I dropped the cookie sheet on the counter. The cookies, or what was left of them, bounced and sizzled, and looked horrible.

"Yuck. What happened?" Alyssa asked.

"I must have gotten something in the recipe wrong," I said, removing my oven mitts and picking up the recipe book. I'd read each line with due care, making sure all of the ingredients were measured correctly and added in the proper order. What I'd missed was the temperature. "Shoot. I read that really, really wrong. It's supposed to be 345 degrees, not 435 degrees. That's way too hot."

The doorbell rang then, startling us both. I turned off the oven and hurried to the front door, glancing out the kitchen window as I went. I didn't see a car in the driveway, and I wasn't expecting anyone.

I opened the door and sucked in a mouthful of air in surprise when I saw Connor standing on the porch. He appeared very calm and his smile warmed me.

"Connor," I said. "Hi. What are you doing here?" A car was parked at the curb, and I assumed it was his.

"I'm sorry," he said. "I didn't mean to just drop in, but you gave me your address, and I was in the neighborhood and thought I'd say hi, see how you were."

"I'm okay," I said.

Connor's nose twitched. "Is something burning?"

"We tried to make some chocolate raisin cookies and failed. Miserably," I said, laughing. "I'm sorry, would you like to come in?"

"Is that okay? Are your parents home?"

"Mom's out running errands, and my step-dad is at work. I'm hanging out with my little sister."

Connor stepped inside, and I closed the door. I led the way to the kitchen where Alyssa was sitting at the breakfast bar, examining one of the burned cookies with a fork. I was a little nervous about Connor meeting Alyssa, but she didn't react strangely to his presence at all. She simply greeted him with a curious stare and then extended her hand.

"I'm Alyssa," she said. "Are you Connor?"

"I am," he said. He shook her hand.

"I'd offer you a cookie, but they're not suitable for human consumption," she said. "Would you like a peanut butter or jelly sandwich instead?"

Connor just blinked, glancing my way, and then nodding. Alyssa slid from her stool and busied herself making a sandwich.

"Wow," Connor said under his breath. "You told me she was smart, but wow."

I invited him to sit at the table, and I helped Alyssa. We made a plate of sandwiches, and I poured glasses of milk. Alyssa peppered Connor with questions, asking about his classes, his hobbies, and his family. There were questions even I hadn't asked him, and I worried that she was getting too personal. He answered them all without hesitation. He got along well with Alyssa, and she seemed to like him. She even offered him the other half of her sandwich, which he accepted.

When Mom came home, she was surprised to see Connor, and also pleased to finally meet him. I'd talked with her about him, and she was curious. He charmed her within minutes, and she invited him to stay for dinner, even though dinner was three hours away. While he and Alyssa put together a puzzle, Mom pulled me aside under the guise of helping her find something in the pantry.

"Did you invite him over?" she asked softly.

"I didn't. I would have asked first."

"It's okay, sweetheart. It's obvious he's interested in you." She glanced at him. He was laughing with Alyssa as she found the missing border piece and snapped it into place. "He seems like a nice young man."

I felt myself blushing. "That sounds so corny," I said.

Mom laughed and patted my shoulder. "Okay, how's this? He's super hot, and he could give Eric a run for his money if I were a few years younger."

"Ewww!" I exclaimed, catching Alyssa and Connor's attention. "Um, whoops. This box of mac and cheese is expired," I said to cover my reaction. They went back to the puzzle.

Mom just laughed. "I'll take care of your sister if you want to hang out with him alone for a bit."

"Thanks."

I asked Connor if he'd like to go for a walk around the neighborhood, and we headed out.

"I'm sorry if my sister offended you," I said. "She's very curious. She doesn't meet new people very often."

"It's fine. She seems like a special kid. She's lucky to have a sister like you who understands her."

He was quiet as we walked, and I realized we were heading for the park. A feeling of nervousness unrelated to Connor crept up my back, and I tried to look around without being obvious.

"Are you expecting someone?" Connor asked.

"What? No," I said quickly.

"Okay. Want to swing?"

We sat side by side and had a contest to see who could swing higher. Of course, he won, because he had longer legs. My face was flushed with exertion, and I laughed. Connor slowed down, and I dragged my feet in the sand to come to a stop. He twisted so that he was facing me, and I did the same.

We sat on the swings and talked, and he elaborated more on the answers he'd given Alyssa. His parents had separated when he was young, and he didn't know his father because his mother had moved them away.

"I'm told Dad had a bit of a drinking problem," Connor said.

His mother had died when he was eleven, so he went to live with his older brother. It was rough at times, just the two of them, but they understood they were family and needed each other.

"Are you and your brother still close?" I asked.

Connor smiled and nodded. "He's incredibly busy now, running his own law firm. But yeah, we keep in touch. I mean, he raised me, kept me safe, made sure I went to school and focused on my studies. He wanted to make sure our mom would have been proud of me."

"Sounds familiar."

Connor ducked his head then. "I'll be honest with you, Aubrey," he said, "I did a little research about you."

"Oh?" I asked, and I could feel the disappointment bubbling in my stomach. I'd heard this before. Whenever I traveled with Dad, I'd come across kids my age who looked me up to see if they could find out anything that would make me like them. They always wanted to be introduced to Dad and try to get on a TV show or in a movie.

"Please don't think badly of me," he said. "I'm not one who follows all that celebrity stuff, but your name sounded familiar. I'm sorry about what happened with your dad."

I stared at my shoes, unsure of what to say. He sounded so sincere. He cupped my chin in his hand and tipped my head up so he could look me in the eye. And then he leaned in, slowly, and kissed me. It was gentle and sweet, and I couldn't believe how soft his lips were. He leaned back, breaking contact, and I opened my eyes. I hadn't even realized I'd closed them.

Connor ran a hand through his hair and gave and uncomfortable laugh. "I'm sorry. Inappropriate timing."

"It's okay. It was...nice," I said, and blushed.

My cell phone chose that moment to buzz, and I pulled it from my pocket to see that I had a new text message from my mom.

"Dinner's almost ready," I said in surprise. I hadn't realized we'd been gone that long.

We stood up from the swings, and Connor patted his pockets and frowned. "I must have left my phone at home. Would you mind if I used yours and let my roommate know I'm not meeting him tonight?"

"Did you already have plans?"

"Nothing important. I was just going to meet some of the guys and play video games and eat a frozen pizza."

"I wouldn't want to keep you from your friends," I said, handing him my phone.

"No worries. You're a lot better looking than they are."

I half-snorted, and coughed to cover it. Connor dialed his roommate, and I moved a few steps away to allow him some privacy. I also took the time to calm my racing heart. I liked Connor. A lot. But was this a good time to start a relationship? With everything going on, I didn't know if it was fair to Connor.

He finished his call and came back to me. He handed me the phone back, and we started to walk back to my house. Along the way, he reached out and took my hand, cautiously at first. I took a deep breath and closed my fingers around his.

I introduced Connor to Eric, and they began talking about the university. Eric was an alumnus, and he shared some interesting stories about his old professors in the science department. As we sat down at the dining room table, I caught the sly smile that crossed Alyssa's face. I shot her a warning glance, and she made the motion of locking her lips shut and tossing away the key. She shook out her napkin and giggled not-so-discreetly into it.

Dinner lasted longer than usual. Mom had whipped up a chocolate mousse for dessert, and while we were enjoying that, Alyssa grilled him some more. He didn't seem to mind answering her, and he even asked her some questions. I saw Mom and Eric tense a little, but Alyssa handled the questions with ease, and they relaxed.

Connor offered to help with the dishes, and Mom refused to let him, instead ushering us out of the kitchen. Alyssa took Connor's hand and offered to show him her room. He was as surprised as I had been by her reading materials, and I could tell he was intrigued by her. I showed him my room, and let him flip through some of my photography portfolios. He told me he was impressed by my photos from Europe, and we talked about Paris, London and Rome. He was well traveled, thanks to his brother, and he wanted to go back.

"Probably not until after I finish graduate school," he said, sounding wistful. He checked his watch and saw it was almost nine. "Wow, I should get going. I have some homework to do before class tomorrow."

"Oh, sure," I said, hearing the disappointment in my voice.

He said goodbye to Alyssa, who hugged him, and then I walked him to the front door. Mom and Eric said their goodbye's as well, and then scooted upstairs. We stood on the porch, and that awkward feeling returned between us, until I couldn't handle it any longer. I stood on tiptoe and kissed him. He was surprised, but soon his arms were around me, pulling me close. I noticed that we fit together nicely, and he was solid and strong against me.

"I really need to go," he whispered, and he sounded very reluctant about it. "Can I see you again?"

"Yes," I answered.

He released me, and hopped down the steps to the sidewalk. He kept looking over his shoulder at me, and he tripped over the edge of the curb. I grinned and waved.

I stayed on the porch after he left, leaning on the railing and staring out at the neighborhood. There was something about Connor that I was drawn to, something other than his good looks. He was smart and ambitious, and the way he spoke about his family was with respect and loyalty. I heard the front door open and close behind me, and then Alyssa was beside me, mirroring my pose. She was dressed in her pajamas and wearing pink bunny slippers.

"I like him," she said.

"So do I."

"Are you going to marry him?"

I laughed and ruffled her hair. It was moments like this that reminded me she was still just an innocent young girl. "Let's take one step at a time, okay?"

Alyssa nodded. Then she tilted her head and looked down the street. "Paul will be jealous."

I followed her gaze and cringed. "We talked about this. He knows he and I are just good friends."

Alyssa shrugged. "That doesn't mean he can't be jealous." She pushed herself away from the railing and turned to go inside.

I stayed on the porch awhile longer, thinking about that. Paul and I had been working together on the float, and I had caught the moments where he casually tried to stand beside me and brush his hand against mine, or when he would pay close extra attention when I spoke. Charlotte had noticed it too, and she'd mentioned to me that Paul hadn't expressed much interest in any other girls before I showed up. Paul had also been entrusted with Alyssa's secret, so that meant I had a special bond with him concerning my family. I just hoped he wouldn't confuse that with anything else.

I sighed and scrubbed a hand over my face. It was all so dramatic, and I hated drama. I remembered despising the way the other girls at school would pine over boys and get all weepy because so-and-so didn't call them back or ask them out again. I hoped I wouldn't turn into that, but if that was normal, then I would take normal.

Chapter Eleven

The finishing touches were being added to the float, and the entire neighborhood was gathered in Len Morris's yard to watch. Mom was passing around a huge container full of cookies, and Alyssa was following her with a wagon filled with bottles of water. I stapled one last foiled star in place and stood back to make sure it was straight.

"Looks perfect," Paul said, his voice full of enthusiasm.

Charlotte finished with her stars and came over to join us. Her dark hair was held back with a headband, but a few wisps had escaped to frame her face, giving her a disheveled look.

"I only stapled my fingers twice this year," she announced with a wide smile.

"How many times did you do that last year?" I asked.

"Seven."

A test firing was done with the confetti cannon, and we all cheered as it dispensed red, white and blue confetti and streamers. Len had some announcements to make about the meeting point for the next afternoon, and who was to be stationed where. He had several plastic bags full of candy and stickers, pencils and little American flags lined up by the float. Those that were walking in the parade would be handing out the goodies to the crowd. There were also going to be people riding on the float, mostly the neighborhood children.

Alyssa was pleased as punch to be included this year. She'd begged Mom and Eric to let her participate, and at first they'd been reluctant, just like always. This time it was Alyssa who told them the best way for her to hide from any secret agency was to be out in public. If she appeared to be a normal eight-year-old girl, there would be nothing to draw their attention to her. They consented, as long as I promised to stay near her. I crossed my heart. I was going to walk behind the float, close to her at all times.

We arrived home, exhausted and with fingers sore from stapling and painting and hammering. There was an unfamiliar car in the driveway, and I panicked for a moment, wondering who it was. When I looked at Mom, she was smiling at Eric.

"What's going on?" I asked.

"Happy birthday, Aubrey," Eric said. "My friend Dan dropped it off for you. It's yours."

I just stared. It was a newer Jeep, and it was black and compact, but not too small. I walked around it, peering inside at the interior and all of the features. Mom mistook my lack of response as disappointment.

"I know your dad would have bought you something nicer," she said, "like a Mercedes or a Porsche-"

I threw my arms around her, cutting her off. "This is perfect!" I exclaimed. She laughed with relief and hugged me back.

"Keys are in the ignition," Eric said, and I hugged him too.

Alyssa ran her hands over the outside. She approved of it, judging by the grin on her face. I asked if I could take it for a drive, and Mom said to go ahead.

"Just be back in an hour. Dinner will be ready then," she said.

I loved the way it drove, and it had recently been detailed because it had that new car smell. I parked in front of Paul's house and honked. He came to the door, very confused at first, then shocked, then excited. I heard him yell to his mom that he'd be right back, then he hopped in, and we were off. I went two blocks north and picked up Charlotte.

This wasn't my first time driving; Dad had let me drive his Jaguar a few times, but this was my first time driving my own car, and it was an exhilarating feeling. I wondered if I would have felt this independent and this excited if I was driving in New York City. Looking at the faces of my two friends, I somehow doubted it.

I circled back and dropped each of them off at their houses. We were all wound up from the car ride, and anxious about the parade the following day. Charlotte wished me an early happy birthday, and when I stopped at Paul's house, he did the same, leaning over to kiss my cheek.

I felt a shiver when his lips touched my face. Even though something deep inside me was a little thrilled at the contact, I stamped down that feeling, thinking about Connor instead. He'd called the day after meeting my family to ask me out on a real date. He said he'd heard it was my birthday soon, and he wanted to celebrate. I was extremely excited about it, but I hadn't mentioned it to Paul or Charlotte yet. I wasn't sure how to approach the subject.

I parked in the driveway behind Mom's van, and as I got out of the Jeep, a black car made its way past the house. At first, I thought it was the neighbor's again. When it slowed to a crawl, I knew it wasn't. I ran down the driveway, and it sped up and turned at the corner. My heart was pounding, and I was having second thoughts about allowing Alyssa to be in the parade. She would be crushed if we told her that she couldn't ride on the float though, so I made sure to tell Mom and Eric about it. We were keeping a record of each time we saw the black car. So far, I was the only one to see it, which made me start to wonder if I was being overly paranoid.

Mom made a special breakfast the next morning in honor of my eighteenth birthday. I was happy and sad at the same time, and I couldn't keep the tears from falling when Alyssa started singing to me. I was thinking of my dad, and how he'd sung to me at the restaurant the night he'd disappeared. Alyssa crawled into my lap and hugged me tight. Then she presented her gift to me, which was another blue poppy anemone. We all watched in wonder as she made it bloom before our eyes.

The rest of the morning passed in a blur to get ready for the parade. We had a light lunch, and then headed out to the meeting point at the beginning of Main Street. All of the floats were lined up, and people were everywhere. Alyssa held my hand as we reached our float, and I swung her up onto it. Eric was driving the truck that would pull the trailer, and Mom was going to ride with him. Paul and Charlotte were walking behind me, and we were all armed with our bags of goodies for the crowd. Soon we were on our way, traveling along to the sound of patriotic music.

I found myself smiling and waving back at the people lining the street. Small children stood with their parents and grandparents, waving little flags and happily accepting the treats being handed to them. Just ahead of me was Alyssa. She was sitting on the back end of the trailer, swinging her legs back and forth and waving a flag in each hand. She caught my eye and grinned, and I knew she was thrilled to be involved in this parade. We turned onto Main Street, Eric steering the trailer around the corner with great care so as not to jostle the people on the float.

As the trailer straightened and continued along the route, there was a sudden boom from the confetti cannon, louder than it should have been. A small explosion followed, and that section of the float was in flames within seconds. Tissue paper, foam and streamers were flying everywhere, and people were jumping from the trailer to get away from the fire. I dropped my bag of candy and grabbed Alyssa's hand, pulling her off and swinging her around onto my back.

It was pure pandemonium, and I felt Alyssa's grip tighten around my neck. I spotted Mom and Eric ahead of us. They had already jumped out of the truck, and Mom was ushering others away. Eric grabbed a fire extinguisher from the truck and worked to put out the fire.

"Get away from here!" he yelled at me.

I turned and ran, following the throng of people. We'd gone a few feet when someone bumped into me, and I tripped and went flying to the ground. I threw both my hands out to brace myself, but I still fell hard. The jolt made Alyssa release me, and she rolled away. My left knee had slammed into the ground, and I collapsed in pain. Alyssa screamed, and I looked up in time to see a dark suited man throw her over his shoulder and take off with her. She was reaching for me, and I yelled at him to stop.

"Aubrey, are you hurt?" Paul asked as he helped me up. I shook free and started limping after Alyssa, ignoring Paul as he yelled, "Aubrey, wait for me!"

They were almost to the black car, and I kept screaming for Alyssa. I was losing ground fast, panic welling up in my chest, when the man was tackled from the side. He and Alyssa hit the ground. Paul sprinted past me and scooped her up.

"Run!" Connor ordered, and Paul did without hesitation. I was frozen to the spot, watching as Connor wrestled with the man, and they exchanged punches. Connor took a solid hit to the face and fell onto the grass. The black car screeched to a halt beside us, and the man jumped in. Before the car sped away, he glared at me.

I saw Conner stumbling to his feet, and I hurried to help him. I grabbed his arm as he swayed a little.

"Is your sister all right?" he asked.

"She got away. You're bleeding."

He touched his nose and his lip, saw the blood and wiped it on his shirt. "I've taken worse."

"Aubrey!"

We turned to see Eric hurrying toward us. The fire on the float had been put out, and people were milling around now. The police officers who had been patrolling the parade route were gathering the remaining people into groups, asking questions, trying to determine what had happened. They paid no attention to us, which shocked me. Hadn't anyone seen Alyssa almost get kidnapped?

"I'm fine," I assured Eric as he started checking me for injuries. "Just my knee. Nothing a little ice won't fix."

He turned his attention to Connor. "I saw what you did, and I thank you for it. You saved my daughter."

Connor shook his head. "I just did what anyone else would have."

"They could have had weapons," I said.

"I didn't think about it," Connor said, wiping at his nose again.

"Come on. Let's go to the house," Eric said. He lowered his voice when he said to me, "Your mother is frantic."

Alyssa was wrapped up in a blanket, sitting at the kitchen table when we got home. Eric was right; Mom was a mess. She was trying to hide her panic by keeping busy cleaning up the kitchen, but it was already pretty spotless. Her face was pale and her hands were shaking. Connor and I limped inside, each leaning on the other. Paul jumped up when he saw me. His gaze went to Connor, and he frowned.

"Oh my gosh, Connor, sit down," Mom said. "I'll get the first aid kit."

"I'm okay, Mrs. Vaughn, really," he tried to tell her. Mom ignored him and started cleaning him up. Connor just smiled at me and shrugged.

"Are you all right?" Paul asked. He pulled me aside and gave me a once over. "I saw you fall."

"Yeah, I just bumped my knee. I'll be bruised tomorrow, but it's nothing." Eric handed me an ice pack, and I pressed it to my knee, wincing at the sensation. "How's Alyssa?"

"She's been quiet since we got here. I don't know what she's thinking," Paul said.

"She's probably scared out of her mind. Some goon just tried to kidnap her. It was the same one I saw two weeks ago. Same car. They must have been checking us out for a while."

"Do you think they caused the problem with the confetti cannon?"

I shuddered at the thought. "A distraction? Just to grab a little girl?"

"A very special little girl," Paul reminded me.

"Should we call the police?" Connor asked. Mom had finished fixing him up, and he now had a bandage over the cut on his cheek. She looked like she was going to object to the suggestion, when Eric spoke up.

"Connor, we appreciate what you did. We'll take care of it from here. Thank you."

Connor nodded and stood up. "Okay, sure, I understand. I'm just glad nothing serious happened. I'll take off then. Thanks for the bandage." He turned to me. "I'll call you later, Aubrey. We can decide then if you still want to go out."

Paul bristled beside me as Connor let himself out the back door. Eric watched to make sure he was gone before he faced us again.

"*Should* we call the police?" Mom asked.

"We don't know if this has anything to do with her abilities," Eric said. "And we don't want to draw attention to her if it doesn't."

"But those were the same guys I told you about," I said. "They know us, they know where we live. I feel like this is all my fault. I wanted Alyssa to be in the parade."

"Aubrey, it's not your fault," Mom said. "Don't think like that."

"It could just be some crazy coincidence," Paul said. The silence that followed his statement was loud enough to suggest that none of us believed that.

"So, what do we do?" Mom asked. She ran a hand through Alyssa's hair. Alyssa just stared at the table.

For the moment, we agreed to do nothing except to keep Alyssa inside and with someone at all times. Paul told us his father didn't remember anything helpful about the company building special labs, so that was a dead end. Paul went home, and we spent the rest of the day trying to keep our minds off of what had happened. Eric left for a couple of hours to make sure the truck and the float were taken care of, and when he returned, he assured us that no one had noticed the incident. They were all running away from the float when it caught fire. He didn't tell Alyssa or Mom, but he shared with me that Len Morris thought the confetti cannon had been tampered with.

"Just some kids playing a joke," Len had said. Eric and I didn't believe that for a second.

I called Connor to reschedule our dinner. He was fine with that, and he expressed his concern for Alyssa. I wasn't surprised when he asked what was going on, and I told him that it was a random thing. I also lied to him and told him we were having it investigated by the police.

"Good," he said. "You never know what kinds of people are lurking out there."

I had to agree with him.

* * *

I contacted Mark for an update. He was still looking into the missing children, and he was on his way to Seattle to meet with a scientist whose sole subject of study was the elements. He also let me know that he'd been unable to trace my anonymous warning email. I could hear the frustration in his voice, and I knew this mystery was starting to get to him.

I was spending a lot of time in my photo studio, enhancing and printing pictures as fast as I could. I had shots of the black car from that day in the park, and I studied them for anything that I could use to track them down. In one picture, there was a partial blurry outline of the license plate. I scanned and emailed copies to Mark, hoping he could use them. Two days later, Paul showed up with an idea.

He suggested using the research library at Hamilton University to see if we could find articles about the Mason family. From what we could tell, they were one of the earliest families to lose a child with special abilities. I was doubtful that we'd find anything more than Mark had while Paul remained optimistic.

"Besides," he said as he drove us to the campus, "I'm going nuts just sitting around, and my mom keeps talking about what happened at the parade."

The library wasn't busy. There were a few students scattered here and there, almost all of them engrossed in their work. Paul took us to one of the private research rooms and logged onto the computer.

"You're not a student, are you?" I asked.

"Nope. Mom has special access, being head librarian at the high school."

He did a search for the names of Jeffrey, Amelia, Travis and Emily Mason and got a number of hits, all articles from newspapers in the Chicago and surrounding areas. He clicked on one and we were shown a picture of the distraught parents, holding a framed photograph of their son. Standing beside them was a young girl, thirteen years old. Her dark hair was pulled back in a tight ponytail that fell over her left shoulder. Her arms were crossed defiantly in front of her, and she seemed to be glaring at the camera.

"Paul," I said, my voice dropping. "I know that girl."

He enlarged the photo and zoomed in on her face. The hair color was different, but I was positive. "Her name is Emily Mason," he said. "How could you know her? They lived outside of Chicago."

"She may have been Emily Mason then, but she's Monica Orson now."

Paul squinted, studying the photo. "Who's Monica Orson?"

I explained how I'd met her on the flight from Chicago to St. Louis when I moved down here. She'd been polite and eager to talk with me, and I hadn't been very receptive to her. I dug through my wallet now, hoping that I hadn't thrown away the paper with her phone number. I found it and stood up, moving away from the computer to make the call. My fingers were trembling, and it took two tries before I was able to type the number in. It went to her voicemail, so I left her a brief message, asking her to call me back as soon as she could. "It's about Chicago," I said.

Paul did another search and found more articles about the alleged abduction of Travis Mason and the following weeks, up to the family's disappearance. He printed them off, folded them in half and stuffed them into my purse.

"Mark already sent me some of these," I said.

"I'm sure he did, but I think we should get out of here."

"Why?" I asked, confused at his sudden need to leave.

"It feels like we're being watched," he said.

He began erasing the search history on the computer. I looked around, an uneasy feeling settling over me. Paul shut down the computer and turned to me. Without a word, we hurried out of the research room and into the main part of the library. A couple of students glanced up at us, and we skidded to a halt, my sneakers squeaking against the floor. Paul put his arm around my waist as we pushed through the double doors and jogged down the steps. As we went, I bumped my elbow against another student heading up.

"Aubrey, hey, what are you doing here?"

"Connor," I said, surprised. "Um, hi."

"Doing some research?" he asked. His cheekbone was still a little bruised from the incident at the parade.

I hugged my purse closer to me, feeling the papers hidden inside.

"Yeah. I'm sorry, Connor, but we kind of need to be somewhere. Can I call you later?"

He shifted his backpack from one side to the other, glancing at Paul while he did. Paul was sweating and appeared antsy, so I'm sure Connor knew something was up. He didn't question us though, just nodded and smiled. Then he kissed my cheek. I felt rather than saw Paul tense beside me.

"Sure thing," Connor said. "Good luck with whatever you're doing."

Paul grabbed my hand and we ran the rest of the way back to his car. My cell phone rang, and I answered it without checking the number while putting on my seatbelt.

"Aubrey. Are you alone?"

"Who is this?"

"Monica."

I smacked Paul's arm and pointed to my phone, mouthing her name. Paul waited before backing out of the parking space.

"Are you alone?" she asked again.

"No," I answered. "My friend Paul is with me. He knows everything."

Silence greeted my ears, and I feared she'd hung up.

"We need to speak in person. Now. Where are you?"

"Hamilton University. Where do you want to meet?"

Monica was quiet again. Paul gave me a questioning look, and I shrugged in response. After a moment, Monica spoke. She gave me an address, and told me to be there as soon as possible. Paul didn't know the area well, and we got lost a couple of times before we found it.

"Are you sure this is it?" he asked, leaning across me to stare up at a small ranch-style house. It seemed innocent and peaceful.

I studied the front of the house. It was white with an attached two car garage and a long front porch. The yard was trimmed, and there was no indication that this house belonged to anyone other than a normal family. I was beginning to doubt that this was the right place, when my gaze fell upon the flower bed. It was small, maybe a foot square, right in the middle of the yard. It seemed out of place at first. What caught my attention was the type of flower it held.

Blue poppy anemones.

Chapter Twelve

I threw open the car door and jumped out, sprinting up the driveway and into the yard.

The flower bed was in perfect bloom, the colors vibrant with life. Paul parked the car at the curb and hurried after me. He stared at the flowers, frowning in confusion.

"This is the right place," I said.

At that moment, the front door opened, and there stood Monica. She beckoned us to come inside, and she pulled me into a hug the second I was in the door. I didn't know anything about this girl, and yet, I felt an immediate connection. I hugged her back, fighting the urge to cry. I couldn't imagine what she and her parents had been through. All I knew was that I didn't want that same thing to happen to my family.

"Aubrey, I'm so sorry I couldn't be up front with you when we first met," she said.

"You knew about me already?"

"We have a lot to talk about. Come on. I want you to meet my father."

She led us down a hallway. Paul and I stared at the framed pictures hanging on the walls. We saw Travis as a baby, a toddler, up to age eight, and then nothing after that. We reached the end of the hall, and Monica knocked once before entering the room. It was set up like some kind of command center, full of electronic equipment. There were three computers, all hooked up to huge monitors, printers, and fax machines. We were greeted by Monica's father, who introduced himself as Jonathan Orson.

"Or, in special company, Jeffrey Mason," he said, shaking our hands.

I introduced myself and Paul, and we sat down. I wasn't sure how to proceed, so I pulled the papers from my purse and handed them to Monica. She flipped through them and passed them to her father.

"Does anyone else know about us?" he asked, pointing to their photograph.

I shook my head. "Not that I'm aware of. We just found that about an hour ago."

"Good," Jonathan said. He swiveled in his chair and ran the papers through a shredder. "Monica and I can't risk being found."

"Found by whom?" Paul asked.

Jonathan tapped some keys on one of his computers, bringing up a screen of information, and we were soon reading a detailed report about an organization named Luminesk Enterprises. It was a legitimate company that dabbled in everything from pharmaceuticals to agriculture. On the top, it seemed harmless. As I read further, I felt my skin start to crawl with fear.

There were several accusations of unapproved scientific experiments being conducted on humans. These experiments related to the four basic elements of earth, water, fire, and air. The authorities had done an investigation and found nothing to support the claims, all of which had been made anonymously.

"I don't understand," I said. "Is this the group that's after my sister?"

"Your sister, and every other child that possesses the same abilities. This is the group that took my son," Jonathan said.

"Who's in charge of it?" Paul asked.

"A man named Simon Foley," Monica said. "A total recluse. There's very little information about him, and he's very careful about being photographed. That may not even be his real name. He funds everything through private investors, which aren't listed anywhere, and he doesn't attend meetings or conferences."

Jonathan brought up another file. "Financial records for Luminesk," he said. He pointed to a line that read, "Procurement Team".

I didn't like the sound of that. "What does that mean?" I asked, even though I was sure I knew the answer.

"Trackers," Monica said. "An elite group that seek out kids like your sister and bring them in for experiments."

I shuddered at the thought. "I think we've seen them. Someone tried to kidnap Alyssa from the Fourth of July parade."

"Black cars, men in dark suits?" Jonathan asked, and I nodded.

Jonathan and Monica exchanged glances, and I saw the frowns and looks of confusion. Monica turned back to me and said, "That's unusual. They've always taken the children from their homes during the night. They don't want any witnesses."

"So they saw an opportunity, and they took it," Paul reasoned. "That's not so unusual."

"Simon Foley has remained under the radar because of his ability to keep his operations hidden. There's no way he would allow such a careless move to happen, at least not without his knowledge," Jonathan said.

I was stumped. Could there be someone else after Alyssa? And if so, why? What piece was I missing from this puzzle?

"Hey," I said, and I realized I'd interrupted Jonathan and Paul. I had no idea what they'd been talking about, and I had probably missed something. I didn't care at that moment because I had a question. "Did you send me the warning email?"

Blank stares all around was my response.

"What email?" Paul asked.

I explained the email I'd received with the "please be careful" warning the day of the incident at the Arch. Mark knew about it, but I hadn't wanted to cause further alarm for Mom and Eric so I hadn't told them. After sending it to Mark, I'd pushed it from my mind. My heart sank as Jonathan and Monica told me they knew nothing about any email.

"The only approved contact I had with you was on the plane," Monica said.

"Approved? What do you mean? How did you know I was going to be on that flight? My plans were changed last minute."

Monica ducked her head a bit and said, "Well, we may have had something to do with that."

I looked to Jonathan. "You changed my flight," I said, and he nodded.

He rose from his chair and crossed the room to a tall file cabinet. He unlocked it, opened the top drawer and removed a folder, handing it to me. Paul and I waited for him to start talking about it. Instead he just leaned against the cabinet and crossed his arms. I opened the file and pulled out several sheets of paper, all of them with a small picture of a blue poppy anemone at the top. We read each page, understanding dawning on each of our faces.

After Travis Mason was taken from his home, his parents asked the public for help in finding him. Against their better judgement, they also revealed to the world their son's abilities in controlling the elements. Their friends thought they were just desperate and in shock, and eventually, ridiculed, the family disappeared.

They had been contacted by a small group calling itself Anemone. At that time, Anemone consisted of just two families who had also lost young children who were capable of controlling the elements. One parent from each family had been employed by Luminesk Enterprises, and they believed Simon Foley was responsible. He had befriended them, hired them, and then stolen their children. Through some investigating of their own, they had found reports dubbing these children as Elementals, a name given to them by Simon Foley himself. The families packed up and went into hiding, all the while, trying to prove that this man and his company were conducting experiments on their children.

The Masons changed their names, moved away from Joliet, and joined Anemone in the fight against Luminesk. Jonathan's wife had passed away a few years ago, and now, Jonathan was in charge. They moved from city to city, wherever there may be a potential case of an Elemental. They never stayed too long and always had the ability to pack up quickly if necessary. Over the years, he and Anemone had helped relocate a dozen other families with stories just like theirs. Monica described it as a sort of witness protection program.

The name "anemone" is of Greek origin meaning "windflower". It's thought to bring luck and protect against evil, and also represents anticipation. It seemed a fitting symbol for this group. I told them that Alyssa had given me this very flower, and they weren't surprised.

"It seems that all of these children are drawn to it," Jonathan said. "We don't know why, just as we don't know why they have these abilities. Travis filled our backyard with them year-round. The ones out front are fake, but we put them there as a sign for others in our group."

"I go back to Joliet a few times during the year," Monica said, wiping an unshed tear from her eye. "Just in case Travis makes his way back."

Looking at her, and how her father hugged her to him, I knew deep down that they would never see Travis again, and yet they were still so hopeful. It broke my heart. I didn't want to see myself or Mom and Eric in this same position.

"We learned about your sister through a source in your area. I wanted to meet you, see if you knew anything. It was very clear that you didn't," Monica said with a half-smile. "I still wanted to give you my contact info in case you ever needed help."

We definitely needed help. Whether it was Luminesk or someone else after Alyssa, I wanted Monica and her father involved. They had the resources ready and available in case something happened. I hoped against hope that it wouldn't come down to us having to leave town and assume new identities. I asked them about their source, curious about who else could know about Alyssa. Jonathan informed me that he couldn't reveal that information, or anything about the other relocated families.

"I apologize, but it's protocol. To keep them safe," he said, and I understood.

Paul and I stayed and talked with them for another couple of hours. Jonathan still did some freelance writing, simply to pay the bills. However his main focus was on finding out as much as he could about Luminesk and protecting the families in Anemone. He knew his way around a computer, and he could break into almost any system he came across. Every now and then, he was able to get through Luminesk's security and grab a file here and there.

Monica really was a college student, studying biology at Hamilton University for the time being. Like me, she didn't exhibit any of the same powers that our younger siblings had. She explained that all of the other missing children were the second children in their families. Jonathan had a theory that the altered genes skipped the first child. The mystery of how this happened still existed, and this was the basis for Monica's studies, although she was very careful not to draw too much attention to her work. I suggested that she and her father meet with Eric and my mom, and they agreed. They also wanted to meet Alyssa and see what she could do.

We made plans to have them over for dinner soon. Jonathan gave me a file for Mom and Eric about Anemone and Luminesk. I was positive they would be interested in both of these organizations.

Paul was quiet as we drove back to my house, drumming his fingers against the steering wheel and frowning. The song playing on the radio fit my mood. I felt hopeful, scared, and melancholy, all at the same time. When I left New York City to move to Hamilton Green, I had pictured my life being simpler. Instead, it was turning out to be more complicated than ever.

I wondered what my father would say, what advice he'd have to give me. Anytime I was confused or just needed to talk, he would stop what he was doing to give me his full attention. It didn't matter if he was working on a business proposal or producing a movie; he always wanted to help. I wished that he could help me now, to understand what was happening and find a solution. It was frustrating to gain new information, and along with it new questions without answers.

"Aubrey."

How could I protect my family without knowing what we were up against? Who was Simon Foley, and what did he want with these children?

"Aubrey!"

I jerked in my seat. Paul's eyes were darting from the road in front of him to his rearview mirror, then to his side mirror.

"We're being followed," he said. "Hold on."

I grabbed the armrest and swiveled around. "I don't see anyone."

"The red Buick. It's hanging about a block back."

I looked again, finally spotting it. Paul took a sharp left turn, and I was thrown against the passenger side door.

"Sorry," he said through gritted teeth.

The car was still there, and it had sped up.

"That can't be them. I've only ever seen them in black cars. Where are we going?" I asked. I didn't recognize the street we were on. "Are you heading back to Hamilton Green?"

He said nothing and turned right at the next intersection. He pulled into a parking lot and urged me to get out. I followed him while he paid the parking attendant, then he grabbed my hand and we ran into the adjacent building. The lobby was professional while still maintaining a bright and cheerful appearance. Just inside the entrance was a large check-in desk. I glanced around, wondering if we were in a hotel, surprised to see a large glass logo on one wall that spelled out "Wilton Labs".

Paul went to the security guard at the desk, told him we were being followed and feared for our safety. While he went outside to check for the car Paul described to him, Paul spoke to another guard and explained that I was Eric Vaughn's step-daughter and we needed to see him right away. The head guard returned and waited with us until Eric arrived.

He was wearing a white lab coat and glasses. I'd never seen him in glasses before. I didn't even know he wore them. His eyes were frantic behind the lenses, almost wild. He saw me and rushed over.

"Where's Alyssa? Is she here? Is she hurt?" he asked.

I shook my head. My mouth was dry when I spoke, "She's okay. We…we have something to tell you, and we're being followed."

Paul nodded his agreement. Eric told us to wait for a moment while he talked to the security guards. We moved aside, and Paul kept his arm around my shoulders. After a couple of minutes, Eric came back to us with visitor badges and guided us to the bank of elevators. He led us inside one, swiping his key card against the card reader on the wall.

"We'll go to my office," he said. He noticed me staring at the card reader, intrigued. It was very similar to what we had in my apartment building in New York, which meant that only a few people were allowed in.

There were no buttons to indicate what floor we were heading to. He smiled a little. "Security is very tight here. Our cards grant us access to certain floors depending on our level of security clearance."

"How much access do you have?" I couldn't help but ask.

"Quite a bit," was all he said.

The elevator slowed to a stop, and the doors slid open. We entered a stark white hallway that hurt my eyes, and then went through another series of locked doors to another hallway. We passed several rooms with computer and lab equipment before reaching a door marked "Director of Genetic Services".

"That's me," Eric said, letting us inside to his office.

Once we were inside, he shook off his lab coat and hung it on the coat rack. Then he phoned his assistant and asked her to hold all of his calls, unless it was Mom or Alyssa. He sat down behind a huge black desk and folded his hands together. Paul and I dropped into the leather armchairs across from the desk, the adrenaline having worn off.

"Tell me everything," Eric said.

Paul and I talked for a good thirty minutes, and I shared with him the file Jonathan had given me. Eric was fascinated with the scientific aspects of Luminesk Enterprises, flipping through the pages at rapid speed, his eyes roving over the data.

"But why steal the children?" he asked. "If Simon Foley's theory is correct, it could change so much for mankind. Surely he would see the benefits of legitimate research." He closed the file and turned his chair to face the windows behind him. The city stretched out below.

"I think you should keep the file here," I suggested. "I'd hate to see it fall into the wrong hands."

Eric agreed. He told us that he kept several important documents regarding Alyssa in his office safe. No one but he had access to it, and the security to even get into his office was strict. His desk phone rang, and he excused himself to answer it. I stood up and wandered around the office. I had no idea that Eric held such a high position, and though I didn't fully understand everything he did and was responsible for, I felt better in knowing that he was well equipped to understand Alyssa and her abilities.

"There hasn't been any sign of that red Buick," he said after hanging up his phone. "The security cameras in the area didn't pick up anything. If you'd like to wait, we can drive home together. It will be about an hour."

Paul and I agreed to wait. Eric offered to have some snacks brought in, which we gladly accepted. He left us then to finish something in one of the labs, and we were alone in his office. An assistant stopped in a few minutes later with gourmet popcorn, fresh fruit and bottled water. It reminded me of hanging out in my dad's office when I was little.

My cell phone buzzed, indicating I had a new text message. I couldn't fight the blush that colored my cheeks when I saw it was from Connor, and I almost choked on my popcorn. He wanted to see if tomorrow night would be okay to take me out for my birthday dinner. I texted back that I would call him when I got home and put the phone away.

Paul got up and went to stand by the window. "So, um, are you and Connor…serious?"

I laughed. "Not even close. We're still getting to know each other."

"He seems like a decent guy," Paul said, and I heard the reluctant tone in his voice. "As long as he treats you well, I mean."

I joined him at the window and hugged him. "It's nice of you to worry about me like that."

"Hey, we're friends, right?"

"Right."

"So that means I'll always be there for you, no matter what."

It was a promise I'd heard before, from my father, and it sent a pang of hurt straight to my heart. Paul must have sensed my mood change, and he coughed and went back for another bottle of water. I straightened and focused my attention on the street below, searching for the car that had followed us from Monica's.

"Omigosh," I said.

"What? Do you see them?"

"No, but we need to let Monica know. She and her father could be in danger."

I called Monica's number, and Jonathan answered. I filled him in on the sighting of the red car and how it had followed us. He was confused, explaining that if Simon Foley was changing things up now, there must be something very special about Alyssa. That thought chilled me to the bone.

Chapter Thirteen

I'd often wondered what a real date would feel like. I'd been out with boys before, but always in a group setting, and never with someone I was genuinely interested in as a boyfriend. My nerves were threatening to get the better of me as I moved from one room to another without purpose. Connor was picking me up in an hour, and I was ready to go. I ended up in Eric's office. He was sifting through papers, reading reports and marking things here and there. Since we'd learned about Luminesk and Simon Foley, Eric had been on a mission to find out more about the experiments. All of his research amounted to nothing but information on Luminesk's legitimate business operations.

"I just don't know what to make of it," Eric said. He leaned back in his chair. "This man is experimenting on children, and there's no record of any of it. I just can't believe that anyone would go along with this. He has to have a research team and medical personnel on staff."

"Maybe they're not willing participants."

"Maybe," he mused. "Have you gotten anything new from Mark?"

We had decided it was time to share everything with Mark O'Donnell, and while at first he was skeptical about children being able to control the elements, he was very interested in finding out all he could about Simon Foley.

"Not yet," I said.

Eric rubbed his eyes, then smiled and said, "Would you like to see something?"

I pulled a chair closer to his desk and he brought up a video on his computer. It was of Alyssa when she was nine months old. She was toddling around the living room on surprisingly steady legs. Mom was calling to her off camera, and she changed direction, giggling and clapping her hands.

"This is what Luminesk doesn't know or care about," Eric said. "These children are innocents, and no matter what, experimenting on them is wrong."

The video ended after three minutes. "What if we look at it from their side?" I asked. "You're a genetic scientist. You're always looking to find a way to make the world better, right?"

He frowned and crossed his arms over his chest. "True. But my lab doesn't do any human or animal testing. We mainly use computer generated analysis."

"I'm not accusing you of anything," I said quickly. "I don't mean to offend you. I'm just saying that something has motivated this man to do something about our world, and to him, the end justifies the means."

"I see your point, Aubrey. I still don't like my daughter being the center of their quest at this moment."

That was understandable, and I agreed with him.

A small report had shown up on the national news about the strange storm that had affected the Arch, and architects and structural engineers had been called in to check out the strength of the building. Jonathan was trying to get into the security footage from the observation deck to see if anyone would notice that Alyssa was the cause of the storm. So far he had been unsuccessful. What he had learned was that someone else had tried to do the same thing, but with no luck either.

Alyssa ran into the room, a huge smile on her face, and a small burst of wind followed her, blowing the papers on Eric's desk to the floor.

"Connor's here," she said breathlessly, just as the doorbell rang. I leapt to my feet and followed her down the hall. She stopped at the landing and gave me a gentle push toward the steps. "You'll be fine," she assured me. "Just be yourself."

Mom had let him inside, and he was waiting in the kitchen, chatting with her about the weather. He saw me and smiled.

"So what do you have planned for tonight?" Mom asked.

"It's kind of a surprise," he said, looking from her to me. "But I promise to keep her safe and bring her home on time."

"Oh, of course. Well, have fun," Mom said.

Connor walked me outside. I could feel eyes on me from the house, and when I turned around, I saw the curtains in Alyssa's room fall back into place. I smiled and waved, knowing she'd see me.

"We have an audience," Connor said as he steered the car away from the curb.

"Yes. She's become very protective of me."

"I think the feeling is mutual."

I picked at a loose thread on my jeans, unsure of what to say now. I'd been alone with Connor before, but this was different. This was a date, and I had no idea what was supposed to happen.

"So where are we going?" I asked.

"You'll see," he replied, unable to hide his smile. "I hope you're not super hungry yet. I made the dinner reservation for a little later."

"Sure, no problem."

We drove into downtown St. Louis, and I was surprised to see we were parking next to a dance studio. I looked around for a movie theater, a museum, even a park, and saw nothing. Connor got out of the car and hurried around to the passenger side.

"Uh, what are we doing?" I asked, even though the answer was staring me in the face.

"I thought it would be fun to take a dance lesson."

"A what?"

He took my hand and guided me to the entrance. Through the tall windows, I could see other couples of all ages inside. Some were mingling, and some were hanging back, obviously nervous.

"I have two left feet," I said.

"So do I. Guess we'll just end up going in circles then."

My mind was flashing back to all of the charity events I'd attended with Dad. I'd taken dance lessons before, and he expected me to use them. At my debutante ball, Dad presented me and we shared a ballroom dance. It was both a memorable event and something I wished to forget because I'd ended up tripping over the hem of my dress, causing us both to fall in front of hundreds of people. Dad had laughed it off, taking all of the blame, but I was devastated when the pictures showed up in the papers the next day with the caption, "Debutante Takes a Dive".

I gripped Connor's arm, slowing him down. "I don't think I can do this," I said. I knew I sounded whiny, and I hated that. He regarded me for a moment, and then nodded.

"Hey, I'm sorry," he said. "I don't want to make you uncomfortable. We can do something else."

We were almost back to the car when I decided I was being childish and told him I wanted to give it a try. He asked if I was sure, and while I wasn't 100%, I was determined to get over my fear of humiliating myself in public.

We were the youngest couple in the class, and while that may have bothered someone else, Connor didn't even seem to notice. The instructor was a beautiful woman named Samantha, and she walked us through the basic steps of the Foxtrot. Connor took me in his arms, and we moved around the room with everyone else.

"You're good," he said.

"I'm not that good. I mean, I took lessons, and I used to dance with my dad, but you won't see me on *Dancing with the Stars* anytime soon."

He laughed, and I had to wonder what this amazing guy saw in me. The lesson ended all too soon, and as soon as Connor released me, I missed the warmth of his touch. He took me to a fantastic Italian restaurant for dinner, and after dancing, we were both starving. He commented that he was pleased to see a girl with a good appetite. I told him I hoped he was prepared for a hefty dinner bill because I was also ordering dessert.

Over a shared piece of tiramisu, we spent another hour at the restaurant, just talking. At one point, he reached across the table and grasped my hand. It was a simple gesture, and it sent my senses into overdrive.

"So tell me more about your parents, your sister," he said. "They seem like great people. What's it like to have such a close knit family?"

"Well, that's an odd question for me, because up until a few weeks ago, I didn't. I was so worried that I wouldn't fit in, or that it would be awkward living with my mom again, but things have worked out fantastic."

Aside from the crazy scientist who is after my little sister, I thought. I took another forkful of dessert to keep from saying that out loud. It was killing me that I couldn't share this with him. If I was going to have any kind of relationship with Connor, I knew that I needed to be honest with him. I also knew my mother and Eric would freak out on me, so I kept my mouth shut on the subject.

"Has there been any news about your father?"

I shook my head. "There hasn't even been a sighting. The investigation has gone cold."

My grandfather had called a few days earlier to discuss with me the possibility of having Dad declared legally dead. There were some issues with the business, and the board of directors was pushing to have this done. I burst into tears, and he promised we'd wait awhile longer.

"What do you think happened to him?" Connor asked.

"I wish I knew. I keep hoping it's something as simple as he got into some kind of accident and has amnesia or something, and he just hasn't been recognized. I refuse to think about the alternatives."

Connor nodded and gave my hand a gentle squeeze.

"What about you? Do you see your brother much? Where does he live?" I asked, refocusing the attention to him instead of me.

"The usual, holidays and such. He's all over the place, traveling for his job. He's a corporate lawyer, so he's pretty busy. I'm busy too, with school and all, and yet sometimes I feel like he's a little too involved with my life. He doesn't want me to make mistakes, but how else am I going to learn?"

I nodded, understanding where he was coming from. "My dad didn't want me to have to struggle with anything, and while he could buy me all of the latest things, he couldn't help me fit in that well in school, or find true friends. I think I've found that here, and it's nice."

Connor wiped his mouth with his napkin and leaned back in his chair a little. "Speaking of friends, Paul seems nice."

I was glad the lighting was somewhat dim in the restaurant to hide the blush that reddened my cheeks. "He's great. A good friend."

"I think he likes you," Connor said. "A lot, and I don't want to ruin a good relationship like that."

"We've talked. He knows he and I are just friends," I said, forcing my voice to sound firm.

Connor nodded. "All right. I'd like to get to know him better. Maybe then he'd know I have only the best intentions toward you." He chuckled a little. "That sounds a little old fashioned, doesn't it?"

I couldn't help but smile. "I think my father would like you. He's old fashioned too."

After dinner, Connor drove us around the city, and I felt a little homesick for New York. It was a similar atmosphere, and I missed it. I decided at that moment that I would keep the penthouse, no matter what the outcome was with Dad. Maybe someday Alyssa would like to visit the big city, and I could show her my life before Hamilton Green.

We arrived back at my house, and I was disappointed that our night was over already. Connor walked me to the front door, and we shared another kiss on the porch. I was falling hard for him, and very fast.

All too soon, he broke our connection and sighed. "I have to go. But I had a wonderful time tonight," he said.

I nodded in agreement. "I'd like to take another dancing lesson sometime. It was fun."

"You got it. I'll call you."

He kissed my forehead and then headed back to his car. I went inside and wasn't the least bit surprised to find my mom and sister sitting in the kitchen, a package of Oreos and glasses of milk in front of them.

"Alyssa wanted to wait up for you," Mom said, and Alyssa shook her head.

"Mom wanted to wait up for you," she corrected. Mom's sheepish expression gave her away.

I just laughed and joined them for a cookie.

* * *

Monica and Jonathan Orson arrived at our house on a Saturday afternoon for lunch, and ended up staying for dinner as well. There was a lot to discuss with them about Luminesk. It was obvious that Alyssa was on their radar, and we had to acknowledge the fact they knew exactly where she lived. The only thing we could do was try and make sure she was safe at all times.

Mom, Eric and Jonathan were instant friends. I suppose the bond of having a child with special abilities was pretty strong. They talked technical aspects of Luminesk, Simon Foley, and Elementals. Monica, Alyssa and I went up to Alyssa's bedroom to hang out. I noticed Monica becoming a little wistful as she listened to Alyssa talk about her abilities and then enthusiastically show them off. Monica was remembering her little brother and how he had been the same way. Alyssa became tired after a while, so we went to my room so she could take a nap.

"She is amazing," Monica said to me. She sat down on my bed and shook her head. "She reminds me so much of Travis. Her excitement and joy at what she's able to do is almost tangible. I remember my brother being the exact same way."

I fiddled with the hem of my comforter, unsure of how to ask, knowing that I needed to. "What happened with your brother? I mean, I wasn't around Alyssa when she started showing her powers."

Monica looked up at the framed and matted flower hanging on my wall. "He started exhibiting some of his abilities when he was just a baby. Mom and Dad absolutely flipped," she said with a laugh. "I thought it was the coolest thing ever, so I was no help. They had him checked out by a doctor, but it was just a checkup really. Nothing to the extent that your mom and step-dad had done with Alyssa. Of course, nothing was found, so we just thought it had to be a fluke."

She paused and stood up, examining the flower closer. "This is beautiful. Did Alyssa do this?"

"Yeah. My first day here."

"Travis made one bloom on his fourth birthday. Out of nowhere, it just sprouted from the ground."

"So how did you handle his abilities after that until he…um…" I trailed off, shifting uncomfortably.

"Until he disappeared?" Monica finished for me, and I nodded. "We worked with him on staying calm, kept him out of loud, crowded situations as much as possible, and just loved him. The hardest part was how we had to stay calm. Anytime we became stressed about even the littlest thing, he could sense it, and he would start to react."

"Alyssa killed my flower when I got excited about a boy," I said.

"That doesn't surprise me. Here, sit down. Let me give you a few tips."

We sat down on the floor, legs folded. She told me to sit up straight and square my shoulders.

"Take deep breaths," she said, "and focus on your posture. Okay, good, now visualize a happy memory, really throw yourself into it."

A smile formed on my lips as I remembered Connor dancing with me, his strong hands guiding me through the steps.

"Must have found a good one," Monica teased me. "As long as that memory can stay there, just in the background, you'll be able to stay calm and pass that calm on to Alyssa."

I exhaled and nodded. "I'll work on it."

"Just keep that memory nearby, and you'll be fine. I still use a special memory every now and then when I need to stay calm."

"What's your memory?" I blurted out before I could stop myself. "I'm sorry. It's none of my business."

"No, it's fine. I remember when Travis was just a baby, and my parents brought him home. I was less than thrilled at the idea of having an obnoxious little brother. Then my mom had me hold him, and he gazed up at me with absolute trust and adoration. I knew that I would do anything I could to protect him."

She sighed. "I think a lot about the last time I saw him. I tucked him into bed that night he disappeared. He was having some issues with the dark, so I made sure to turn on his lamp for him. It was his favorite, a frog shaped lamp that sat by his bed. Then we read a story, and I kissed his forehead. He told me I was the best big sister in the world." Her joyful expression faded into one of sadness. "And then I woke up in the middle of the night with a strange feeling, and I went to check on him. His room was dark, and he was gone. But do you want to know the weirdest part?"

I swallowed and nodded.

"Whoever took him also took his lamp. We never found him or the lamp."

"Do you think he's still out there somewhere?"

I wanted to smack myself for being so insensitive. The words just came rushing out. Monica assured me it was fine.

"I always hold hope. If I allow myself to be honest, I believe he's gone, and I think, so does my dad. He'll never say it though, because saying it out loud will make it real. I think my mother died of a broken heart. After so many years of helping other families who had gone through what we had, she was just too devastated to go on."

I glanced toward the direction of Alyssa's room and shuddered. It had been difficult enough to believe that Alyssa had special abilities, and even more difficult to accept that someone wanted to take her away from us. I was having a harder time dealing with it now because I personally knew someone who had experienced just what we were trying to prevent. In just a short time, I'd gone from having a little sister I didn't know or care too much about to being sickened at the thought of losing her.

Monica told me more about Anemone, the organization that helped other families like ours. She shared with me the escape plan if Alyssa was taken and Mom, Eric and I needed to disappear. She explained to me how we would leave the area and be set up with a new life. Anemone had several other families located around the world, each of them ready and willing to help another in the same situation. Even though the plan was sound and made sense, I knew my mother would never in a million years go into hiding. Monica gave me an encrypted flash drive with all of the information we'd need, and I hid it in the bottom drawer of my dresser, along with all of the documents about Dad.

After Monica and her father left, and everyone had gone to bed, I closed my bedroom door and the bathroom door, making sure they were both locked. Then I crawled into bed with my laptop computer and typed in

"Wendell Benton" in a search engine. A few hundred thousand hits came up, most of them old articles reporting on some new movie he was producing, or how much money he'd given at some charity benefit.

Of course, the major news organizations were doing their follow-up stories, asking the same old question, "Where is Wendell Benton?"

I wished they were able to answer it. It was so frustrating not knowing anything. I realized there were similarities between his disappearance and that of the Elemental children, and for a crazy moment I wondered if there was a connection. Then I shook my head. There couldn't be. Dad never showed any type of powers, and he wasn't Alyssa's father, so even if he had, he couldn't have passed them on. His work dealt with movies, television, newspapers and magazines, not scientific experiments on children.

Still, I thought it was odd that he went missing, and there was the scary possibility my sister could as well. I closed the lid on the laptop and put it back on the desk. As I did, I looked out the window, giving a cursory glance up and down the street. Everything appeared normal, and I allowed myself to relax enough to go to sleep.

Chapter Fourteen

I was not pleased with the reflection staring back at me from the mirror. I had already changed my outfit four times, and a quick glance at my bedside clock told me that Paul was going to be here in ten minutes to pick me up. I was frustrated with myself for being this nervous. Every new school year brought some anxiety, sure, but this was completely foreign territory to me. I was going to a brand new school with people I'd never met before. Paul and Charlotte would be there, and that made me feel a little better.

At Radcliffe, we had uniforms, so it wasn't difficult to decide what to wear. Sure, we all added our own flair, but basically everyone appeared the same. Now I was faced with having to decide how I wanted to present myself to the other kids at school. Would they judge me based on my clothes? Would they know right away that I was a rich girl from the big city? What had they already heard about me? I knew it was silly to worry about something like this, but I'd never been the new kid before.

Alyssa had helped me pick out jeans and a light sweater the night before. It was the first outfit out of about ten I'd tried on, and I decided she'd been right. She just loved looking through my closet, running her hands over the different fabrics and commenting on the colors and patterns. I saw a budding fashion consultant in her, and I made a mental note to take her shopping in New York City sometime. We would just need to get past her issues with crowds first. And oh yeah, make sure some mad scientist wasn't out to get her anymore.

I hurried to change, and then raced downstairs to grab something to eat. Mom was just as nervous as I was as she flitted around the kitchen.

"I was about to call for you," she said. "What would you like for breakfast?"

I saw Alyssa's half-eaten plate of scrambled eggs and bacon, and I felt my stomach roll. There was no way I could eat anything.

"First day jitters," I said. "I'll just grab something at school."

Even the word flustered me. I shoved some notebooks, pens, a calculator, my wallet and my cell phone into the new backpack I'd gotten and zipped it up, slinging it over my shoulder. We heard the car pull into the driveway, and everyone turned to see Paul coming up to the house. He waved and grinned before stepping inside.

"Ready to go?" he asked.

I nodded, trying to feel confident. Alyssa turned in her chair and balanced on her knees to reach up and give me a kiss on the cheek.

"Have a good day," she said.

Mom hugged me and handed me a blueberry muffin. She saw Paul eyeing it and gave him one too. He hungrily bit into it.

"Thanks so much," he said, his mouth full.

He held the door open for me as I climbed into his car, and soon we were on our way to school. I ate half of my muffin and gave the rest to Paul. My mind was full of uncertainty as we got nearer and nearer, and I wanted to just go home and hide out with Mom and Alyssa. I hadn't been in this situation since my first day of kindergarten, and I wasn't sure how to handle it. I tried to remember my first day at Radcliffe Elementary, and it seemed so long ago. Dad had taken me himself, walking me to the classroom and helping me to find my seat. He stayed as long as he could, and I remembered how proud and sad he appeared at the same time as he backed away, leaving me to embark on a new adventure without him.

Somehow, I knew he would be proud of me today.

"Are you okay?" Paul asked. "You're not going to puke, are you?"

I laughed at his weary expression and shook my head. "Not yet. Let's see what's for lunch first."

I was instantly seen as the new girl, and I hated the feeling. I knew people were talking about me, about who I was and why I was there. I plastered a smile on my face, and said hello to everyone, determined not to be considered a snob, and walked with Paul to find our lockers. Mom had taken me to register for classes a few weeks earlier, so I didn't need to check in at the main office. I already had a locker assignment and a class schedule. It matched Paul's for the most part, and the classes that Paul and I didn't have together were ones that Charlotte was in. I felt safe in that respect.

During first period English Literature, a note was passed my way. Paul was sitting beside me, focused on what the teacher was saying. I glanced behind me to see where it had come from. A group of girls huddled in the corner, whispering amongst themselves. I knew that clique. I'd seen it a thousand times at Radcliffe. They were the popular girls, the ones with more money than they knew what to do with, and parents with prestige and titles. Cautiously, so as not to be caught by the teacher, I unfolded the note and saw a picture torn from a magazine taped to the paper. It was of my dad and me attending a movie premiere the year before. We were standing beside the stars of the film, the leading man's arm wrapped around my shoulders. Dad had been an executive producer of the film.

Beneath the picture in flowery handwriting were the words, "Can you hook us up with him?" and an arrow pointing to the good looking movie star.

My face flushed hot. I looked back at the girls, who were regarding me with expectant and starstruck eyes. I crumpled the paper and tucked it into my backpack, then turned and faced front, slumping in my seat. I heard the indignant huffs from the girls, and the new whispers started.

Even at Radcliffe, I'd hated that kind of attention I received from the other students. I was proud of my dad and his involvement in things like that, but it made the other kids at school look at me differently. None of the celebrities I met were close, personal friends, and to be honest, they didn't care who I was. Yet everyone seemed to think these famous people were on my speed dial. I realized how foolish I was to think that these kids wouldn't be like that.

The bell rang, signaling the end of the class, and everyone started to leave the room. I picked up my backpack, and got up to follow Paul. Someone bumped me from behind, knocking me against a desk.

"Oh, I'm so sorry," one of the girls said, her voice dripping with false concern. She passed with her friends, all of them giving me evil looks.

"What was that all about?" Paul asked.

"Nothing. Forget it."

Word spread quickly, and by lunchtime, I was pretty much a leper. I had received two more notes of similar inquiry, and I'd thrown both of them in the garbage. Charlotte met us in the cafeteria, her tray loaded with food. I couldn't understand how someone so small could eat so much.

"Geez, Aubrey, you sure made an impression," she said.

I drowned my French fries in ketchup. "I didn't do anything. If people are upset because I'm not going to help them hook up with Robert Pattinson or Channing Tatum, that's their problem."

Paul frowned and threw a glance around the room. "People are jerks. There's more to life than celebrities. Just because your dad knew people doesn't mean you do."

Charlotte shook her carton of milk before opening it and taking a long gulp. "Well, I like you for who you are, not because of who you've met."

Such a simple statement, and yet it meant so much to me. We finished our lunch with fifteen minutes before the next period. I excused myself to use the restroom, and Paul and Charlotte went to the library. I told them I'd meet them there.

When I came out of the stall, I was surprised to see a girl with dark brown hair leaning against one of the sinks. She appeared to be waiting for me, and she seemed familiar, but I couldn't place her.

"I thought that was you," she said. "You're the girl from the mall."

My eyes widened as I pictured her with pink hair. She'd knocked into Alyssa in the food court, and shortly after, the gust of wind had come through.

"I like to change it up every once in a while," she said, pointing to her hair. "So you go to school here now?"

"Yeah," I said. I couldn't tell by her tone what she wanted with me. I eased around her to wash my hands at another sink. She continued to stare at me.

"So what the heck happened that day?" she asked.

"What do you mean?" I countered, playing dumb.

"You know what I mean. How did you do that?"

I shook my head and dried my hands on some paper towels, then tossed them in the trash. "I don't know what you're talking about. I've got to get to class."

I turned to leave, and she grabbed my upper arm and squeezed. I winced and tried to move away.

"I saw you there," she said, "and I know you had something to do with that...that force. Or whatever it was. There's something weird about you. Some of the other kids think you're just a rich snob. I think it's something else."

"Really, I don't know what you're talking about. Now let me go before I scream," I said.

She glared at me for a moment more before releasing me. I rubbed my arm, knowing it was going to bruise.

"See you around," she said with an ominous smile. Then she left.

I waited another minute before leaving the restroom. Kids were streaming out of the cafeteria, on their way to their next class. I didn't see Paul waiting for me, and when he reached out to touch me to get my attention, I whirled on him, smacking his hand away. He jumped back, startled.

"Whoa, what's wrong?" he asked.

My heart was pounding. I had no idea who that girl was. I was nervous about what she thought she'd seen that day at the mall, and what she was going to do. I scanned the group of students milling past, spotting her as she climbed the stairs to the second floor. I pointed her out to Paul, asking who she was.

"Carly Grand," he said. "Her dad teaches genetic biology at Hamilton University. Why? What's going on?"

I promised to fill him in later, on our way home. I didn't want to talk about it around others, and he immediately understood it had something to do with Alyssa. By the end of the day, I was ready to go home and call Mark O'Donnell. I had some questions about Carly Grand and her father.

Paul was curious about her as well. He said that she'd lived in Hamilton Green her whole life, and that her parents were both teachers. She'd been friends with Paul and Charlotte when they were younger. Then during the second grade, things changed and she didn't want to hang out with anyone anymore. She became rebellious, and even at that young age, she changed her appearance and her attitude. By middle school she was hanging out with a bad crowd, dying her hair and smoking. She'd been busted for shoplifting twice and stealing a car. Her parents sent her away to a juvenile camp in Wyoming two summers ago, and while she hadn't been in any more trouble with the law, she still had a reputation.

I wanted to know more about what her father taught, and if it had anything to do with Alyssa or other Elementals.

"She never showed any interest in school," Paul said as he drove me home. "Her dad is a real brainiac though. Her mom teaches too."

"What does her mom teach?"

"American history at the middle school. Do you think she knows something?"

"She thinks that what she witnessed at the mall has something to do with me. I'm just afraid she'll start asking questions and attract unwanted attention."

I got out of the car and closed the door, then leaned down into the open window. "I'll call you later if I get anything," I said. "Thanks for the ride. I'll pick you up tomorrow."

"Sure thing. Good luck."

I took a moment before going inside to clear my mind. I didn't want to alert Alyssa, so I was using the deep breathing and concentration method that Monica had taught me.

Mom and Alyssa were upstairs in Alyssa's room, finger painting. They asked me about my first day, and I chatted with them for a little while before Mom decided to go start dinner. Alyssa offered to help. I told them I'd be down soon, and I went to my room to call Mark.

He took down the information I gave him about Carly and said he'd have a full history for me in twenty-four hours. I had no idea what he would find out, but I wasn't going to take any chances of Luminesk finding Alyssa if I could help it.

* * *

Carly cornered me again the next day, this time in one of the second floor hallways. I was on my way to the library to meet Charlotte during our free period. Carly grabbed my backpack and swung me around, slamming me into a row of lockers. I tasted blood and touched my lip. I turned to face her. She was glaring at me with pure hate.

"You're having someone check up on my family?" she shouted at me, poking me in the shoulder.

I couldn't hide the shock from registering on my face. "I don't know what you're talking about," I stammered.

"Don't lie, sorority girl," she said, "you're no good at it. Stay away from my family."

"Then stay away from mine," I said, standing up straight. We were the same height, and she somehow managed to tower over me. I stood my ground though, refusing to back down.

Other students were steering clear of us, watching, but from a safe distance.

"I don't know what you think you know," Carly hissed, "but you've got it all wrong. You have no idea what you're up against. You need to back off."

I narrowed my eyes at her, confused. I wasn't sure what she was getting at. I took a step toward her, and she shoved me again. This time, I shoved back, knocking her off balance. She flailed and cried out, falling to the floor. I saw the fire in her eyes as she charged at me. I raised my hands in front of me to stop her attack. Her balled up fist connected with my chin, and I went down. Before she could land another punch, someone pulled me to my feet, dragging me away.

"Aubrey! Are you hurt?" Paul asked, standing in front of me.

"I'm okay, I just-"

"Miss Benton, Miss Grand, come with me this instant!" a deep voice yelled over the noise in the hallway.

Paul and I both looked up to see the assistant vice principal, Mr. Bridges, glaring down on us. He already had one hand on Carly's shoulder, and I could tell that he was expecting me to follow.

I glanced at Paul, who shrugged helplessly, and then I went with Mr. Bridges. He took us right to his office, sat us down, and demanded to know what we'd been fighting about. Neither of us said a word. The nurse had given me an ice pack, which I held to my face.

The vice principal tapped his pen against the desk, dissatisfied with our lack of cooperation. He gave a heavy sigh.

"Miss Benton, I understand that you've recently moved here after dealing with some personal issues, and I apologize. However, this does not allow you to lash out in such an inappropriate manner," he said. "And you, Miss Grand. What can I say about you?"

Carly examined her fingernails, uninterested in the conversation.

"Well, our school has a zero tolerance policy for fighting," he continued. "On that note, you're both suspended for two days. Please wait outside while I contact your parents."

He held the door open and waited for us to leave. I sat down in one of the hard plastic chairs, still holding the ice pack. Carly chose to stand near the vice principal's door. I couldn't believe I was being suspended. This would never have happened at Radcliffe, because I would never have gotten into a fight. I was always the good girl, the quiet, meek girl who did as she was told. A small giggle erupted from me as I thought about what my old classmates would think of me now.

"What are you laughing at?" Carly asked.

"Nothing," I said.

She glanced at the secretary typing behind the counter, then she came to sit next to me. I shifted away from her.

"Hey, I'm sorry," she said, her head bent and her voice soft.

I didn't have time to say anything back. Mr. Bridges came out of his office and told me my mother had been called, and I was to go straight home. I picked up my backpack and left the administration office. Paul was waiting for me in the hallway.

"I skipped class," he said, walking with me to the parking lot. "You got suspended, huh?"

I nodded. "Two days, and I have to leave right now. Can you get a ride home today?"

"Sure thing. I'll just wait for Mom."

It started to rain just as I got into my car. I looked up at the sky that had been clear and blue a minute before and wondered if Alyssa knew I was in trouble and was upset for me. I drove home as slowly as legally allowed. I wasn't in a hurry to face my mom, and I was not surprised to find her waiting for me on the porch. The expression on her face was a mixture of worry and disappointment.

"If it makes you feel any better," I said, "I didn't start it."

She sighed and shook her head. "If you're upset about something," she said, "Alyssa, your dad, whatever it is, please tell me. We can work through this."

"Mom, it's not what you think. I'm not rebelling or anything, and I'm fine with Alyssa. I'm doing better about Dad, and I'm adjusting great with you and Eric."

"Then what is it? What happened?"

"This girl, Carly Grand, she saw us at the mall that first day. She was there, and she witnessed what happened. She asked me about it yesterday."

Mom's eyes widened. "Does she suspect anything?"

I told Mom that she was asking questions, and that I'd called Mark O'Donnell the night before to find out more about her. I explained that she'd jumped me at school today, warning me to back off.

"What does that mean?" Mom asked.

I had no idea. "Where's Alyssa?" I asked, realizing she wasn't around.

"She's taking a nap."

"Is she sick?"

Mom stood up then and we went inside the house. "Yesterday, she said she didn't feel well, but it passed.

Today, the same thing happened, and she caused the bathtub to overflow. She said she thinks that we're in trouble, that someone is watching us."

"We haven't seen those black-suited guys in weeks. And Monica would have warned us if they'd heard anything."

"I know that, sweetheart. I think all of the new information is making her a little nervous."

My cell phone vibrated, causing us both to jump. I dug around in my backpack to find it and checked the caller ID. It was Mark.

"I can't talk long," he said as soon as I answered. "Can you come to the city tomorrow?"

Something in his tone frightened me, and I gripped the phone tighter with both hands. "What's wrong?"

"If you can, meet me at the place where I first met your father. Alone."

The definite click of the call ending was all I heard next.

Chapter Fifteen

I wasn't sure what to make of Mark's call. I just knew I needed to get back to New York to talk to him in person. Mom was not pleased, and she refused to let me go. When Eric got home, he reasoned with her, arguing that if this was in regard to Alyssa, it was imperative that I meet with the private investigator. He was worried too, but I promised to be careful, and if there was any trouble, I would contact the police.

I booked myself a one way ticket on the first flight out the next morning, and I tried calling Mark back on his cell phone and his private office line. I didn't reach him at either number, and that concerned me. I didn't want to call his home phone number in case someone was there and I frightened them. He must have come across something very important, and he was afraid to pass it along by phone, email, or fax.

Paul called me when he got home from school, and I told him what was going on. He wasn't thrilled at the idea of me going alone, so he booked himself on the same flight. I protested, assuring him I would be fine. He refused to listen to me and told me he'd pick me up. We'd go to the airport together.

"What about school? Your mom?" I asked. "I don't want you to get into trouble."

"She'll understand," was all he said.

I didn't sleep well that night. Every time I would drift off, I would picture black cars following us, and faceless men from Luminesk trying to kidnap Alyssa. Finally, I gave up and got myself ready. I packed my bag with my wallet, camera, and cell phone. There was no telling what the day would bring, but I was determined to face it.

I was curled up on the couch in the family room with a mug of hot tea when Eric came downstairs a little while later. He sat down beside me. "Do you have any idea what Mark found out?"

"Not a clue. It's got to be big though. I've known Mark for years, and this is the first time he's ever been cryptic."

"You'll call us as soon as you get there, and after you talk to him?"

"Of course."

He was quiet for a moment, and we watched the sun come up.

"This might sound strange," he said, looking at me, "and you may disagree, but I think the best thing that could have happened to Alyssa was having her big sister come into her life."

Eric hugged me then and wished me luck. When Paul arrived, my mom tried to talk him into letting her call his mother and explaining things. He shook his head and said he had it taken care of. Everyone stood on the porch and waved us off as Paul backed out of the driveway. We got breakfast at the airport, then boarded the plane.

I thought I would feel relief when I was back in the city. Instead, all I felt was apprehension and fear. Mark hadn't specified a time for us to meet, but I figured he'd be watching the place.

Dad and Mark had met outside a hotel near Times Square. Mark had been hired to follow Dad and take pictures to make sure he wasn't cheating on his then-girlfriend. He hadn't been cheating, and he paid Mark double to turn around and prove his girlfriend was the one doing the cheating. They'd been friends ever since.

I didn't want to go there right away, just in case we'd been followed. We hailed a cab and headed toward Central Park West, to the apartment I'd shared with Dad.

We got out four blocks away and walked, taking side streets and going in through the back entrance to avoid the doorman.

"Why do I feel like I'm in a spy movie?" Paul whispered as we stepped onto the elevator. I inserted my special key card that would take us straight to the apartment.

"I don't want to take any chances."

"I totally agree."

The elevator doors opened into the foyer of the apartment, and Paul hung back, taking it all in. I tugged at his sleeve, pulling him further inside. A large gallery displayed my father's collection of art. Paul stared, open-mouthed, as he gazed around in wonder.

"My whole house could fit in this space alone," he said.

"That's a bit of an overstatement," I said.

"This is amazing. I can't believe I know you."

"All right, stop," I said, feeling myself blush.

I didn't have many people over, but whenever someone new visited, they always reacted like this, and it made me uncomfortable. Dad was successful, yes, and we lived very nicely. I just hated thinking that people judged me because of my lifestyle. Paul seemed to sense my discomfort, and he nudged me in the side.

"Don't worry," he said. "I know you're not a spoiled little rich girl. But can I still get a tour?"

I smiled and showed him around. To the right of the gallery was the dining room, library, living room and the master bedroom. To the left was the kitchen, and down the hallway were two guest rooms and my room.

We went back to the library where Dad's desk was, and I booted up the computer to check his private email. I thought maybe Mark had left me some communication there. I tried not to feel disappointed that there was nothing but junk mail. As I shut down the computer, I checked through his desk drawers, searching for anything that could help me, knowing it was pointless. Judging by the fine layer of dust that covered everything, no one had been in this room since the day I left. I knew we still had a cleaning service, but it appeared they had become lax in their duties. It angered me because I didn't want Dad to return and see that his home hadn't been taken care of.

I opened the bottom drawer which contained a single item, a polished black metal lockbox.

"Do you know what's in there?" Paul asked, looking over my shoulder.

I shut the drawer. "Dad's gun."

"Do you have the key?"

I nodded and stood up. "I know where it is, but I don't want to use it. I don't like guns."

"Understandable," Paul said. "So where to next?"

"Let's swing by Mark's office."

"You really think he'll be there?"

I knew he wouldn't be. I just wanted to see if there was any activity. Before we left the apartment, I went into my room and selected a stuffed animal from one of the shelves for Alyssa. It was a pink elephant that Dad had given me when I was little and afraid of the dark. I tucked it into my bag.

We took a cab downtown to Mark's office building. We hung out in the lobby for twenty minutes, just waiting and watching. Paul chatted with the security guard and learned that Mark hadn't been there in two days. This worried me. As we were walking out of the building, I called Mom to let her know what we were up to. She warned us to be careful and watch our backs. Alyssa took the phone from her to tell me that she didn't feel like she was in any danger today.

"But I think you might be," she whispered. "Please be safe, Aubrey."

Her words sent a chill of fear down my back, and I looked up and down the street, searching for anything out of place. I had been so positive we hadn't been followed, and now I wasn't so sure.

Paul and I bought lunch from a vendor, and while he was excited for his first New York City chili dog, I was too nervous to eat. At around one o'clock, we ended up at the Ramsey Hotel. There was a coffeehouse across the street, so we went there first, ordering drinks and sitting at the window to watch for Mark or anyone suspicious. An hour passed, and then I spotted him coming out of the hotel. He checked out his surroundings, his gaze landing on the coffeehouse. I stood up and waved, and he saw me and nodded.

Paul threw some money down on the table, and we hurried outside. Mark was watching for the light to change so he could safely cross the busy intersection. He frowned when he spotted Paul with me. I had forgotten Mark said to come alone, and I feared he wouldn't meet with us. After a moment, he motioned for us to wait for him. The "walk" signal changed, and he started toward us. He wasn't smiling, and even from that distance I could see he was scared. That added to my already high level of anxiety.

He was halfway across the intersection when a familiar black car came speeding down the street. Paul and I spotted it at the same time, and we started screaming at him to move out of the way. He, along with others crossing the street with him, turned and saw it. He jumped back just in time so that the car missed him. I gripped Paul's arm, relieved that he hadn't been hit, and we ran to meet him.

As we neared, we saw the color drain from Mark's face. His legs buckled, and he crumpled to the pavement. A woman screamed. Some people ran away, and some gathered around to see what was going on. A pedestrian reached him before we did, rolling him over to reveal blood all over his chest. I saw two distinct bullet holes in his white shirt. I wanted to throw up. Paul moved closer while I stood, frozen to the spot and biting my knuckles to keep from screaming. He returned a moment later, shook his head and swallowed hard. Then he grabbed my hand, steering me away.

"We need to get out of here," he said.

I nodded, glancing back at Mark's body lying in the street. His black leather jacket had fallen open on both sides, and I saw a yellow envelope peeking out from an inside pocket. Was that what he wanted to show me? I jerked away from Paul and dashed back, snatching the envelope and shoving it in my pocket. I took Paul's hand again, and we ran as fast as we could for several blocks before getting a cab and heading back to the airport.

I wasn't hysterical yet, but I was shaking pretty badly. Paul held me tight, his lips pressed together in a thin line. His jaw twitched, and each mile that took us closer to the airport also took us farther away from Mark.

"Do you think anyone saw us?" Paul whispered.

I wiped tears from my eyes. "I don't know. Paul, I feel awful. Mark was a friend."

"I know. We'll get them, Aubrey. We'll get them. I promise."

At that moment, I didn't think we would.

We purchased tickets for the next available flight and boarded a plane that would take us as far as Chicago, where we'd have to transfer. Once we reached Chicago, I called my grandfather. I wasn't sure how to explain what I knew, and luckily I didn't have to. He told me that Mark had been in a terrible accident near Times Square, the victim of a drive by shooting.

He had known Mark only through Dad, but it was heartbreaking to hear it was true. Somehow, I'd hoped that maybe it had all been a dream, that this entire situation was just a terrible dream. My grandfather didn't give me details, and for that I was grateful. I had witnessed it. I didn't need to hear about it. I asked him to let me know about funeral arrangements for Mark.

"Of course. I've already spoken to the police, and the surveillance cameras in that area were all malfunctioning at the time," my grandfather said. "There's no footage of the shooting, which hurts their chances of finding the person responsible."

My throat constricted as I realized this was both a blessing and a curse for us. I wanted the people who'd killed Mark to be caught, but I was also a tiny bit relieved that we wouldn't be showing up on any surveillance footage. It would end up leading to too many questions, and we had no answers. What I knew for sure was that somehow, Simon Foley was responsible for the entire thing.

Eric was waiting for us at the St. Louis airport when we arrived. I'd called him from an airport bathroom stall at LaGuardia, right after I'd puked. He was understandably anxious and wanted to get us home as soon as possible. The second he saw me, he pulled me into a hug. It was similar to the hugs Dad gave me after a bad day, strong and soothing. I swallowed the lump in my throat and let Eric guide us outside. No one had spoken yet. I was still reeling from what had happened, and I cried almost the entire way home. Paul drove his car back to our house, and I rode with Eric. I kept checking behind us to make sure Paul was still there. I was terrified that something horrible was going to happen to someone else that I cared about.

Very little was said on the short drive. The gravity of the situation was sinking in, and my heart was heavy. Before today, the dangers of Luminesk and Simon Foley were only partially acknowledged. He and his company were unknown, faceless entities. They may have tried to take Alyssa before, but they had failed. Now someone was dead, someone I knew, and the guilt I felt was worse than anything I'd ever experienced.

Mom and Alyssa were sitting in the living room. When Alyssa saw me, she hurried into my arms, and I held her tightly, the tears streaming down my face. None of us were surprised when it began to rain outside and stopped once I had my emotions under control.

Paul did all of the talking, and while he filled in Mom and Eric, Alyssa and I went to sit on the deck. I didn't want to listen to the recounting of Mark's death. Alyssa patted my hand. I pulled the pink elephant from my bag and passed it to her.

"This is cute," she said. "Was it yours?"

"My dad gave it to me. He said it was supposed to keep the monsters in my closet and under my bed from coming out to get me."

"Did it work?"

I squeezed her hand. "It did."

Alyssa hugged it close and we lapsed into silence. We stayed like that, staring into the yard until Eric asked us to come back inside.

"Aubrey, can we see the envelope that you took from...from...that you have?" Paul asked, stumbling over his words.

I had forgotten about the envelope. I pulled it from my pocket and handed it to him. He smoothed it and using a kitchen knife, he sliced open one end. Inside the envelope was a single piece of paper. He unfolded it and scanned the page, his eyes widening and his mouth dropping open.

"What is it?" Mom asked.

Eric took the paper from Paul and examined it, frowning at first, and then his eyes narrowed. "It's a photocopied page from an accounting ledger. Your father's personal ledger," he said, pinning me with a hard stare.

"What? Are you sure?" I asked. "Why would Mark have wanted to give us that?"

"See for yourself."

Something in his voice frightened me, and I realized that Eric was angry. My fingers shaking, I accepted the paper and studied the information. I didn't have much experience with my father's accounting, having caught glances of it on his computer screen now and then, but not really paying close attention, so it took me a moment to find what Eric had seen. When I did, I was stunned into silence.

Halfway down the page were several entries for wire transfers to an offshore account in the Cayman Islands. Not unusual on their own, since Dad had accounts everywhere to protect his assets. However, the name on the account caused me to suck in a hard breath.

Simon Foley for Luminesk Enterprises.

Chapter Sixteen

"I don't...there's no way...how could he..." I stammered. I dropped the paper as if it were on fire and covered my face with my hands.

Paul examined the envelope again, shaking it to see if anything else would fall out, then ripping it open to see if there was anything written inside.

"Nothing," he said with a sigh.

"Why was Dad sending money to Simon Foley?" I groaned, sinking into a nearby chair. "How could he be doing business with a monster?"

"You really had no idea about this?" Eric asked. Mom reached out and placed a hand on his arm. His tone softened. "I mean, he never mentioned anything about the businesses he invested in?"

"I thought your father dealt in media," Mom said.

"That's all he ever did," I assured her. "Television, movies, newspapers and magazines. Certainly not kidnapping children and experimenting on them."

The room was spinning, and I couldn't breathe. This had to be some kind of mistake. Dad would never be involved in something like this. Had Simon Foley tricked him? Blackmailed him?

"How did your friend get this?" Eric asked.

I shook my head. "I have no idea. Mark had his ways. Legal or otherwise, he never shared with us how he got his information."

And that information had gotten him killed. I jumped up and ran for the bathroom, making it in time to vomit into the toilet. This was an absolute nightmare. I sat on the bathroom floor, my head in my hands as I tried to sort through the chaos going through my brain. Dad had never once mentioned anything about Simon Foley or Luminesk. He'd never once mentioned taking on new business opportunities. I wondered if this was why he'd gone missing. I wondered if my grandfather knew about this.

I stood up on shaking legs, rinsed my mouth out, and emerged from the bathroom, still feeling sick. I was also determined to get some answers. My family was where I had left them, in the kitchen, gathered around the table. I asked Eric to call Jonathan and see what he could find. There had to be another reason for Dad to have been sending money to Simon Foley. I knew that Jonathan would immediately distrust us due to this connection. He needed to be informed, nonetheless.

Then I excused myself to go up to my room where I dialed my grandfather's direct office line. Even though the work day was done, I figured he'd be there rather than at home. Any other time, I would have gone through his assistant. However, I felt this was a valid reason to skip company protocol.

"Aubrey," my grandfather said, surprised to hear from me again so soon. "I haven't gotten any new details about Mark's funeral, but I've arranged to take care of all the expenses. Your father would have wanted that. His family will be taken care of."

My heart lurched. "His family?"

"He had a wife and two small children, a boy and a girl, I think."

The lump in my throat rose again, threatening to choke me. I squeezed my eyes shut. Another family destroyed. When would it end?

"Is there something else you needed?" my grandfather asked. "Are you all right?"

"I need you to be honest with me, please," I said.

"Of course," he said, sounding confused. "What's going on?"

"Did Dad ever mention a company named Luminesk? Or a man named Simon Foley?"

There was a brief pause, and then, "It doesn't sound familiar. Is he a movie or television producer? Your dad had a couple of new projects lined up for a cable network in the fall."

"Was he thinking about investing in scientific experiments? Genetics or anything along those lines?"

My grandfather gave a little laugh. "No offense to your dad, but he wasn't the smartest when it came to science. Did you know he failed biology three times?"

"No, I didn't," I said. It seemed there was a lot about him I didn't know. "Would you have been made aware if he had an interest in anything new like that? You're responsible for making all of the financial decisions now, right? If he'd been investing in something not in the media field, it would be recorded?"

"Well, for the most part, yes, I have the final say in any new or continuing projects in his absence. I haven't seen anything out of the ordinary. We've had a team of forensic accountants going through every business transaction, as well as his personal accounts, as part of the investigation of his disappearance. I would have been alerted by now."

I took a deep breath, relaxing ever so slightly. Could this paper have been forged? A red herring from Simon

Foley himself to throw us into utter confusion and suspicion and break our relationship with Jonathan and Monica? But then why kill Mark?

"Aubrey, what's going on? Why the questions?"

I shrugged, even though he couldn't see me. "I've just been thinking a lot about Dad and trying to figure out new angles to check. I want to find him." This was true.

"We all want that, sweetheart. If your grandmother were still alive, this would surely have killed her, not knowing. You're an extremely strong young woman. He would be so proud of you."

I felt myself tearing up. We chatted for a few more minutes, and he told me he'd call as soon as he knew more about Mark's funeral. I was going to attend no matter what and thank his wife and children. I owed them that much.

Mom and Alyssa were reading a book in the family room, while Paul and Eric were in Eric's office. They had contacted Jonathan, and as expected, he was less than pleased. I spoke with him and told him this had to be a fake, according to what my grandfather had told me.

"Or your father had a very secret account that he wanted absolutely no one to know about, not even you, and he was funding some very depraved stuff," Jonathan snapped, and I felt his anger through the phone like a slap to the face. I couldn't talk to him anymore and handed the phone to Eric.

I couldn't blame him. Luminesk had taken his son, done who knows what with him, and left nothing behind but questions. Well, I had my own questions. If my dad had been involved in some way with Simon Foley, was this the reason he'd disappeared? What if he'd changed his mind and wanted out of it, and Simon Foley had him killed? I shuddered at the thought.

Paul caught my attention, gesturing me back to the phone. I took it and placed it to my ear. A heavy sigh greeted me, and then Jonathan said, "Aubrey, I want to apologize. I don't believe your father knowingly set out to hurt anyone. Please, understand that Monica and I have been dealing with years of frustration and guilt in not knowing what happened to Travis."

"Of course. We're on the same side. This just strengthens my need to find my dad and get some answers. I feel like he's the key to this whole thing now."

"I agree. I may not be as good as your PI friend, but I can do a little digging and see where your father's investigation is at. Was there anything else your friend was working on?"

I thought for a moment, and then remembered the other thing I'd asked Mark to look into for me. "A girl at school," I said. "She threatened me in a not so direct way. She was asking about Alyssa. I don't know what he found, but she cornered me yesterday and yelled at me for looking into her family."

"What's her name?"

"Carly Grand."

Jonathan was silent for a moment. "Are you sure?"

I frowned. "Positive. Do you know her?"

"Do you remember when I told you we learned about your sister through a source in your area? She was our source, Aubrey. She's an Elemental."

My eyes widened, and Paul and Eric were instantly by my side. I replaced the handset and put Jonathan on speakerphone so he could explain to them as well.

"She and her parents refused Anemone's help years ago. Her parents didn't believe their daughter could control the elements. They thought she was just depressed and delusional. They tried treating her through medical methods. Therapy, medication, and counseling. Something must have worked, because she stopped displaying powers. I personally contacted her parents to see what they had done, and they refused to talk to me. They ignored it and went on with their lives. They were on Luminesk's radar for a short time, and they haven't bothered with her since."

"She was an only child," Paul said. "I grew up with her, and she never had any siblings. I thought Elementals were second children?"

"She *was* a second child. Her parents had a little boy about three years earlier. He was stillborn."

After a moment of stunned silence, Eric said, "We've got to talk to her."

"She seemed spooked about something," I said.

"We haven't heard from her in a while. See if she's willing to meet with us," Jonathan urged. "She may have some answers that could help us."

Chapter Seventeen

Paul rang the doorbell for a second time, and then knocked on the door. I stood beside him, nervously bouncing from foot to foot. After we hung up with Jonathan, we called Carly's home number. We received no answer. Eric had insisted on driving us over to her house. I glanced back to the street and saw him sitting in his SUV, waiting for us.

"Isn't it strange that there are two Elementals in the same town?" I asked.

"Yeah, a little."

"Why do you think that is?"

Paul shrugged and said, "Could be anything. Maybe your mom and the Grands are somehow distantly related. Maybe it has something to do with being near large monuments. Or it could just be a total fluke. Evolution is like that, you know." He frowned. "It doesn't seem like anyone's here."

"They might be out having dinner," I said. "We could leave them a note."

Paul rang the bell again. "If I remember the Grands, they hate eating out. They've always been very private people. Now I understand why." He walked along the porch and pressed his face against the window, peering inside. "Hey, check this out. It's empty."

I blinked in surprise. The curtains had been drawn, just not quite all the way. The living room was void of furniture, not even a lamp or book in sight. Goosebumps rose up on my arms. I turned and motioned for Eric to join us. We split up and went around the house. Eric and I went one way, and Paul went the other. Each window we peeked into revealed empty rooms. We met in the backyard, feeling very confused and a little scared.

"This is not good," Paul murmured, running a hand through his hair. "What the heck happened?"

Eric shook his head. "I don't know."

"Do you think Simon Foley has them?" I asked.

"Why would he clean out their house?" Paul wondered.

I shrugged. "Maybe to make it look like they just skipped town. It would be suspicious, but wouldn't raise as many questions if just the family disappeared." I shivered, even though there was no breeze. "Can we leave now? I'm getting creeped out."

Eric led the way back to his SUV and we all climbed inside. Just as Eric was pulling away from the curb, Paul's cell phone rang. It was his mother, and boy was she mad. We could hear her screaming at him, asking him where he was, why he skipped school, and telling him to get home this instant.

"Uh, Mr. Vaughn? Do you think you could drop me off please?" Paul asked, sounding a little sheepish and ducking further into his seat.

"What will you tell your mother?" Eric asked. "Do you want me to talk to her?"

"No, that's okay. I'll figure it out," Paul said.

"What about your car? It's still at our house."

"I'll come get it tomorrow."

I thanked Paul for going with me, and gave him a hug before he turned and walked inside his house. I felt bad knowing he was in for some major trouble with his mom. Eric and I were quiet as we drove the rest of the way home. It was a short drive, and yet my mind was able to race through the events of the past few days before we were back to our house.

I went right upstairs to my room to do some thinking. Sitting down at my computer, I started looking through all my notes that I had about Alyssa, Luminesk, Simon Foley, Anemone, and the other Elementals. I added new information about Carly and my father to the document. Had Carly Grand really been able to stop her powers? Or had she just become very good at suppressing them? Had she and her family been threatened by my arrival in town? Maybe they'd felt safe knowing they were of no interest to Luminesk anymore, and when I showed up, it brought Simon Foley back.

And the biggest mystery of all was still looming above me like a big, black thundercloud. What had happened to my father?

I knew I had to go back to school, act as though nothing was out of the ordinary. I also wanted to see if anyone else who knew Carly would talk to me.

And I needed to call Connor. My fingers froze over the keyboard. I wondered if I should even keep seeing him. Was it fair to bring him into this mess? I could barely keep it straight, and I knew I wasn't spending much time with him. He was such a decent guy, and I didn't want to hurt him.

"I think he would understand, you know," a small voice said behind me.

I yelped and whirled around. Alyssa was leaning against the doorframe, her arms crossed over her chest. She stepped inside and climbed up on the bed.

"You have got to stop scaring me like that," I said. I tried to get my heart rate under control again.

"Sorry."

"What did you say?"

"I think Connor would understand, about us. About me. He might react at first out of fear, but I think he would be okay with it. He cares about you."

"I just don't want to burden him with this. We don't have a lot of answers. If anything, we just have a million more questions now."

Alyssa nodded and pulled one of my pillows toward her. She set it on her lap and picked at the hem. "I heard Dad tell Mom about the Grand's house. That's so weird. Dad called Mr. Orson, and he's very concerned." She rolled her eyes. "So of course, Mom and Dad are freaking out and don't want me to set one toenail outside of this house without one of them with me." She threw the pillow aside and bit her lower lip. "I'm so tired of this!" she said, her voice rising with each word. "If he wants me, why doesn't he just come and get me?"

Outside, the sky suddenly darkened, and a crack of thunder boomed in the distance.

"Alyssa," I said, trying to remain calm. I held my hand out to her. She ignored me.

She jumped off the bed and went to the window, staring into the street. The thunder became louder, and the wind picked up. I knew it would be a matter of seconds before it began pouring down rain. I touched her arm, hoping that would bring her attention back to me. She slapped my hand away, glared at me, and then stomped through the bathroom to her room. Her door slammed shut with such intensity the whole house shook.

Outside, lightening was flashing, thunder was rumbling hard enough that all of the neighborhood dogs were barking and howling, and the rain came down in fast, angry sheets so thick I couldn't see the house across the street.

Mom and Eric came barreling up the steps. I assured them Alyssa was fine, just upset. She wouldn't let them into her room, having locked both doors. She told us to go away and leave her alone for the rest of the evening.

We had no choice but to agree.

* * *

The weather was still terrible when I returned to school. An umbrella did no good because the wind just whipped it inside out. Broken tree limbs littered the streets, and at least three power lines had fallen in our neighborhood alone and had to be repaired. One power line had been hit by lightning, causing a nearby tree to catch fire. Luckily, it had been stopped before the fire spread to any houses. The weather forecasters were stumped. They had no explanation for this freak storm that had appeared out of nowhere and showed no signs of leaving.

The real reason for the weather, Alyssa's foul mood, could not be changed. She stomped all through the house, slamming doors and glaring at no one in particular. She got angrier when my grandfather called to tell me about Mark's funeral arrangements, which were set for Saturday morning. Eric insisted on going with me this time, and I didn't argue. We were leaving Friday night and returning Sunday morning. My grandfather offered to let us stay with him.

Mom and Eric were stressed to the max, and Eric was taking some time off. We weren't scared of Alyssa. We were just unsure of what to do to help her. She felt responsible for everything and helpless to fix any of it.

I hugged her before leaving for school. She responded by scowling at me and stabbing her pancakes with her fork. I met Paul by our lockers. I hadn't heard from him since we dropped him off at home, and when I called his house, his mother told me he was unavailable to talk.

"She's pretty pissed at me," he told me. "I haven't seen her this mad in ages. She even called my dad."

"What did he say?"

"Not much. Boys will be boys and all that. I'm kind of under house arrest, and I have to ride to and from school with her."

"For how long?"

He looked heavenward. "Probably until I graduate college."

I gave him a reassuring hug and then opened my locker, grabbing the textbooks I would need for the morning.

"My mom said the whole town is talking about the Grands," Paul said as we walked to class. "Mr. Grand packed up his desk and walked out. Same for Mrs. Grand. No one knows when they left, or where they went."

"Jonathan couldn't find anything out either. They're just gone."

We fell silent for a moment until Paul mentioned the crazy weather.

"Yeah, guess who else is pretty pissed?" I said.

"No way. She's doing this? Wow."

Charlotte came running up to us then, so all talk of the Grands and Alyssa stopped. She handed me a folder.

"Here's your homework from your missed days. I was going to bring it by, but I don't like driving in bad weather," she said.

"Thanks. So what did I miss while I was out?" I was hoping she would tell me what everyone else was saying about the Grands.

Instead, Charlotte launched into the latest gossip about who was dating whom, who had been dumped and the fight that had broken out in the cafeteria that left a broken window and one boy with a black eye.

"Totally nuts!" she said. "And then of course, Carly Grand just vanished into thin air. There's a rumor going around that she killed her parents and ran away. I don't think that's true, do you? And this rain! It's doing nothing for my hair!" She gestured with her hands and hit my arm, knocking my books to the floor.

My biology book skittered across the hall, the cover opening and revealing an unmarked white envelope taped inside. I dove for it before anyone else could grab it. Paul caught my eye and distracted Charlotte with picking up my other books. I tore into the envelope, surprised to see a handwritten note from Carly.

Skipping town. He's nearby. If you're smart, you and your family will do the same. Sorry for being a jerk. Just needed to see what you knew. Carly.

Was the "he" Carly was referring to Simon Foley?

I surveyed the busy hall filled with students and teachers. Could he be here at the school?

"I'm so sorry," Charlotte said. "I'm such a klutz."

Paul handed me back my books. "It's no problem," I said. "Hey, we better get going. The first bell is going to ring soon."

Charlotte bounded off ahead of us, spotting another student, a boy named Max who was in our gym class, and started a conversation with him. Paul and I hung back.

"It's from Carly," I said, keeping my voice low. "She and her family left town because 'he' was nearby."

"Foley?"

"It's definitely possible."

Paul's expression was grim, which sent a ripple of fear through my stomach. Simon Foley was close.

Chapter Eighteen

I was sitting in my British Literature class when I received a message to go to the principal's office right away. It was like that day at Radcliffe all over again, when the detectives came and told me that my father was missing. Heart pounding, I gathered my things together and ran down the hallway. Mom was waiting for me with Alyssa.

"What's wrong?"

We moved a few steps away from the curious ears of the school secretary.

"Eric's been in an accident," Mom said, lowering her voice.

"What? I thought he wasn't going into work today."

"He didn't. He went for a jog and someone tried to run him down."

"What? He went jogging in this rain?"

"You know how dedicated he is to his running."

"Did he see who it was? Is he okay?"

Alyssa clutched Mom's hand, and I saw the tear tracks down her cheeks.

"He didn't see the driver, just the car, and he's at the hospital now getting checked out. The doctors don't think it's anything serious, just some minor cuts and bruises from when he dodged the car, maybe a sprained ankle. We're on our way over there, but I wanted to stop and let you know in case we're not home when you get out of school."

"Yeah, no problem. Tell him I'm glad he's okay." I tucked my hair behind both ears, leaned in closer to Mom and whispered, "Do you think this is related?"

"I'd rather not think about that right now," she whispered back, and I could see the worry in her eyes. She was thinking the same thing I was, that Eric was lucky he hadn't been shot like Mark. "I'll call you later," she said.

I bent down to hug Alyssa. She seemed very small, and I assured her that Eric was going to be just fine. She nodded and kissed my cheek. I watched them go, wondering why Luminesk would have gone after Eric. Was this supposed to scare Alyssa? If so, it was definitely working. Or was it supposed to scare me? He wouldn't be able to go with me to Mark's funeral now, and there was no way I was going to miss it. Was this a way to separate me from my family? The hair on the back of my neck stood up, and I shivered.

My class was out when I left the office, so I went to my locker instead and found Paul waiting for me. When he saw the look on my face, he knew something was wrong. I told him about Eric, and Paul was convinced that Luminesk was behind it. When I showed him Carly's note, it further solidified his belief.

"I can't focus," I said, shoving my books into my locker. I folded the note and put it in my pocket. "Mom and Alyssa went to the hospital. I should be there too."

"We only have two classes left. I'll cover for you if you want to take off."

"That would be fantastic, thank you." I hugged him, grabbed my backpack and headed for the parking lot. As I was starting my car, I got a text message from Connor asking how my day was going. I called him, letting him know it was pretty darn rotten.

"Everything all right?"

"Eric's been in an accident," I said. "Nothing serious, but we're all a little shaken."

"Do you know what happened?" he asked. A small thrill went through me at the concern in his voice.

"Mom said he was out jogging, and he was almost hit by a car."

Connor told me to call him if I needed anything. I backed out of my parking spot and turned toward the hospital. I arrived at the hospital and asked for Eric's room. He was sitting up in bed, his left leg elevated and his ankle wrapped, and there were cuts across his face. He looked up in surprise as I entered the room.

"Aubrey, aren't you supposed to be in school?" he asked.

"I skipped. I was concerned," I added, seeing the disapproving look cross his and Mom's faces. "I'll take the punishment."

Mom came over and shook her head, hugging me. "I'll clear it with the principal."

"So, how are you?" I asked. "And what the heck happened?"

He motioned for me to close the door. "I had my music on, and I wasn't paying attention to my surroundings," he said, sounding angry with himself. "I saw the car coming at me, and I jumped out of the way. It clipped me in the leg, and I rolled away, unfortunately right into a thorny bush. That's all."

"Did they have guns? Was it someone from Luminesk?"

"No guns, and I didn't even see the driver."

"Did you tell the police?"

Mom nodded. "We already spoke to them and filed a report."

A knock came at the door, and a nurse poked her head in. "I'm sorry to interrupt, but these just came for you, Mr. Vaughn." She set a basket of fruit and a flower arrangement on the tray table.

Mom reached out and stopped the nurse before she left. "Who brought them?"

"Just a delivery guy," the nurse said, shrugging. "They're from a local florist."

I searched the baskets for a card, shaking my head at Eric when I didn't find anything. The nurse left, and Mom closed the door again.

"Who else knows about the accident?" I asked.

"Just the police."

"And I told Paul," I added, "and Connor. He texted me, and I called him back."

Alyssa stood up from the chair in the corner and checked out the arrangements. After a moment of quiet, she peeled the cellophane from the fruit basket and popped a grape in her mouth. We all yelled out, "No!"

"Relax," she said. "It's safe."

Eric reached out and pushed the tray table away. "I don't care. We're not taking these home. Aubrey, will you please get rid of them?"

I grabbed both baskets and took them out of the room, passing by the nurses' station. A large trash can with no lid sat against the counter, and I dropped everything into it. This earned me a few strange looks, to which I said, "Allergies," and faked a sneeze. As I walked back to Eric's room, I had the distinct feeling that I was being watched. I paused at the water fountain and took a drink, taking the opportunity to glance around. There were only doctors, nurses and patients in the hall, yet I couldn't shake the feeling that someone else was there.

"What are you doing?"

I jumped back from the fountain, startled at the voice. Alyssa stood with her hands on her hips, her head cocked to one side.

"Just getting a drink," I said, wiping water from my mouth. "How are you holding up?"

She sighed and said, "I was scared when the police came by the house. I knew it was about Dad. I just couldn't feel what. I imagined how you must have felt when your dad disappeared."

I held her hand and walked with her to the nearby waiting area. We sat down, and I waited for her to talk. I sensed there was something more going on, and I didn't want to push her. She twirled her hair around her fingers, took a deep breath and said, "I feel responsible for what happened to Dad, and to your friend. Luminesk is after me, not any of you. I don't know what to do," she said.

Her lower lip began to tremble, and soon the tears were falling. Pulling her into my lap, I cradled her close. I had no words to say, so I simply held her while she cried. It wasn't fair for her to feel such a burden. Sometimes, because of her abilities, I forgot that she was eight years old.

Across the hall, I watched as the flowers in the trash can wilted, and the fruit rotted.

"Don't go to New York," Alyssa said after a moment. "Please don't. Dad can't go with you, and I'm afraid for you."

"I have to," I said, even though I was afraid now too. "Paul's mom won't let him out of the house except for school, so I'll just have to make the trip by myself. Maybe I can come back right after the funeral."

Alyssa sat up straighter and said, "What about Connor? Could he go with you?"

My heart gave an extra little thump. "I don't know. Maybe." I shook my head. "We've only been on one date. I think it may be a little too soon to ask him to go away with me."

"It wouldn't be a romantic trip," Alyssa said, her voice serious. "He could protect you, like he protected me at the parade."

I thought about it, finally conceding that she did have a point. He was big and strong, and I felt safe with him. But would he be weirded out if I asked him to go to New York with me? For a funeral, of all things?

"You'll have to ask him to find out," Alyssa said. She slid off my lap, all traces of the scared little girl she'd been just a few minutes ago gone. She walked back to Eric's room.

I took my time following her, thinking it over. When I rejoined my family, Mom and Eric had already decided it wasn't a bad idea. I glanced at Alyssa who shrugged.

"I told them," she said.

"It would make me feel better," Mom said, nodding.

"I'll ask him. If he says no, I'm still going," I said. I left and went back to the waiting room to call Connor.

He answered on the first ring. "How's your step-dad?" he asked. "How bad was he hurt?"

"He's got some cuts, a few bruises here and there, and a sprained ankle."

I paced around the empty waiting room, trying to figure out what to say.

"Did the police catch who did it?" he asked, breaking into my scrambled thoughts.

"Not yet. Um, Connor? Can I ask you something?"

"Sure, anything."

I took a deep breath and squeezed my eyes shut. The words just spilled out in a jumbled mess, and I sank into a chair and cringed. There was a moment of silence, and then a confused, "You want me to go to New York City with you this weekend for a funeral?"

I tried to explain it was for a family friend without going into too much detail.

"Eric was supposed to go with me. Obviously, now he can't. And my mom doesn't want me going alone. She worries about me going missing, like my dad," I added, which was probably true. "I have to be there. I'll pay for your ticket, and we don't need a hotel because we can stay at my place."

I felt my cheeks burn at the thought of staying anywhere overnight with Connor.

"I, um, well, this is unexpected," Connor said.

"It's all right if you say no. I know we haven't been seeing each other long."

"Aubrey, it's all right. I'll go with you. As long as you and your family are okay with it."

"They are. It was actually Alyssa's idea."

Connor's soft laugh sent my pulse racing. "She's a smart kid."

"You don't know the half of it."

"Just tell me where I need to be and when. I didn't have plans this weekend anyway."

I breathed a huge sigh of relief and we chatted for a few more minutes before we hung up. I would swing by his place after school on Friday, and we'd fly out on a 6:30pm flight. I was smiling, nervous and excited to be going to New York City with Connor. And then I felt like the worst person in the world.

Mark's funeral was nothing to be giddy about, and here I was acting stupid because Connor was going to attend it with me. I actually hated myself at that moment.

* * *

Paul was granted a reprieve from his punishment and picked me up for school the next morning. He noticed my sullen mood, left over from the events of the previous day. Thankfully, I couldn't control the weather. It was still gloomy, but Alyssa had calmed down a lot after Eric came home with us.

"Everything okay?" Paul asked. "Well, I mean, you know. Relatively speaking."

"We're all tired. No one slept much last night."

"Understandable."

He headed toward school while I kept a lookout for any black cars.

"So is he going to be able to go with you to Mark's funeral?"

I inwardly cringed. I didn't want to talk about this, so I just shook my head.

"I can try and talk to my mom. Maybe she'll go easy on me if I beg. I mean, look, I'm out and about today."

"No, you don't have to," I said, a little too quickly.

There was a pause, and then Paul said, "You're not going by yourself, are you?"

I bit my lip and sighed. Paul's grip on the steering wheel tightened, and I saw the muscle in his jaw clench.

"I get it," he said.

We rode the rest of the way in an awkward silence. Even though I had tried to convince myself that Paul knew we were just friends, it was pretty obvious how he felt. We arrived at school, and Paul said he'd meet up with me in class. He needed to go talk to one of our other teachers first. I knew he just needed to get away from me, and I felt bad.

I went to find Charlotte, spotting her hanging a sign for an upcoming pep rally. She stopped and hugged me, asking about Eric.

"The neighborhood is so freaked out," she told me. "Nothing like that happens around here."

The rest of the day passed in a blur. Paul was polite to me, just not as warm as he usual. When he dropped me off at home, he apologized, even though he had nothing to be sorry for.

"I guess I'm a little jealous," he admitted. "Okay, a lot jealous."

"I'm the one who should be sorry. I don't want to hurt you. I think you're a great guy, and I'm glad we're friends," I said.

"I'm glad we're friends too. I'll get over it. But if he ends up hurting you, I'm going to have to hit him."

He smiled at me, and the tension disappeared. My cell phone rang, interrupting us. It was my grandfather, wanting to go over the details of our trip. Paul said goodbye, and I got out of the car. Mom had filled in him on what had happened to Eric, and that I would be traveling with Connor instead. My grandfather was not pleased, and this surprised me.

"What do you know about this boy?" he asked. "What is his interest in you? Does he know about your background?"

Ouch. That stung a little. "We're seeing each other," I said. "He's really smart, and I think you'll like him."

"Are you still staying with me?"

"I thought we'd stay at the apartment," I said. "I miss it."

There was a beat of silence and then, "Aubrey, this is not a social visit."

I bristled at his tone. I knew that. Mark's funeral was not going to be easy for me. I felt incredible guilt over his death, and I was torn between telling the authorities what I knew and keeping my sister safe. One could argue that by involving the police I could also help Alyssa. Yet somehow I doubted that they'd be able to keep Simon Foley away. He seemed to be everywhere and nowhere at the same time, and that terrified me.

"Grandpa, Connor isn't after my money or any company secrets. We're arriving Friday night and leaving Sunday morning. Mom and Eric just don't want me traveling alone."

"You should stay with me. I have excellent security."

"I know. I just...I want to stay at home," I said, and the word sounded strange to me. Was that my home anymore, or was my home here? With Mom and Eric and Alyssa?

My grandfather sighed. "There isn't anything new about your father. My team of investigators haven't found anything, and neither have the FBI. We're going to have to talk about what to do next."

I squeezed my eyes shut. "Soon," was all I said. He let the subject stop there.

He arranged for a car to pick us up at the airport and take us to the apartment. He was also having it cleaned and stocked with food for the weekend.

"I'll pick you up Saturday morning. After the funeral, we need to stop by the offices. Now that you're eighteen, there are some papers you need to sign."

"What papers?"

"Your father had a trust fund set up for you. You gain partial control of it at age eighteen, and complete control at twenty-five. We can discuss this in person."

I agreed to that. No way did I want to talk about money now. I didn't have a need for it. Not unless I could use it to find my father and keep my sister away from Simon Foley.

These thoughts swirled around in my head for the rest of the week. What if I could use the money for those exact reasons? Jonathan Orson was very good at finding information, like Mark had been, and Anemone wasn't a publicly funded organization. It was always in need of funds to keep it going.

Of course, I had no idea how to have the money routed to Anemone, and involving my grandfather could be tricky. He would want to know every last detail, and I couldn't reveal Jonathan or Monica, or what they did. He wouldn't understand.

I just knew that Anemone deserved to be on the same level playing field as Luminesk, and if it took my trust fund to do it, then so be it.

Chapter Nineteen

I parked the Jeep in front of a three story apartment building and double checked the address again. Just as I was digging out my cell phone, the front door opened and Connor stepped out, a duffel bag slung over his shoulder. He waved and jogged over, then tossed his bag into the back and climbed in, leaning over to kiss me.

"I wish this trip was under better circumstances," he said, his voice low and soft. "I'm glad you asked me though."

His hand curled around mine, and I knew I would be all right with him along. I drove us to the airport, and he carried our bags inside. Soon we were on the plane and heading to New York City on a direct flight. He held my hand for most of the trip, and we just talked. He had heard about the Grands disappearing and was as intrigued as everyone else.

No one knew anything. They had left no forwarding address, and none of the neighbors remembered seeing any moving vans or trucks come to the house to remove the furniture. They had simply vanished. It was making me uneasy, and I wondered if everyone I had contact with would just disappear without a trace.

Mom, Eric, and I had a long talk before I left about Connor. I wanted to tell him everything, but they were hesitant. They wanted more answers before involving anyone else. I didn't like keeping this from him, especially because I felt that we were starting to become a couple. I agreed to wait a while longer.

My grandfather had a car waiting for us, as promised, and we were whisked away to the apartment I shared with my dad. I was surprised to learn that Connor had never been to New York City before, and he was fascinated by it. He was shocked into awed silence, like Paul had been, when we arrived at the apartment. The refrigerator and the pantry were filled with food and drinks, and there wasn't a dust bunny to be seen.

It was late when we arrived, and we had to be up early the next morning. I showed Connor to one of the guest rooms, and he left his bag on the bed. I gave him the grand tour, ending in my dad's office. I stood and stared at the desk, at the chair that sat empty. A lump formed in my throat as my gaze fell on the silver frame sitting on one of the bookshelves. It was a picture of Dad and me at a friend's wedding reception. What I loved about it was that it hadn't been posed. The photographer had been walking around, capturing moments of all the guests, and he'd caught us laughing about something. I made a mental note to take it with me back to Hamilton Green.

Suddenly, Connor's arms were around me, and I melted against him. The stress of everything, Dad's disappearance, Eric's accident, Paul's disappointment at me not feeling the same for him, and of course, the danger that Alyssa was in, seemed to all crash down on me at once. Before I knew it, I was sobbing. Connor lifted me and carried me down the hall to my room. He placed me gently on the bed, and then crawled up beside me.

I fell asleep tucked in his embrace, waking a few hours later. Connor was still beside me, asleep. One arm was across his face, the other still around me. I tried to get up without waking him, and I failed. He sat up straight, eyes wide, his hands clenched into fists, like he was ready to fight.

"Whoa, it's just me," I said, shrinking away from him.

"What happened?" His voice was deeper, rougher.

"We fell asleep." I glanced at the clock on the bedside table. "It's almost three. You must have been dreaming."

He rubbed his eyes. "Sorry. Sometimes I have nightmares."

"I can relate. I have nightmares too."

He half-smiled. "I should go to my own room, let you get some rest."

I reached out and touched his hand. "You don't have to. You can stay here. I feel...safer with you here."

He studied me for a moment. "What are you afraid of, Aubrey?"

It was on the tip of my tongue, to tell him everything about Alyssa and Luminesk and Simon Foley. I forced all of that away.

"I'm afraid of never finding out what happened to my dad," I said, and it was true. I scooted closer to him, resting my head on his shoulder.

We just sat there for a moment. It felt natural and very nice.

"I promised your mom I would be on my best behavior," he said in a whisper. I almost didn't hear it.

"What?"

"She made me swear not to take advantage of you."

I blushed to the roots of my hair and buried my face in a pillow. Mom and I were going to have a serious talk when I got back. I took a deep breath and raised my head to look at him.

"Well, she didn't make me swear not to take advantage of you," I said, and leaned over to kiss him.

I have no idea where that came from. I had never been that bold before, and I was surprised at my actions. He resisted at first, then he was pulling me closer, kissing me deeper. We fell back onto the bed. I ran my hands through his hair, down his neck and along his shoulders, savoring the feel of him. He was solid. Strong. After a few minutes of serious making out, he lifted his head away from me.

"You're making it difficult to keep my word, and I'm a man of my word."

Sighing, I propped myself up on my elbows. I knew that I wasn't ready for anything else to happen anyway. "Can you still stay with me? I don't want to be alone."

He pulled the comforter and sheet back, and we moved beneath them. I felt more relaxed than I had in weeks, and I got a restful night of sleep.

I woke the next morning to find that he'd made breakfast. He kissed me as he handed me a plate of waffles. I shivered at his kiss, wishing again that we were here for different reasons. I told him more about Mark, explained that he had been close with my dad and had been doing his own investigation about Dad's disappearance. Connor said he was sorry for not getting the chance to meet Mark in person.

As we were getting ready to head downstairs, my cell phone rang. It was my grandfather. He told me that there were several reporters waiting for me. I hadn't dealt with any reporters since I'd been in Hamilton Green. For some reason they had never ventured out to follow me, even though I knew Dad's disappearance was still a top story. I wondered if my grandfather's influence had somehow protected me. My stomach flipped as I hung up and informed Connor of the situation.

He frowned. "How did they know you were here?"

"Someone must have tipped them off. My grandfather is out front though, and they've already seen him, so there's no point in trying to sneak out. I'm so sorry. Are you okay with this?"

He pulled a pair of dark sunglasses from the inside pocket of his suit jacket and slipped them on. He looked so handsome and a lot like a bodyguard. I trusted him with my life at that moment. "Let's go," he said, extending his hand to me.

I put on my own sunglasses and grabbed my purse. We rode the elevator down to the main lobby, and as soon as the doors opened, I could see the mob of people standing outside. The building's security team was holding them back as best they could. I squared my shoulders and walked past them, Connor right beside me. The flashes from the cameras were blinding. I'd forgotten how bright they were. Questions were yelled out to me, asking who Connor was, if I knew anything more about what happened to my father, and if Mark's death was in some way related.

I stumbled at that question, and Connor had to steady me as I got into the car, his hand firmly at the small of my back. The driver shut the door behind us, cutting off the attack. My heart was racing. I didn't want to think about that. My grandfather had assured me there was no business being done between Benton Media and Luminesk, but then where had that ledger come from? Jonathan was unable to learn more from the banks in the Cayman Islands, so we were at a standstill with that information. We had no way of knowing for sure if it was true.

I blinked, removing my sunglasses when I realized that Connor had introduced himself to my grandfather.

"Vultures," Grandpa said, shaking his head in disdain. "They have no decency."

Connor agreed. I bit my tongue to keep from pointing out that a few of the reporters were from papers that Benton Media owned or dealt with. He always hated it when I said something like that, whereas my dad would just chuckle and nod.

The service for Mark was small and private. But because it was found out that he'd been a close personal friend of Wendell Benton, the press were all over it. I felt horrible that Mark's family couldn't grieve in peace. My grandfather, Connor and I sat a few rows back from Mark's wife and children in the church.

I reached over and took Connor's hand. He gave me a comforting squeeze, and I was so glad that he was here with me. When the service ended, we got back into the car to follow the hearse to the cemetery. Everyone was quiet as we walked to the gravesite. A large tent had been set up to shield the mourners from the intruding cameras surrounding the cemetery. My grandfather had also lined up extra security to keep out anyone not associated with the service.

As the pastor spoke of Mark's devotion to his family, and how his life had ended too soon, I felt a wave of emotion roll over me, and soon the tears were flowing. Connor put his arm around me and pulled me close. I cried against him, feeling helpless.

I was in control of myself when I spoke with Mark's wife, offering my condolences. She knew who I was, even though we'd never met, and she thanked me. She also thanked my grandfather for his help with the funeral plans. Staring at the faces of the children, my guilt rising to the surface again. I had to get some air, so I excused myself and stepped toward the opening flap of the tent. I peered outside, saw the reporters lined up around the fence of the cemetery.

A flash caught my attention. It wasn't the flash of a camera, it was something else. I looked to my left, and it flashed again. My mouth dropped open in disbelief. I recognized it. My father always wore a shiny silver Rolex Submariner watch, and I would joke about being blinded by its glint. I searched the crowd of reporters and onlookers, my gaze falling on one in particular who was standing right by the fence. He was bearded, wearing sunglasses and a ball cap with the bill pulled low, and he was holding a camera with a telephoto lens. He adjusted his grip on the camera, and the sun bounced off the watch on his left wrist, causing that familiar flash of light.

My heart lurched as I whispered, "Dad."

Chapter Twenty

I know he spotted me too, because he lowered the camera and hastily backed away from the fence before turning toward a group of parked vehicles. Without thinking, I started running in his direction, through the large gates and into the path of the bystanders. He glanced over his shoulder at me, then jumped onto a motorcycle and sped off. I came to a stop in the road, staring after him.

I was swarmed by reporters, cameras clicking, and questions being fired at me from all directions. I shielded my face with my hands and tried to get away, but I was trapped. Connor pushed his way through and put his arm firmly around my shoulders. He steered me through the crowd, straight for our car. He instructed the driver to take us to the Benton Media offices in Times Square.

"Your grandfather will meet us there. He wanted me to get you away from here."

I was shaking. My snowflake pendant felt icy against my skin, and a thousand thoughts were pinging around the walls of my brain, seeking answers and finding none.

"What happened?" Connor asked, his tone gentle. He passed me a bottle of water. "What did you see?"

I couldn't speak.

I was positive I had just seen my father.

Which meant that he was alive.

Connor reached out and touched my face, startling me. "You look like you're about to go into shock," he said, shrugging out of his jacket and draping it around me. "Do you need a doctor?"

I shook my head. "No, I just..."

How could I say it? Would he believe me?

"I thought I saw someone I knew," I finished lamely. The adrenaline left me at that moment, and I sank back against the seat, exhausted.

"You looked like you'd seen a ghost."

He wasn't far off. We hit some traffic and slowed to a crawl.

"Aubrey, are you sure you're all right?"

I shook my head. "Yeah, I'm fine. This is just a really stressful time for me." I reached over and covered his hand with mine. "I'm glad you're with me."

I was trying not to freak out, when all I wanted to do was find out for sure if that had been my dad. My first thought was to call or text Mark to start investigating, and then the realization that I'd never be able to do that again washed over me, and I felt like crying again. Connor didn't ask anymore questions, just kept glancing at me every now and then. I could tell he wasn't buying my false bravado.

We arrived at the offices and were ushered inside. Paparazzi were waiting for us there too. I couldn't understand what was so newsworthy about me showing up for a friend's funeral. Weren't there other things going on in the world that deserved more attention? I almost stopped and whirled around to yell at them to track down Simon Foley and all of the missing children he had kidnapped.

My grandfather's office was down the hall from my dad's, and we were told to wait there. He would be joining us shortly. Connor admired the view, whistling at the awards and trophies lined up on shelves that covered an entire wall.

"How long as your family been running this company?" he asked.

"Grandpa started it right before my dad was born. It was small, just a single newspaper then. Grandpa grew it, and my dad expanded it. Dad's the one who used his contacts in Hollywood to branch out into movies and television."

"You sound very proud."

I nodded. "I am. My family has worked hard to become successful."

"And all of this will be yours someday?"

"Eventually. Of course, I don't know what I'm doing yet."

My grandfather came into the office then, followed by two very stressed out assistants.

"I want to know which reporters are running stories, and how soon they'll hit," he said, heading straight for his desk. He shrugged out of his suit jacket and handed it to the nearest assistant. "I also want an update regarding Wendell's investigation, the contract negotiations with that news station in Connecticut, and can we get some food in here please? Oh, and the trust papers for Aubrey."

His assistants nodded, scribbling furiously as they rushed out the door. Connor's eyes were wide, and I stifled a grin. I had seen this side of my grandfather many times, so I was used to it. When he meant business, he meant business.

"Please, have a seat, both of you," he said, motioning to the two chairs across from his desk.

Connor sat, his back ramrod straight as if expecting to receive orders of his own. Five minutes later, the assistants were back. One pushed a cart of food and bottled beverages, and the other a stack of files. Everything was arranged neatly on the desk, and then they were gone. They had yet to say a word.

Connor and I helped ourselves to a snack. I hadn't realized I was even hungry until then. My grandfather flipped through some papers, shuffling things here, signing something there. When he reached for a thick manila envelope, he paused before opening it.

"Connor, I truly appreciate what you've done for Aubrey by being here with her, but if you don't mind, this is family business," he said.

Connor snapped to attention, getting to his feet and nodding. I half expected him to salute.

"Of course, no problem."

"Speak with Melinda, and she'll show you around the offices."

Connor retreated, closing the glass door behind him.

"I think you scared him," I admonished.

"Good. He was getting too comfortable with you." His voice was rough, but I caught the teasing glint in his eyes. "Anyway, would you care to share with me why you ran out of the funeral tent toward the cameras and reporters?"

Oh shoot. I had hoped he wouldn't ask me that. Would he think I was crazy for running after someone who had a watch like Dad's?

"I thought I saw him," I said after a long moment of silence.

"Who?"

"Dad. I thought I saw Dad."

He regarded me with an expression that revealed nothing. After a few seconds, his shoulders sagged, and he suddenly appeared older and more tired than I'd ever seen him.

"Sweetheart, I think I see him all the time too. And trust me, I've notified the authorities each time. Nothing has come of it."

My throat tightened as tears welled in my eyes. I forced them back, refusing to cry again. I was crying entirely too much these days.

"I'll let the lead investigator know about your sighting as well. Just please don't expect too much."

He took notes as I explained why I thought it was Dad, what he was wearing, and I described the motorcycle. Dad had been a novice motorcycle enthusiast, becoming interested in them just before he disappeared. Grandpa promised to keep me informed. Then he cleared his throat and opened the envelope, removing a stack of papers. He slid the stack across the desk to me, and I flipped through the pages.

My eyes felt like crossing, and I hadn't even read any of it. I'd seen legal documents like that plenty of times before, and none of it ever made sense to me. I could never be a lawyer.

"Can you just give me the shortened explanation?" I asked, and Grandpa frowned.

"You should read this over yourself," he said. "However, given the subject matter..." His voice trailed off. "Your father had a sizable trust fund set up when you were born. He never told you about it because he didn't want you to be like those other trust fund brats. He wanted you to learn the value of a dollar. He also wanted you to be taken care of if such a situation called for it."

He continued talking, and I tried to focus, but after a few minutes, I was zoning out, catching about every third word. Something about monthly stipends deposited directly into my bank account, I could do with the money as I pleased, and there would be no monitoring of the funds once they were released to me. That last part definitely caught my attention.

"And when you turn twenty-five, you gain complete control of the trust. It is quite large, Aubrey," Grandpa warned. "It was your father's hope that by the time you receive control of it, you'll have established yourself financially on your own and will have little need for it. That it will be a backup for you if necessary. He did not want you to blow it. Do you understand?"

I nodded, feeling numb. I could think of just one use for the money. I was going to find Simon Foley.

* * *

After signing papers for the trust fund, I went in search of Connor, locating him in one of the large conference rooms on the seventeenth floor. He was staring out the windows, his expression thoughtful. He heard me enter the room and turned around.

"Everything all right?" he asked.

"Peachy."

I walked right into his arms, and he embraced me tightly.

"Can you keep a secret?" he asked.

"You have no idea."

"Your grandfather scares the bejeezus out of me."

I laughed. "Well, you're going to have to get over it. He wants to take us out to dinner tonight."

Connor groaned and shook his head. "This sounds like a bad decision."

"Don't be silly. You'll be fine. Actually, he said he thinks you're a fine young man, and he's pleased I met you."

Connor eyed me with suspicion. "Did he really say that?"

"Err...let's go do something fun," I said, changing the subject. "This morning was rough."

He agreed and we headed back to my apartment, pleased to find no reporters waiting for us. Grandpa would pick us up for dinner at seven, so we had some time to ourselves. Connor wanted to see more of the city sights, so we changed from our funeral attire into more casual clothes. We took a cab to Times Square and walked around. Connor was trying not to act like an excited tourist, but I could tell from his expression that he liked the area. I had my camera with me, and I took several shots of him. He was reluctant at first, and then he got into it, posing and making silly faces.

When we passed the theater where my dad and I had spent the evening before he went missing, my heart clutched a little at the memory. I slowed to a stop and stared up at the marquee, remembering how excited I was to be attending with him. It had been a perfect evening, and now the memory was tarnished.

"Has anything new been found?" Connor asked.

I shook my head. "Grandpa said the authorities are backing off the investigation. The case will still be open. There won't be as many people involved though. It's just so frustrating."

"Do you think he's still alive?"

I bristled at the question. No one had asked me that yet, so I wasn't sure how to respond.

"Twenty-four hours ago, I would have said no," I said, and it was true. I had begun to give up hope. I just couldn't tell my mom or my grandfather that. They were still so confident he would come back.

"What changed your mind?"

"I...I thought...I thought I saw him," I said, my voice getting softer with each word. I stared at my camera, focusing on a tiny speck of dirt on the lens. I brushed it away.

Connor's eyes widened, then narrowed in confusion. "When? Where?"

"This morning. At the funeral. That's why I ran out of the tent. I told my grandfather about it, and he said he'd pass the information along. I guess he's been having sightings like that too, ever since Dad disappeared. Stupid, huh?"

"It's not stupid to want to see your loved ones again. Sometimes I swear I see my mom, even though she died when I was just a kid."

We hadn't talked much about his childhood, and I hesitantly asked about it as we continued walking. He was uncomfortable answering, but he did, and I appreciated that.

"Mom was diagnosed with pancreatic cancer when I was nine. Two years later, she was gone. My brother says she gave up, that she quit," Connor said. His jaw tightened. "I told him he was dumb to think that. Mom was just so tired, and she didn't have any fight left in her. It was hard to accept at the time, and I don't think my brother ever really has. This has always been a sticking point between us."

He sounded a little wistful, as though he regretted not having a better relationship with his brother. I vowed to maintain and build my relationship with Alyssa. That meant not just being there as a big sister, but also protecting her from harm, whether it be something as simple as falling off her bike, or as huge as keeping her away from the clutches of Simon Foley and Luminesk.

At seven, we were back at the apartment, waiting for Grandpa to arrive to take us to dinner. There were no reporters watching us as we climbed into the car and headed out. Grandpa was scrolling through messages on his phone, still business as usual.

"Where are we going?" I asked.

"We have reservations at Valbella. I know you love it there."

The name was like a shock of cold water. Connor felt my reaction and placed a hand on my knee.

"Something wrong?" he asked, sounding concerned.

Grandpa glanced up from his phone, his brows furrowed. And then it hit him.

"Aubrey, I'm so sorry. I forgot," he said. "I'm sorry. We can go somewhere else."

Connor looked to me, and I shook my head.

"No, it's all right. You already have the reservation. It's fine." I turned to Connor to explain. "This is the restaurant my dad and I went to the night before he disappeared."

He nodded his understanding. We pulled up in front of the restaurant and headed for the entrance. It was true that I loved this restaurant, and Dad had enjoyed it as well. My heart was pounding, and my palms were sweating. Connor held my hand and gave it a reassuring squeeze as we walked inside.

We were seated and handed menus. Grandpa selected a wine and shifted in his chair, straightening his tie and adjusting his cufflinks. These were telltale signs that he was uncomfortable with the situation. I glanced around the room, at the sloped ceilings, the soft lighting and the wine racks that lined the walls. The linens were perfectly arranged on the tables, crisp and clean, and all of the plates and glasses were sparkling. Everything was just as I remembered from that night.

A server came around to take our order, and I tried to focus on my menu. We ordered appetizers of fried calamari and caprese. I decided on a traditional Caesar salad and the filet mignon while Grandpa chose the veal. We both glanced at Connor, who seemed to be struggling with his decision.

"Sorry, I don't usually eat this nicely," he said with a shy smile. "I'm a college kid on a limited budget."

Grandpa smiled. "I remember those days."

"What would you recommend, sir?" Connor asked.

Grandpa browsed the menu again. "The lamb chops are delicious."

"Works for me."

While we waited for the appetizers, Grandpa and Connor talked about Connor's classes and his career path. They chatted easily, filling up the time. I sat there, thinking about what I'd seen at the cemetery. Could it have really been my dad? If it was, what was he doing there? If he was in trouble, why hadn't he contacted me?

Maybe he was staying away to protect me. Maybe he had sent the warning email.

I sat up straight in my chair, knocking the table hard enough to rattle the silverware. Connor and Grandpa looked at me in alarm, and I assured them I was fine. I just needed a minute. Excusing myself, I stepped outside and took a deep breath. Couples strolled past me, arm in arm, on their way to a nice dinner or a show at the theater. Everything was normal, just like the night I was here with my dad.

A hand touched my shoulder, and I jumped.

"Just me," Connor said. "I got worried about you. Are you all right? Are you sure you want to stay? We can go somewhere else you know. Your grandfather feels terrible."

"No, I'm okay. Just...thinking."

He pulled me into his arms, wrapping me in his jacket against the coolness of the night. He kissed me then, and I melted against him.

"Don't tell your grandfather I did that," he said close to my ear, and I laughed.

"It feels nice," I said after a moment.

"What does?"

"Being with you. Here." I tipped my head up. "It means a lot that you came with me. I don't think I could have gotten through this alone."

He dropped a kiss on my forehead and sighed. "I just wish I could help you more."

"You're doing great."

After a minute, he leaned in closer and whispered, "You're stronger than you think you are."

"What?"

"You heard me. With all you've been through, the disappearance of your dad, leaving your home and moving in with your mom. Any other person would have given up by now. But you, you just keep fighting and refusing to give up. I admire you."

I tipped my head up to look at him. "Are you serious? I'm hardly what anyone would call a role model."

"Now why do you say that?"

I chewed on my lower lip until he gently took my chin in his hand and ran his thumb over my mouth.

"You're not some spoiled rich girl," he said. "Regardless of the lifestyle you may have had a few months ago-"

"And technically still do," I said. "I'm still Wendell Benton's daughter, Russell Benton's granddaughter-"

"But you're Aubrey Benton first," he said, interrupting me. "You're a strong young woman who cares very much for her family and friends." He paused for a moment, as if he were pondering his next words. Then he smiled and said, "Don't lose that."

His words touched me deeply, and I tucked them away. We stayed outside for a little while longer, and then re-joined my grandfather. Our food had arrived, and he didn't say anything about my abrupt departure as we sat down and began to eat. As our entree dishes were being cleared away, he reached over and gave my hand a reassuring squeeze. That was all he needed to do. That one action strengthened my resolve to find out what had happened to my dad, to find Simon Foley, and to end all of this madness.

We finished our dinner, and Grandpa took us back to the apartment. He hugged me goodbye, kissing my cheek and promising to stay in touch. The paperwork for the money in my trust fund was already being processed, and I was eager to use it.

While Connor was packing his things in the guest room, I went to mine and closed the door. I called home and spoke with Mom and Alyssa for a few minutes. I didn't tell them about my sighting of Dad.

"So is he a nice kisser?" Alyssa asked, and I told her I loved her and hung up.

Chapter Twenty-One

After we got back from New York, I dropped Connor off and went straight home. Mom quizzed me about everything we did, and I had to convince her we'd done nothing more than kiss and cuddle. She seemed relieved with that. I scolded her for telling Connor to keep his hands to himself, and she said that's what mothers do. I didn't have much to say to that. It felt nice to have a mother who really cared.

Not long after we returned, pictures of me showed up in the tabloids. They were from outside my apartment building and at Mark's funeral, when I had my freakout moment. One showed Connor with his dark sunglasses and steely expression as he guided me into the car. The blurb that went with it asked if he was my new personal bodyguard, and if I needed him to protect me because of possible leads in my father's case.

I was disgusted by the pictures, and even more annoyed by the way the kids at school looked at them and whispered behind their hands whenever I walked past. I'd always thought attending a public school would be easier and more relaxed. I thought I'd be able to blend in and lead a normal life. I guess I hadn't considered that I'd need a normal life first.

There were rumors going around about my supposed bodyguard, and the popular girls wanted to know who he was and if we were dating. I ignored all of it and focused on my schoolwork and the Anemone organization.

I let Jonathan and Monica know of my plans to use my trust fund money to help them, and they were stunned at my generosity. Jonathan was also very excited, already planning out uses for the funds. I turned over all of Mark's research to him, including the stuff about my father. He was impressed, but he let us know that the families Mark had been speaking to were not families of Elemental children. The last family that Anemone had helped had gone into hiding just over a year ago. Jonathan wondered if there were less Elementals out there, or if they had just become better at keeping themselves hidden.

I hadn't heard from Connor in a couple of days, so I sent a few text messages and left him voicemails, apologizing for having thrown him into the spotlight. I hoped it wasn't causing problems for him. He didn't call me back, but he did reply with short text messages, saying he had stuff going on. I was considering stopping by his apartment to talk to him in person when Alyssa told me he was probably busy with school. We'd all been busy lately, and I reasoned that she had a point. Her birthday was coming up, and with all of the drama regarding Luminesk, we'd kind of forgotten about it. Mom remedied this by baking a huge cake and inviting Paul and his mother, and Charlotte and her family over for an impromptu party. I invited Connor as well, but didn't receive a response.

Eric was still at home, recovering from the jogging incident, although his injury didn't stop him from working the grill. He was happy for the opportunity to be with us, although he wished it were under different circumstances. Alyssa was still upset over what had happened to him, but he was working with her to get past that.

Paul, Charlotte, and Alyssa were playing a game of Scrabble on the deck after dinner, and the others were enjoying coffee. I was helping Mom to frost the cake and add the candles when Eric came into the kitchen with Connor. I was surprised and pleased that he'd shown up. I had missed him.

"Hey, Connor," Mom greeted him. "You're just in time for some birthday cake."

"Oh, thank you, Mrs. Vaughn, but unfortunately, I can't stay. I just needed to speak with Aubrey."

Something in his tone didn't sit well with me as we walked outside to the front porch. I asked him if he wanted to sit down, and he declined, saying he'd rather stand. He ran a hand through his hair and squared his jaw. My heart did a flip.

"I'm sorry I haven't called you back," he said. "I just needed some time to think."

"It's been kind of crazy around here," I said, forcing my voice to remain calm. "I had no idea those pictures would end up in the tabloids. I never meant for you to be dragged into the mess with my father. That's not why I asked you go to with me at all, even though I truly do appreciate it-"

He held up his hand to stop me. I realized I'd been babbling because I didn't want to hear what I was sure was coming. I could tell from his expression that he was breaking up with me. Could I call it breaking up? We'd only gone on a few dates, and yeah, we'd kissed, and he'd gone to New York with me, but we weren't serious. Were we?

"I'm sorry," he said, "I just think that now isn't the right time. You're obviously involved with something with your family, along with dealing with your dad's disappearance."

I fought the tears, refusing to cry in front of him. He looked like this was hurting him, and I felt there was something else going on.

"I thought we had fun together," I said, annoyed with how pitiful that sounded.

"We do. We did," he corrected himself. "I just think that well, maybe you're a little young for me."

Aha, I thought. *There it is.*

I turned away, grateful that it was semi-dark outside and he couldn't fully see my face. I felt his strong hands touch my shoulders and he leaned down to drop a kiss on my cheek.

"Bye, Aubrey, take care of yourself," he said, and then he walked down the porch steps and to his car.

I watched him drive away, and then I sat down on the swing. I don't know how long I was there, and I wasn't sure what emotions I should be feeling. We hadn't known each other more than a couple of months, but I'd thought we had a connection. I cared about him, and I thought he cared about me. How could I have been so wrong?

Mom stepped out onto the porch and glanced around. "Did Connor leave?"

I nodded. The swing moved as she sat down beside me. She patted my leg, and I leaned into her.

"I'm sorry, baby," she said. "I know you liked him."

Mom just held me in a comforting embrace, like I'd held Alyssa at the hospital.

"Do you want to talk about it?" she asked.

267

I shook my head, wiped my tears and sat up. "Not yet. Please don't say anything to Alyssa. I don't want to spoil her birthday."

"Relationships are tricky," Mom said. "Just look at your dad and me. We were so in love at first."

I bit my lower lip and touched my snowflake pendant. "What happened? I mean, no one's ever really told me about it."

She shrugged. "We grew apart, that's all. We met just after he won the Oscar, so everyone wanted a piece of him. I didn't fall in love with his money or his fame, but his heart. He has a good heart, Aubrey. Then he stopped acting and went to work with your grandfather, and he was always so busy, taking on his new role as a CEO, and modeling wasn't what I thought it would be. There were a lot of other girls out there, younger, prettier, who would do things I wouldn't. I was being passed up for jobs, and I didn't want to use your dad's name to boost my career. I wanted children, and he agreed."

"So I was like a business decision?" I asked, looking at her sideways.

"Of course not. He was very involved with you. He loved you more than anything." Mom sighed. "We fell out of love, Aubrey, but we always cared for each other. He tried to keep me updated on what you were doing. We talked at least once a week."

I was shocked. "I never knew that. He never told me."

"He didn't want to upset you. He knew you weren't my biggest fan, and he hoped you would come around on your own."

I wondered if I ever would have if Dad hadn't gone missing. I hated to admit I probably would have gone on with my life as usual, with Mom staying a tiny blip on my radar.

We rejoined the party, all smiles. Eric was about to ask where Connor was, but Mom stopped him. We enjoyed cake and ice cream, and after everyone left, I helped Eric clean up while Mom got Alyssa ready for bed.

"So, your mom told me about Connor," Eric said as I wrapped up the rest of the cake and put it in the refrigerator. "I wish it hadn't turned out this way for you."

I shrugged. "What's life without a little heartbreak? I wouldn't be a real teenager if I didn't experience some loss."

"I think you've experienced enough loss, in my opinion," Eric said. "Besides, you're still young. You don't want to get tied down now anyway. You have college ahead of you, a bright future where you can do anything you want."

I was a little embarrassed by this pep talk, so I changed the subject. "What I want to do is find this Simon Foley character and get him off our backs."

That was Eric's goal too, and he was taking advantage of his time at home to reach out to some colleagues in other states. I was on my way to bed when Alyssa called out to me. She was sitting on her window seat, staring out into the front yard.

"I'm nine years old now," she said as I grabbed a blanket from the foot of her bed and wrapped it around myself before joining her.

"Congratulations," I said.

She half-smiled. "No, that's not what I meant. I'm older than the other children that went missing. Perhaps this means that I'm no longer valuable to Luminesk." I didn't say anything, and she sighed. "It's a nice thought, but probably implausible."

"We'll figure this out," I said. "Simon Foley won't get you."

We sat together, just looking out the window. The street lights were on, and there was no activity, save for one of the neighbors walking his dog. It was peaceful, and I wanted nothing more than to hang on to this moment.

"It's too bad about Connor," she said.

I didn't ask how she knew about that. I just shrugged and pulled the blanket tighter around me, reveling in its warmth.

"You know, Paul is still interested."

I wasn't sure if Paul even knew Connor had stopped by. And if he did and guessed what had happened, he was too polite to mention it during Alyssa's party. I rolled my eyes and nudged her with my knee. "Is that your way of telling me to move on?"

She giggled. "Maybe." She scooted closer and put her head in my lap. I stroked her hair, remembering how Mom used to do that to me when I was little. "I just think that if Connor can't see how great you are, then he doesn't deserve you."

"You're getting very wise in your old age," I teased.

She didn't laugh, and I felt her tense a little.

"I wish I were stronger," she said.

"What do you mean?"

"I'm getting more powerful. I can feel it. If I were stronger, maybe I could fight off Simon Foley. Or maybe if I somehow forgot how to use my powers, he would leave us alone."

I shifted my position, and Alyssa sat up and faced me. Even in the dark, I could make out the brightness of her eyes.

"None of this is your fault. You know that right?" I asked her.

"I know, but I can't help feeling helpless."

She wiped a tear from her eye and sniffled.

"Wait here," I said. I left her wrapped in the blanket while I ran downstairs. Alyssa smiled when she saw I was holding a plate with a piece of cake and a single candle stuck in the middle. I sat beside her and offered her the plate.

"Did you bring a match?" she asked.

I simply smiled. Alyssa moved closer, staring at the candle. She placed her hands above it, fingers outstretched as though she were warming them over a fire. Within a few seconds, the wick ignited.

"Make a wish," I said.

"You too," she said.

She folded her hands, closed her eyes and blew out the candle, and I knew that she and I had both wished for this to end.

Chapter Twenty-Two

My photography had taken a backseat in my quest to find out more about Simon Foley, and I wanted to get back to it. I had a lot of pictures to edit, so I made myself spend at least a few hours a week in my photography studio. It helped to take my mind off of the crazy things going on. While music played in the background, I was able to edit the photos and add effects. There were some great ones of Alyssa's birthday party, and I spent days working on those to put into a special photo album for her.

Then I came to the photos of my trip to New York City with Connor. I thought about just deleting them all.

What was the point of keeping them? I flipped through them, remembering each moment, and wishing it hadn't ended as awkwardly as it had. I still felt like our age difference was just an excuse, and there was something else that was bothering him. I moved all of the photos to a separate folder and didn't look at them again. Maybe someday I would get rid of them, just not today.

Alyssa knocked on the doorframe before moving to stand beside me. Her expression was serious. Dark. It frightened me a little.

"What's wrong?"

"You need to come upstairs," she said. "Now."

I followed her up to the family room, where Mom and Eric were sitting on the sofa. Their gazes were fixed on the television. Frowning, I turned and saw they were watching the news. A female reporter I recognized from a local station was standing outside what appeared to be police headquarters, just not the Hamilton Green police headquarters.

"Reports are still coming in, but investigators have confirmed the bodies of two adults, one male and one female were inside the car found in a vacant lot a week ago," the reporter said. "We are told that the victims are Carl and Suzanne Grand of Hamilton Green, Missouri, who were reported missing by relatives several weeks ago, along with their teenage daughter, Carly. The daughter has not been found. The cause of death is not being released at this time, pending further investigation."

I couldn't believe my ears. Mr. and Mrs. Grand, Carly's parents, were dead?

The phone rang, and Eric stumbled getting up to answer it.

"Yes, we just saw it," he said. "No, I don't understand how. Do you think it was...all right. We'll see you soon." He hung up and scrubbed a hand over his face tiredly. "Jonathan and Monica are on their way. They have something to show us."

Alyssa curled up next to Mom. I was frozen in place. Where was Carly? Who had done this?

The news report didn't give us any other information. Mom turned off the television and hugged Alyssa tighter. A few minutes later, Monica and her father burst into the house, startling us all. Jonathan had a laptop computer with him, and he pushed aside things on the coffee table to set it up while Monica connected it to our television. Soon we were looking at photographs from the crime scene.

"Don't worry, the graphic ones aren't in this set," Jonathan assured us when Mom gasped and covered Alyssa's eyes. No one asked how he had gotten them.

He flipped through several before stopping on a particular one. I watched his jawline harden and his eyes flashed with something akin to absolute hate, and I shivered a little. He stood up and pointed at the television.

"Do you see it?" he asked.

We all stared harder, trying to determine what it was he was seeing. The photo was of the trunk of the car the Grands had been found in. I scanned the screen, taking in three suitcases, a duffel bag, a cooler, two pairs of sneakers, and...

"A frog lamp," I breathed. The room started to sway a little bit, and I had to steady myself.

"Not just any frog lamp," Jonathan said, his voice bubbling with anger. "My son's lamp. The one taken from his room the same time he was."

"How do you know it's the same one?" Eric asked.

Jonathan tapped the television screen. "See those markings on the lampshade? Travis decided he needed to add some color to it with a red marker. He drew a heart and his initials on it."

"But what does it mean? Did the Grands have something to do with the abduction of your son?" Mom asked. "I would never believe it. They were good people."

Monica shook her head, and Alyssa said, "It's a message from Simon Foley. He's telling us he knows about all of us and that he can get to us. That he can get to me."

Silence descended upon the room. No one knew what to do, and it was obvious. I moved toward the deck door and peered outside. The leaves had turned colors and some were falling to cover the backyard. The sky was bright with sunshine, and I wondered how, on such a perfect day, there could be a real monster lurking somewhere out there. He was watching and waiting for the opportunity to take my sister. And do what? Experiment on her? Ultimately kill her?

As I watched the leaves fall, the sky started to darken as clouds moved to block the sun. A light drizzle began, and then a mist of fog. I turned and looked at Alyssa, who was sitting up and staring out the window in confusion.

"It's not me," she said.

The fog thickened, the rain came down harder, and everyone gathered around me to peer outside.

"There was no report of bad weather today," Mom said.

The face that pressed itself against the glass door appeared so suddenly that we didn't notice it at first. Then Alyssa screamed and pointed. Eric grabbed the fire poker and held it up like a baseball bat, and he and Jonathan jumped in front of us.

"It's Carly!" Alyssa exclaimed, pushing past her father and pulling at the door.

Carly fell inside in a heap, sopping wet and shivering. Mom ran to get some towels while Monica and I helped her to a chair.

"Carly, what happened? Where have you been?" I asked.

"My parents," she stammered. "They're dead. He killed them. He killed them."

"Were you there?" Alyssa asked.

Carly's gaze shifted and settled on Alyssa. They stared at each other, sizing each other up. Then Alyssa shook herself and stepped over to hug Carly.

"How awful for you," she whispered. "To have to deny who you are."

"We need to get her out of here," Jonathan said. "Monica and I will take her to our place." He motioned to his daughter who began gathering up their things. He turned to Mom and Eric. "It's not safe to call or email through regular channels, but we'll be in touch. I'm positive we're being monitored. Use this to contact us. There's one number programmed into it. It's mine." He handed Eric a nondescript cell phone.

He helped Carly to stand, and with a towel wrapped around her shoulders, she appeared very frail and scared. Before they left, Monica told us to watch our backs and hugged each of us in turn. I was not comforted at all. We watched them drive away until they disappeared in the fog.

"She's had a rough time," Alyssa said. "Her parents were hard on her, made her think she was crazy for the things she could do. They forced her to go to therapy and subjected her to all kinds of medication. Finally, she told them what they wanted to hear, that she made it all up. That she couldn't really control anything. This made them happy, but it made her miserable."

"That's why she acted out, got into trouble," Eric said, nodding in understanding. "How did they manage to stay off Simon Foley's radar?"

Alyssa shook her head. "They didn't. He's always kept tabs on them, watching and waiting for Carly to show what she can do."

"You got all of that without her saying a word," I said, and Alyssa nodded.

"I'm picking up more than feelings now. I can read actual thoughts, but just in bits and pieces. I fill in the rest."

This scared me. She was getting stronger, which made her that much more of a prize to Simon Foley.

After about thirty minutes, the fog lifted, and the sunshine returned. We had all collapsed onto seats in the family room and hadn't moved. What could we do? Who should we tell?

"I really want to talk to Carly," I said, breaking the heavy silence. "She could be the link to this whole thing."

Eric nodded. "I agree." He was still holding the cell phone. He dialed the number and listened. After a moment, he hung up. "Jonathan says we should come tonight, and try not to be followed."

We waited until sunset, and then Alyssa conjured up her own screen of fog to hide our departure. Eric drove us to Jonathan and Monica's house and parked in the garage. Monica met us at the door to the house and quickly ushered us inside. All of the curtains were drawn and the lighting was very dim in the living room where Carly was sitting in a recliner. She was wearing clean clothes and wrapped tightly in a blanket. She couldn't seem to stop shivering.

"She's been very quiet since we brought her here," Monica explained. "We're moving her out of state first thing in the morning. Another Anemone family has agreed to take care of her."

Alyssa went to stand beside Carly, and again, they just eyed each other, as if having a silent conversation. Then Carly opened her arms and enveloped Alyssa in the blanket. She soon stopped shivering.

"Where's your dad?" I asked Monica.

She glanced over her shoulder. "Holed up in his office, adding additional security to his computer system. He thinks he may have been hacked, and that just makes him crazy."

"Is he all right? I mean, after seeing the frog lamp?"

"He's coping," was all Monica said, and I could tell from her tone that he wasn't coping very well.

Jonathan joined us, and we gathered around Carly, questions on all our minds, and not one of us wanting to ask them. After a while, she took a deep breath and said, "I wasn't with them when it happened."

Mom reached out and placed a hand on her knee. "Take your time, sweetheart."

Carly gulped hard and then told us her story. She was the second child of Carl and Suzanne Grand, born three years after her brother, Leo. Her parents were still very upset over his death, and she always felt she disappointed them, especially after she started showing her abilities.

"I was so scared, and my parents didn't know what to do. They thought I was crazy. They didn't want to believe I could do anything like that, and I didn't want to believe it either. Then one day, this man came to our house. He introduced himself to us as Simon Foley, and he was very polite and professional, even nice looking. I wanted to like him. When he told my parents he could help me, I trusted him. All they would need to do was sign over custody to him, and he would make me better."

The complete disbelief that I knew was on my face was also evident on everyone else's.

"My parents said no," Carly continued. "They thought he was nuts too. He said he understood and left. Then weird stuff started happening."

"What kind of weird stuff?" I asked.

"We kept seeing these black-suited guys all over town, following us. The grocery store, the gas station, even at church. They never approached us, just watched our every move. It kept freaking me out, and so I kept causing small fires and storms. My parents were so angry," she said, shaking her head. "Not at them, but at me. They believed me, even though they didn't want to. They sent me to all kinds of doctors and therapists, hoping I could be cured somehow. I figured out that if I wanted any of this to stop, I had to control my powers.

So I learned to not use them. Then that just made me angry, and I started acting out in other ways. It just went from bad to worse, but those guys stopped hanging around."

"Then we showed up, asking questions," Jonathan said. "Her parents told me to stay away. They refused to relocate or admit that Carly was different."

"But I wanted your help, just in case," Carly said, nodding, "so I kept in touch." She turned to us. "I knew Alyssa had powers, too. I could see all the signs, even though you did a great job of trying to hide them. When I found out Aubrey was coming here, I panicked. I thought your celebrity status would attract unwanted attention, so I contacted Anemone for help."

"Did you send me a warning email?" I asked. "I got it not long after I found out about Alyssa. I was warned to 'please be careful.' Was that you?"

Carly frowned. "Sorry, it wasn't me."

"Why did you run, Carly?" Eric asked.

"My parents found out someone was checking into our family, and they thought it was Simon Foley again. They said we had to run. We took what we could, but we left everything else. It must have been him who emptied our house."

My mouth went dry. I had asked Mark to do a background check. It was my fault the Grands had gotten scared and left town, and it was my fault they were now dead.

"Please don't blame yourself," Carly said, knowing what I was thinking. "I tried to tell them we should tell Jonathan and Monica. They wouldn't listen to me. They never had before, why start now." There was bitterness in her voice, along with great sadness.

I couldn't speak for the guilt that was choking me. I listened to the rest of Carly's story, feeling worse and worse. They had left in the middle of the night, no destination in mind, just knowing they had to get away. After a few days of travel, Carly had sneaked away from their motel for some time alone to think. When she returned, her parents were gone. She was able to track them to the vacant lot and found them, dead.

She'd been on the run alone ever since, trying desperately to make her way back to Hamilton Green, the only place she'd ever felt somewhat safe.

"My parents had nothing to do with your son's disappearance," she said to Jonathan. "I don't know how that lamp got there."

"I believe you," he said, wiping tears from his eyes.

"Carly, you can be a huge help to us," Monica said then.

"I don't see how."

"You've seen Simon Foley. You can help us put together a picture. Maybe we can find out more about him, identify him and see if that's even his real name."

"It was so long ago, I don't know if I remember that much detail."

Alyssa nodded. "I can help. We can do it together."

Carly locked eyes with Alyssa, and a small smile tugged at her lips. "Okay, let's give it a try."

Carly explained that after the children turned nine, their powers increased, just as Alyssa's had done. Simon Foley wanted the children before that so he could use them the way he saw fit. He wanted control to mold them into his own vision. Whatever that vision was, however, was still somewhat of a mystery. Carly said she thought he wanted to change the world for the better, just at a very high cost to the safety of those involved. At first, he'd started out simply asking the parents for the children. He probably thought they would be glad to be rid of them. When they refused, he had found it necessary to resort to stealing the children.

"How did you control your powers?" Alyssa asked Carly.

"I tried a lot of simple methods," she said. "I had a rubber band around my wrist and I snapped it whenever I felt the urge to do something. I kept a thumb tack in my pocket and poked my finger. I chewed gum, ate candy, took up running. I did everything. I even kept a diary, recording every instance where I wanted to use my powers. My parents destroyed it when they found it," she added, much to everyone's disappointment. "They were afraid it would be found and I'd be taken away and locked up somewhere."

Her lower lip began to tremble, and she clenched her jaw tight to stop it. "They were always so scared," she said. "I used to think they were scared of me, but then I realized I had misunderstood. I'd made a huge mistake in judging them my entire life. They were afraid *for* me, not of me."

The tears were flowing freely now, and Alyssa went to her side, comforting her. After a few minutes, Carly was calm again, and she and Alyssa seemed to share a silent conversation. Jonathan suggested they go to his office to put together a sketch on his computer, and the rest of us huddled around the kitchen table, hashing out further details. I still hadn't said much, and I excused myself to step outside for a moment. The Orsons had a small patio at the back of the house with a picnic table. I sat down and took a deep breath. The sky was clear, and the stars were shining bright. Monica came with me, and we sat together, heads tilted up, just staring.

"Where will she go?" I asked. "Will she ever be safe?"

"She's going to stay with a good family. They're very qualified to help. As for being safe, I don't know if that will ever be possible for any of us as long as Simon Foley is out there plotting away. We need to stop him."

I nodded, more determined than ever. I also felt immense guilt, a feeling I was becoming accustomed to these days, unfortunately.

"It's not your fault, you know," Monica said. "Carly's parents took a risk. They were offered our help and they refused."

"Don't tell me you can read minds now too."

"Ha. No, but it's not hard to see what's written all over your face."

"They didn't deserve to die."

"No," Monica said, shaking her head. "They certainly didn't."

I don't know how long we stayed outside. No one bothered us until my mom came to the door, asking us to rejoin them.

"The sketch is done," she said.

The black and white image was computer-generated, and according to Carly, was pretty darn accurate to what she remembered from those years ago. Alyssa was able to use Carly's emotions to give more precise details, such as the lines around his eyes, and the slight arch of his brow. We all stared at the picture, wracking our brains to try and remember if we'd ever seen him.

"I've got nothing," Eric said. "He doesn't look familiar at all."

Mom agreed. "I've never seen him before."

We were all in the same boat. Simon Foley had never been seen by any of us, except for Carly. Jonathan was hopeful that he'd be able to run the photo through some facial recognition software and get a hit through one of the many databases around the world.

"It's worth a shot," he said, taking the photo.

The sun was starting to rise when we left. We each hugged Carly goodbye and wished her the best of luck. We didn't know where she was going, but she promised to try and keep in touch through Jonathan and Monica once she was settled.

When she reached me, she embraced me as an old friend would.

"She's very special," she whispered to me, and I knew she was talking about Alyssa. "Keep her safe."

"I will," I promised. "Take care."

Carly and Alyssa used their powers together to drop heavy fog over a fifty mile radius to disguise our departure. It was very early Sunday morning, and once we returned home, we all went right to bed. I crawled wearily beneath my covers, anxious to put the previous evening behind me. Just as I was about to drift off to dreamland, my bedroom door creaked, and Alyssa padded into the room. She had changed into pajamas. I raised the blankets and she crawled in beside me.

"I'm really scared," she said, her voice soft. "I think something bad is going to happen. I feel it."

I wanted to tell her there was nothing to worry about. We had a picture of Simon Foley, and we were even more alert than before. I wanted to assure her that she was safe, that Mom, Eric and I would never let anything happen to her. All of those words were right on the tip of my tongue, and I couldn't utter a single one.

Alyssa sighed and snuggled against me. She yawned and said, "It's okay. I'd rather you didn't lie."

Her breathing became deep and even within a few minutes, and she rested peacefully beside me. I was wide awake though, unable to get past the fact that I couldn't guarantee anything anymore.

Chapter Twenty-Three

The school cafeteria was crowded as usual. Students hurried back and forth across the room, grabbing bottles of water, fruit cups, or bags of chips to go along with their sub sandwiches, before scarfing it all down in record time to get to their next class. Conversations were going on all around us. Silverware was dropped, wrappers crunched up, trays stacked as they were returned.

Paul and I heard none of it. We sat at a small table near the windows, picking at our food. I glanced outside, wondering if the weather was nice wherever Carly was. I hoped she was coping with the death of her parents. I hoped she was safe from Simon Foley.

After I was sure Alyssa was asleep, I had left her in my bed and slipped downstairs to call Paul. I felt he deserved to know what was going on, and he said he'd be right over. When he arrived, I told him everything, and he was shocked. He was also without any possible solution, just like the rest of us.

Now we were back in school, instructed by Mom and Eric to act as if nothing had changed. Everything was normal.

Except it was the furthest thing from normal.

I pushed my tuna and noodles around my plate. It hadn't been particularly appetizing when it was plopped onto my tray, and now it looked even worse. With a sound of disgust, I shoved my tray away and pulled out my cell phone to check for any new voicemails or text messages. Of course, there was nothing.

Charlotte startled us both when she dropped her backpack on the table with a thud, rattling everyone's trays.

"Whoops, sorry," she said. Her face was flushed, and she was out of breath. "You will never guess what just happened to me."

I forced myself to smile and leaned forward. "What happened?"

She sat down and grabbed my hands excitedly.

"Max Harper just asked me to Homecoming!"

I blinked several times, my brain trying to figure out the appropriate reaction, settling on excitement.

"That's awesome, Charlotte!" I said, looking over at Paul. He grinned and nodded.

"Yeah, that's cool," he said.

Thankfully, Charlotte was too caught up in her own thoughts to notice how lame we were.

"Oh my gosh! The dance is Saturday! Where am I going to find a dress on such short notice? And shoes? Oh my gosh, what am I going to do?"

Her pretty features twisted into panic, and she gripped my hands harder.

"Will you help me? Please, Aubrey?"

"Sure, I can help you. We can go shopping after school for a dress."

"No, no," Charlotte said, shaking her head. "I've never been to a dance with a boy. I've never been to anything with a boy. I need you there."

"Where?" I asked, dumbfounded.

"At the dance!" Charlotte wailed. "You have to go!"

My eyes widened at the thought. "Um, er, I..." I stuttered.

Across the table, Paul sat up and cleared his throat. "We could, uh, go together," he said. He was blushing as he spoke. "Strictly as friends," he added.

Charlotte squealed in delight. "Yes, that's perfect! Oh, thank you, Paul!"

She released me and ran to Paul, throwing her arms around his neck in a hug. Then she grabbed her backpack and took off, yelling at us that she had to tell Max.

"What just happened?" I asked.

"It looks like we're going to Homecoming together," Paul said. "If that's all right with you."

I raised a brow at him. "Is that really what you think we should be doing right now? Going to a school dance?"

He shrugged. "What else will you be doing this Saturday night? Come on, it'll be fun. It'll show Simon Foley that he can't stop us from having a good time."

I pondered this for the rest of the day, and came to the conclusion that he was right. We deserved a little fun. After the last bell rang, I met Charlotte outside by Paul's car. He was going to drop us off at my house.

"Do you want to come with us? Don't you need a suit or something?" I asked him.

"I've got a couple already. You girls go have fun...doing what girls do," he said, sounding confused.

Mom and Alyssa were waiting for us at home. "Mind if we tag along?" Mom asked.

"How did you know?"

"Charlotte called her mother and told her about you and Paul. Then Paul's mother called me. Paul's mom is thrilled and has agreed to let him go since she'll be chaperoning the dance. I'm so happy for you!"

Alyssa was grinning. "Mom said we can go get you a pretty dress!"

We all climbed into Mom's van and she drove us into the city. We scoured all the stores that carried fancy dresses. This close to the dance, they had pretty much been picked over, but there were still a few good ones left. Charlotte was a mess. This was her first ever date, and she had no idea what she was supposed to do. I helped her choose a dress, a long navy blue one with spaghetti straps that showed off her figure. She emerged from the dressing room, timid and trying to cover herself.

"You're perfectly respectable," Mom assured her.

She stood in front of the mirror, taking in her appearance. I pulled her hair back and held it up off her face.

"And with your hair up like this, you'll knock off Max's socks," I said.

"You're a total hottie, Charlotte," Alyssa said, which caused us all to laugh. "What? Is that not right?"

Alyssa chose my dress, and I didn't think it was my style.

"Trust me, it's you," she said to me, pushing me toward the dressing room.

It was deep purple in color, strapless and with simple beading on the bodice and a short layered chiffon skirt. I tried it on and found that I actually liked it. It was more feminine and flirty than I would have picked out, but Alyssa had been right, of course.

We found shoes and jewelry to go along with our new dresses, and when Mom offered to do our hair and makeup for us, we gladly accepted. I had been to school dances before, and I had been presented at the debutante ball when I was sixteen. Those had all been so formal and stuffy, and I found I was excited to attend this one. Before we left the mall, Mom said she wanted to stop at the cell phone store.

"We're going to get a phone for Alyssa," she explained. "Just in case."

I completely agreed, and wondered why we hadn't gotten her one before then. As we stepped into the store, my feet turned to lead when I spotted Connor at the counter. He was speaking with a customer service representative about all of the details of a nationwide service plan. He looked up when the bell above the door dinged, then focused on me.

"Awkward," Alyssa muttered, scooting off with Mom to check out the display of phones.

Charlotte, having never met Connor but knowing who he was, followed them, leaving me to stand alone. Connor excused himself and came over to me.

"Hi," he said. "How have you been?"

I swallowed hard, determined not to sound nervous. "Fine. Good."

He nodded at the huge garment bag slung over my arm. "New dress?"

I looked down, forgetting it was even there. "Homecoming dress."

"Yeah? Do you have a date?"

I heard the curiosity in his voice, and I squared my shoulders. "As a matter of fact, I do. Paul and I are going together."

Connor was visibly surprised. "Oh, well, that's nice. He's a good guy."

"Yes, he is."

Connor coughed. "Well, I'll just finish up what I'm doing and be on my way. It was nice seeing you, Aubrey."

I only nodded. He went back to the counter, and I forced myself to take steps toward my mom and Alyssa.

"What did he want?" Alyssa asked, crossing her arms over her chest and scowling. "He has no right to be jealous. He dumped you."

"Alyssa," Mom scolded, then turned to me. "Are you okay, honey?"

"I'm fine, can we just hurry up and go?"

Alyssa chose a simple phone, one that allowed text messaging, and Mom went to pay for it. Connor was still at the counter. He was purchasing a new phone, and the customer service rep was showing him all the bells and whistles.

I turned away, unable to look at him. I tried to ignore his perfect profile, or his strong hands, or his hair that was still that beautiful dark brown, and how it was longer than the last time I'd seen him and was curling a little at the nape of his neck. I was staring blankly at a wall of cell phone accessories when I heard him leave the store.

Tears threatened to fall, but I held them back, focusing on my anger at how he'd hurt me.

A hand touched my shoulder. It was Mom, and they were ready to leave. We stopped for dinner at a fast food place, where I ordered a salad that I didn't eat. We dropped off Charlotte, and then headed home ourselves. Alyssa had already acquainted herself with her new phone, programming in important numbers and changing her ringtone. She bounced out of the van to go show Eric her phone.

"You have every right to be upset," Mom said as we walked inside after her.

I sucked in a breath, held it for a few seconds, and then let it out with a whoosh.

"I know. I just thought, well, I guess I don't know what I thought," I said.

"You thought you had real feelings for him," Mom said. "And you probably did. That doesn't mean you should let those feelings control how you handle the rest of your life. Especially your love life."

Mom reached out to ruffle my hair and hug me. It made me feel a little better.

Chapter Twenty-Four

I was nervous all day Saturday, thinking about the dance. Every now and then, an image of Connor popped into my head, and I shook it away. I was trying to follow Mom's advice and not let Connor barge into my thoughts too much. It was difficult, considering I still liked him.

Eric got a message from Jonathan that was disappointing. There had been no matches to the sketch of Simon Foley. It was like the man didn't exist except as a name on a piece of paper. If Carly hadn't met him, we would have thought that was exactly the case.

Charlotte arrived a little after four in the afternoon, and Mom did her hair and makeup first so she could go home and show her parents. Max was picking her up and then they were coming back to my house for some pictures.

I was seated on a chair in the bathroom facing the mirror while Mom curled my hair. Alyssa sat on the counter, her legs swinging back and forth as she played assistant, holding out bobby pins, hairspray, and the curling iron.

"Will you take lots of pictures?" she asked. "I want to see the decorations and the other dresses."

"I will."

"And the music," she continued. "Tell me about the music. I want to know what songs are played, and which ones you and Paul dance to."

"I will."

"And if he kisses you-"

"Alyssa," Mom scolded. She positioned the final pin in my hair and stood back to admire her work. "Perfect."

I stood up, and Alyssa pointed me toward the hallway. "Go get your dress!" she said. "Never mind, I'll get it for you."

She took off for my room. Mom unplugged the curling iron and started gathering up all the stuff scattered across the counter.

"I've never seen her so excited about anything," she said. "Not even Christmas."

Alyssa returned with my dress and proudly held it out to me. I changed into it with Mom's help so that I wouldn't ruin my hair and makeup, then slipped into my shoes. I faced her and Alyssa, my arms extended.

"Well? How do I look?" I asked.

"You look beautiful," Alyssa breathed. "Like a princess."

I hugged her tightly and laughed, feeling happy and lighthearted for the first time in a long time. Paul arrived just as Max and Charlotte did, and Mom absolutely delighted in positioning us in front of the fireplace for pictures. I had to admit, Paul was quite handsome in his suit. I quickly squashed that thought down. We were just very good friends.

I wished my dad could have been there. He would have had fun taking pictures with Mom. Before we left, Eric told me to forget about everything else that was going on and just enjoy myself. I promised him I would.

We enjoyed a nice dinner at a local restaurant, and then headed over to the school for the dance. The DJ was rocking out on stage, and almost everyone was on the floor dancing and having a good time. I tried to take as many pictures as possible to share with Alyssa. I knew she wanted to hear all about my night and would be waiting up for me until I got home.

I had never had so much fun at a school dance. Radcliffe Academy was famed for its lavish and extravagant parties and formal gatherings, but to me, they always seemed a little too perfect and forced. No one seemed to genuinely laugh or smile, and at the end of the night, there was always an underlying feeling of disappointment. Homecoming at Hamilton Green High School was unlike anything I'd ever experienced. The gymnasium looked fantastic, decorated simply yet tastefully by the student council. All of the tables were covered in pretty tablecloths, with bowls holding floating candles and flowers as centerpieces, and the vintage disco ball hanging from the ceiling twirled and cast a rainbow of colors on the floor.

After a while, we tired of dancing and decided to take a break. Paul and Max went to get us some punch. Charlotte and I were sitting at one of the decorated round tables, discussing our opinions of some of the other girls' dresses when my silver, sequined clutch began to vibrate. I had a new text message from Alyssa, and as I read it, I could feel my hands getting clammy.

HELP THEY R HERE

The phone slipped from my grasp and hit the table with a thud, just as Paul and Max returned with our drinks. Even in the flickering light of the school gymnasium, Paul could see the color had drained from my face.

He grabbed my cell phone, read the message and his eyes darted back to meet mine. I stood up with such force that my chair fell backward. Paul quickly righted it and apologized, giving an excuse about a family emergency, which wasn't exactly false. He told Charlotte we'd call her later, then guided me across the floor toward the exit, ignoring the confused looks as we bumped into couples on our way out. We managed to sneak past Paul's mother who was overseeing the punch bowl.

"Are you okay?" Paul asked.

I nodded as I got into his car, and he made sure I was buckled in before handing me my cell phone.

"Call her back."

I dialed and listened to the phone ring. Alyssa's cheerful voice greeted me, and I took a deep breath, only to be disappointed when I realized it was her voicemail message. No one answered, so I called Mom's cell phone and Eric's. They both went straight to voicemail, and the house phone rang without the answering machine picking up.

"Don't panic," Paul said. He kept one hand on the steering wheel as he drove, and one hand on my arm to comfort me. "I'm sure it's nothing. Maybe she's just playing a joke."

"Right. Alyssa's just playing a joke."

Paul cringed at my tone. "I'm sorry. That was stupid, and I'm sorry."

"What if something's happened? What if Simon Foley got her? Got them?"

Paul squared his jaw, put both hands on the steering wheel and drove faster toward our neighborhood. He braked hard and threw the car into Park in front of my house. I flung my door open and was racing across the lawn before Paul had unbuckled his seatbelt. I stumbled on the grass, my heels sinking into the lawn, which was softer than usual. Damp, I realized as I fell to my knees, staining the dress that Alyssa had chosen for me. My heart was pounding so hard I could hear it, and I fought back tears as I pushed open the front door.

"Mom? Eric?" I called out, hurrying inside. I tripped over an end table turned on its side and crashed to the floor.

Paul came in behind me and helped me up. "Oh no," he murmured, looking around.

The living room had been trashed. The sofa had been ripped apart, stuffing all over the floor. Every book had been pulled off the shelves, and lamps were knocked over. My mother's favorite crystal vase lay in slivers on the floor, the flowers flattened, water pooling on the rug.

"Mom!" I yelled again, going into the kitchen.

"Aubrey, wait for me," Paul said, grabbing my arm. He pulled a knife from the butcher block sitting on the counter and held it in front of us.

Together, we checked out the rest of the first floor and found the same results. Every room had been destroyed, every drawer opened and its contents spilled all over the place.

"There's no one down here," Paul said, his voice shaking.

I was panicking as I ran to the steps. There were small dark colored drops on the carpet and a smear on the wall that resembled a handprint. I took the steps two at a time, following the trail. It was definitely blood, and that freaked me out as I worried about who it belonged to. I went into my mom and Eric's room, and a scream erupted from my throat. Paul was beside me in an instant.

"Come on, let's go," he said, moving to stand in front of me, shielding me from the sight.

But I couldn't look away. There was a huge blood stain at the foot of the bed, surrounded by broken glass from the window.

"Paul, where are they?"

"I don't know. But we need to get out of here. Now."

"Shouldn't we call the police?"

"This is way above what the police can do. Come on, let's go. We'll go back to my place and form a plan."

He pulled me out of the room and down the stairs. We both screamed and jumped at the sight of Alyssa standing in the front doorway. Her eyes were bright with unshed tears and her blonde hair was hanging wildly around her face.

"Alyssa!" I dropped to my knees and starting checking for injuries, and Paul put down the knife.

"I'm not hurt," she said. "They got Mom and Dad. I ran away and hid."

"Whose blood is that upstairs?"

"I don't know."

Paul glanced up and down the street. "I don't mean to be rude, but we should leave now."

I scooped Alyssa into my arms and carried her across the lawn to Paul's car. I buckled her into the backseat and got in.

"We can't go to your house," I said.

"Why not?"

"If Luminesk has been here, you can bet they've been to or at least know where you live. They could be waiting for us."

"Mom's chaperoning the dance, so she won't be back until late," he said, sounding relieved. "Where can we go?"

Alyssa patted my shoulder, and I turned to face her. "Monica can help us," she said.

Paul did a U-turn and headed for the highway.

"Can you call her?" he asked. "See if she's home?"

I dialed Monica's cell number and got her voicemail. I didn't leave a message. Even if she and her father weren't there, Monica had given me the alarm code to get into the house in case of an emergency. We were just outside of Hamilton Green when Alyssa tapped my shoulder again.

"We're being followed."

I looked through the back window and sure enough, there was a black Lexus with dark windows about three car lengths behind us. Paul sped up and passed the car in front of us. I watched as the Lexus kept up.

"What do we do?" Paul asked, just as my cell phone rang.

"Aubrey, where are you?" Monica asked. "Are you in trouble? Is Alyssa with you?"

"We have her, and we're on our way to your house. We're being followed. Now I don't think we should come."

"No, keep going. We can help you. Where are your parents?"

I gulped. "I-I don't know. We went to the house. They weren't there. The house was wrecked, and there was blood."

"The people following you, are they close behind?"

I checked again. "No, they're keeping their distance."

"That's good. It means they don't want to cause a scene. Just keep going at a steady pace. Pull right into the garage when you get here."

When we arrived in Monica's neighborhood, I pointed out her house, and Paul steered the car into the garage. Monica was waiting for us and grabbed Alyssa's hand, taking her inside. Paul and I looked over our shoulders to watch the Lexus continue past as the garage door dropped shut behind us. Jonathan was waiting for us in the kitchen.

"The car drove around the block and parked at the end of the street," he said. "I can't see anyone inside."

He gave me a comforting hug.

"Okay, so now what?" Paul asked. "We've got to move Alyssa somewhere they can't get to her."

Paul and Jonathan began discussing a getaway plan. I wasn't listening. I was watching Monica with Alyssa. She'd pulled a package of cookies from the pantry, poured a glass of milk and made Alyssa comfortable at the kitchen table.

"She'll be fine," Monica said, coming to stand beside me. "Everything's going to be ok. She said they took your parents, and she ran away and hid in a neighbor's yard. She tried to slow them down by making all the water in the ground come to the surface."

"It was wet when we got there," I said, nodding.

I gripped the edge of the kitchen island to hide my shaking hands.

"Why don't we get you some different clothes?" Monica suggested, guiding me down the hall to her bedroom. "I think we're the same size. That's a very pretty dress, by the way."

"I know you're trying to keep me calm, and I thank you," I said. "But my mom and step-father are missing, bad guys are outside, and I don't know what to do."

I continued to babble about Luminesk and Simon Foley, and while I did, Monica was handing me clean jeans, a T-shirt, sweatshirt, socks and sneakers. She gently pushed me to the bathroom to change.

"Take a few minutes and join us in the kitchen," Monica said with a gentle smile, pulling the door shut behind her.

I turned away from the door, catching my reflection in the mirror. I looked like crap. My perfect up-do, that my mother had so painstakingly done for me, was hanging down in strings, and my makeup was smudged and smeared. I changed clothes, washed my face and ran a brush through my hair, working out the bobby pins and tangles.

When I went back to the kitchen, I was calmer, but still anxious. Monica handed me a hair tie, and I pulled my hair into a ponytail. I noticed Paul had changed as well into clothes borrowed from Jonathan, judging by the oversized shirt.

"So what's the plan?" I asked, taking a seat next to Alyssa. She offered me a cookie, which I accepted as my stomach growled.

"Simon must be getting desperate," Jonathan said, drumming his fingers on the countertop. "He took your parents, but didn't stick around to grab Alyssa. He either plans to use them as bait, or he wants to study them and see how Alyssa came to be."

Or he's killed them like he did the Grands, I thought. Alyssa sniffled, and I knew she'd heard me, even though I hadn't said it aloud.

"Both situations suck," Paul said flatly.

307

"They've been following us for months now. We thought that if someone stayed with Alyssa at all times, there'd be no way they'd get to her. Now that seems pretty stupid," I said.

"They must have known that tonight she'd be vulnerable," Monica said. She narrowed her eyes as she thought. "May I see your cell phone?"

I pulled it from the back pocket of my jeans and handed it to her.

"Has this been out of your sight at any time since you moved here?" she asked, flipping it over and examining it.

I shook my head. "You think it's been bugged or something? But the back doesn't even come off. Wouldn't it need to be opened to plant a bug?"

"These days it's possible to bug a phone without touching it. Someone would only need to be near enough to clone the signal, but to be absolutely sure the cloning was successful, the person may have wanted to hold it next to a special device." Monica raised her head to look at me. "Has anyone else used this?"

I thought about the past several months. I'd had the same phone the entire time, not wanting to get a new one or change my number in case Dad tried to call me. Not even Paul or Alyssa had used it to make a call. Then my heart clenched in my chest, and I reached out to grab the counter so I wouldn't fall over.

"Who?" Jonathan asked, pushing himself away from the counter and stepping closer. "It may mean nothing at all, or it could mean everything, Aubrey. Who was it?"

I opened my mouth to speak when another voice interrupted me. I stared in horror as Connor entered the kitchen through the garage and said, "It was me."

Chapter Twenty-Five

Jonathan immediately positioned himself in front of us all, his arms outward.

"Who are you?" he demanded. "What do you want?"

Connor stepped forward, followed by six men dressed in dark tactical gear. They fanned out around us, and I jumped when I saw they all had high-powered rifles aimed at us.

"Stand down," Connor ordered. "Do not fire."

A chill crept up my back as I realized he was in charge of this group. Connor was dressed in a black suit with a grey shirt, and his stance reminded me of a soldier. He wore a shoulder holster beneath his jacket, and I could clearly see a gun.

"Get out of my house," Jonathan said.

I took a couple of steps to my left, and Alyssa slid from her chair to press herself against me. She was shaking like a leaf, or maybe it was me. I couldn't tell for sure.

"We know who you are," Connor said to Jonathan and Monica, "and you are not a threat to us. We're here to collect Alyssa."

"You'll have to get through me first," Paul said. He took a swing at Connor. Connor easily deflected the punch and grabbed Paul's wrist, twisting and spinning him to the floor. He pressed a knee into Paul's back and held him down.

"This isn't about you," Connor growled. "Now stop acting stupid before you get yourself killed." He jerked his head toward the men and they began to move toward us. "Take Aubrey as well," he ordered.

At that moment, everything seemed to happen at once. One second, we were all frozen in place, and then the next, all of the men with guns had been knocked to the floor by a great gust of wind, and the spout popped off of the kitchen faucet. Water began spraying everywhere, hot and cold. Connor was flung backward against the wall, and Paul hurried to his feet.

In the confusion, Jonathan grabbed Alyssa and ran down the hallway with her. Monica, Paul and I followed close behind. We made it to Jonathan's office, and Monica locked the door. We started shoving furniture against it, just as the pounding started.

"Aubrey, don't do this!" Connor shouted, and I shuddered at his voice. It wasn't the Connor that I had developed feelings for. It was someone else, a monster sent to hurt us. I wanted to throw up.

"This way," Jonathan said, ushering us to the closet at the back of the room. He and Monica moved aside some boxes to reveal a hidden door in the floor. Together, they lifted it, and we stared down at a narrow ladder.

"At the bottom, turn left, and there's a path that will lead you out to the backyard. The hatch is hidden under the rose bushes," Monica explained as quickly as she could. "Go. We'll hold them off."

"What about you?" I asked. "We can't leave you! They have guns!"

Jonathan removed two handguns from a drawer and handed one to Monica. "So do we," he said. "Now get moving!"

Paul went first, helping Alyssa. I was torn between going with them and arguing with Monica and her father to join us.

"We don't have time," Monica said, as the pounding in the hallway got louder. "Please go. We'll catch up."

She hugged me and shoved me away. With tears in my eyes, I climbed down the ladder. Jonathan closed the door above me, dropping me into darkness. With Alyssa between us, Paul and I ran down the short tunnel and came to another ladder. Paul hurried to climb it, pushing up the hatch and peeking out.

"It's clear," he said, and disappeared outside. Alyssa was right behind him, and he helped her the rest of the way.

I glanced back toward the tunnel. I could hear loud banging noises and then a gunshot, and I feared for Monica and Jonathan's safety. I took a few steps in their direction.

"Aubrey, now!" Paul hissed.

I decided there was nothing I could do to help them. I was unarmed. I turned and scrambled up the ladder, reaching out to Paul to have him pull me up. But it wasn't Paul who clasped my hand.

Connor yanked my arm with such force that I screamed at the shock. He crushed me to his chest, and I struggled to get away from him. I saw Paul and Alyssa had been caught, a darkly dressed goon on either side of them.

"Let them go!" I yelled. "Help! Someone, help!"

Connor pressed a hand over my mouth, muffling my screams, and I bit his finger. He cried out in pain and released me. One of the men holding Alyssa stepped away from her and grabbed me, raising his hand to hit me. I braced myself for the blow, squeezing my eyes shut. It never came. I opened my eyes to see Connor had the man's fist in his hand, and he was crushing it.

"Don't you dare. They are not to be harmed, do you understand me?" he asked, his voice like ice.

The other man nodded, wincing, and Connor pushed him away. "Let's go."

We were hustled to a huge SUV and forced inside. The windows were blacked out, making them impossible to see through. Connor climbed in with us while the other men rode in a separate vehicle. The bench seats faced each other, and while Paul, Alyssa, and I huddled together on one, Connor sat across from us. Alyssa stared at him with a curious expression.

"They're fine," Connor said to her. "Momentarily stunned, but unharmed. They'll be okay. They were not the objectives of this mission."

"Just what is your mission?" Paul spat. "To act all chummy with us and make us trust you?"

Connor's face was difficult to read. His eyes were like stone, and his jaw was clenched.

"I'm not at liberty to discuss this information with you."

Alyssa studied him, unblinking. "How did you fool me?" she asked. "I never sensed any danger from you. Nothing that would indicate you were a bad person."

He was rigid in his seat, unmoving as he avoided her gaze. "I've become very good at hiding my true intentions," he responded.

We were traveling at a fast speed, and as much as I squinted to try and make out where we were going, I couldn't see anything. I had a million questions, but I was afraid of the answers, so I kept quiet. I could feel Connor's eyes on me, and it was difficult to avoid looking at him. Instead, I focused on Alyssa. She had tear tracks on her face, and her nose was running. Connor saw it too, and he handed her a tissue. She accepted it without a word and wiped her nose.

Sixty minutes passed, or it could have been ten. I had no sense of time in the darkened SUV. It came to a stop, the doors opened, and we were pulled from the vehicle. From what I could tell, we were in some kind of warehouse district.

"Blake, take them inside," Connor ordered the guard that had come out to greet us. I recognized him as the one who had been hanging around our neighborhood, and also the one that had tried to take Alyssa from the Fourth of July parade. "I'll meet up with you after I debrief." He caught my eye, almost appearing sad, and then he walked away, leaving me very confused.

Blake nodded, and as soon as Connor was gone, he grinned at me and licked his lips. He, along with two other goons, roughly pushed us into what appeared to be a typical storage building from the outside. They marched us through several corridors, down this way and that way. I tried to remember the route, but I lost track as we passed several doors. Some of the doors had windows in them, and I tried to peer inside, gasping when I saw what appeared to be examination and operating rooms. Blake held me in his iron-like grip and seemed to take pleasure in squeezing harder with every step we took. I bit my tongue to keep from wincing.

They stopped us in the middle of a large room where a circular platform stood about three feet above the ground. A man was on the platform with his back to us. He was staring intently at a series of large television monitors mounted in front of him.

"You're proving to be quite the prize, Alyssa," he said without facing us.

Alyssa flinched beside me.

"Don't talk to her," I said, attempting to sound as loud and brave as possible. "Talk to me."

The man turned, grinning as he stared down at us with eyes of cold blue.

"Miss Benton," he said. "It's a pleasure to finally make your acquaintance. I admire your courage in this unfortunate situation, but I assure you, it's not necessary."

"Who are you?" Paul demanded. "What have you done with Mr. and Mrs. Vaughn?"

The man smiled and extended his hands to us, palms up. "Why, I've done nothing. I simply had them brought here for safekeeping."

He and pushed a button on a computer keyboard and pointed to one of the monitors. It flickered and came into focus. The picture was grey but clear, and I could see my mom and Eric in what looked like a concrete room. There was one door and no furniture. On a wall hung a mirror, like one from a police interrogation room. Mom sat beneath the mirror, while Eric limped around on his still injured ankle.

"Mom!" Alyssa said, taking a step forward. The man that held her jerked her back hard, eliciting a yelp of pain. She clamped her lips shut and stayed quiet.

I looked up at the man. "Are they hurt?"

"Superficial wounds. They fought back quite valiantly." He came to the edge of the platform and bent down toward us. "I'm sorry, how rude of me. I haven't even introduced myself. My name is Simon Foley."

I had to admit, I was surprised. He didn't match the picture Carly and Alyssa had created, and in my mind, Simon Foley was a monster, someone who hunted and destroyed in the name of science. This man before me was younger than I'd expected. He was attractive and elegant, dressed in a charcoal-colored suit. He would have easily fit in at a law firm or on Wall Street.

I shared a confused glance with Paul. I knew he was thinking the same thing. Simon Foley grinned and said, "Do you really think I would go and meet with the families myself? I have more brains than that."

Of course. Carly and her parents had met with someone claiming to be Simon Foley, but if they ever tried to identify him, they would only have a description of a random stranger.

"What do you want with my family?" I asked.

"I just want to examine Alyssa."

317

"Study her," I said.

"Learn about her."

"Experiment on her," Paul said.

Simon straightened and crossed his arms in front of him.

"Young man, I merely want to observe what she can do," he said. "Nothing more."

Paul struggled to move away from the goon that held him back. "We know you've done experiments on other Elementals. We know that you want to harvest their powers, and we know that you've failed. And you're going to fail again." He spit toward Simon, a glob landing on the edge of Simon's shiny black shoe.

Simon narrowed his eyes as he examined his shoe. He said nothing as he turned around to the table behind him, opened a case and removed a gun.

I swallowed hard as he faced us again, the gun aimed at Paul.

"Please don't," Alyssa said. "Don't kill him. He's just scared. We all are. Please don't kill him."

Simon regarded her for a moment before saying, "Because you asked nicely, dear."

The three of us breathed a sigh of relief, and I looked to Paul to share a supporting glance with him. The shot that rang out registered in my ears a second or two after I saw Paul's head snap to the left, and his body spun in the same direction. Then he fell to the floor with a thud and lay motionless.

Alyssa screamed, but mine drowned out hers. I wrenched free from Blake and threw myself down beside Paul. I reached out to him, calling his name, but I was pulled back before I could touch him.

"Put her in the room next to the parents," Simon ordered.

"And the little girl?"

"The surgical room."

Alyssa flailed against her captor and grabbed onto my hands. I held on as tightly as I could, telling her over and over again not to let go. But we were separated and I watched in horror as my little sister was dragged away, kicking and screaming.

Simon stepped down off the platform and stopped in front of me. He grabbed me by the chin and forced me to my feet.

"You have no idea what your sister is capable of, do you?" he asked. "She has the ability to save this planet. She can prolong growing seasons, reverse the pollution that is destroying our air and our water. Do you understand what this means for mankind?"

"But to do that, you have to use her like a lab rat, maybe even kill her," I said through gritted teeth, "and I won't let you."

He sneered at me and squeezed my chin harder. "You don't have a choice."

He released me and handed his gun to one of his men. He then pulled a syringe from his jacket pocket.

"What is that?" I asked.

"Just a little something to help calm your nerves."

"I don't need it."

Of course, he didn't listen to me. He came at me with the syringe, and I tried to duck away, even managing to kick him in the shin. He didn't even flinch. He grabbed my arm, and I cried out as he twisted it. It was then I thought I saw Paul move. I didn't get the chance to examine this further, as the needle was plunged into my skin and I felt a fierce burning begin to course through my veins.

And then there was darkness.

Chapter Twenty-Six

I woke up shivering and with a pounding headache. I thought I had left my bedroom window open, and I tried to get up to close it. My balance was off, and as I pushed through the fog in my head, things started to come back to me. My mom and Eric. Alyssa, and Paul. Monica and her father. Connor.

I sat up too fast and regretted it. Gripping my head, I slowly took in my surroundings. I was in a room just like the one I'd seen my mom and Eric in; one door, no furniture, and a mirror on the wall. My reflection was hell, and I figured that was appropriate, since that was where I was. I used the wall to help me stand, and after a few minutes of swallowing back the nausea, I was able to hold myself up on my own.

I had no idea how long I'd been out, and that horrified me. What if Alyssa was already dead? Had I really seen Paul move? Was he still alive somewhere, in a room like this?

Frustrated and fighting back tears, I pounded the wall with my fists. Everything had gone so wrong, and I didn't know how to fix it. If Alyssa was still alive, she surely didn't have much time left. I also knew that the rest of us were in huge trouble because there was no way Simon Foley would let us leave. I began to pace the room, trying to come up with a plan for escape, but my thoughts were jumbled and still a little fuzzy from whatever drug I'd been dosed with.

The door was locked from the outside, and no matter how hard I tugged on the handle, it wouldn't budge. Pounding on the door did me no good either, as I guessed it was solid steel. It was going to take more than my little fists to make it move. I paced again. It was all I could do to keep myself from going insane.

I was overcome with the thoughts of my family's safety and the fact that Connor had only been interested in me because of my sister. That made my heart ache a bit too. I sank to the floor, going over every conversation and private moment I'd spent with Connor. We'd almost slept together that night in New York, and my stomach churned at the memory. He hadn't liked me in that way, and so he had stopped before things went too far.

"How gallant of him," I said aloud, the words echoing around me.

Tears stung my eyes as I realized my family was in terrible danger, all because a handsome boy had paid attention to me.

Loud clanging noises came from the door as the locks were slid back. The door creaked upon opening, and I jumped back. Two armed men stepped inside first, followed by Simon Foley. My hands immediately clenched into fists at my sides.

He held out his hands to show me he wasn't holding a gun or another syringe. "I just want to talk," he said. He motioned to one of the guards, who stepped forward and placed a bottle of water on the floor in front of me. Then both of the guards left, pulling the heavy door shut behind them.

Simon Foley stood against the opposite wall, leaning back and crossing his arms over his chest. He was still dressed in the same charcoal gray suit, so I guessed I hadn't been out that long. This was good. Maybe there was still a chance of getting my family out of here.

He motioned to the water. "Go ahead, drink it. You must be very thirsty."

I left the bottle where it was, not trusting him at all.

"Where is my sister?" I asked, not caring if I sounded desperate at this point. "Is she still alive?"

"You must think I'm some kind of monster, Miss Benton. But I assure you, I'm not," he said.

"Is she alive?" I repeated.

He smiled then. "Of course. I haven't seen all that she can do. Why would I kill a valuable asset to my cause?"

"She's not an asset," I said. "She's a child. A scared little girl. And you're right. I do think you're a monster."

He shrugged one shoulder nonchalantly. "I suppose I will never be able to convince you otherwise, no matter how hard I try."

"You would be correct in that assumption," I said, matching his tone. "You separate children from their parents and destroy their families. For what? Because you want to play God?"

"I've made some extraordinary advances within the past few years, Miss Benton. These children have no idea what they're capable of. Their parents just want to hide them and stifle their abilities." He shook his head and made a sound of disbelief. "These children can do so much if their powers are harnessed. They just need to be taught."

"You think you're the one to do that? What happens when you go public with your results? You'll be arrested. You've committed murder."

He made a face, as though I'd said something unpleasant. "I release those from my program who are no longer useful to me. That's all, Miss Benton."

I hated the way he said my name. It made my skin crawl, but I refused to cower in front of him.

"Travis Mason," I said. "Carl and Suzanne Grand. You're saying you simply 'released' them from your program?"

"The Grands made their choice by deciding to turn against me. I left them alone when they asked, when I believed their daughter was of no use to me. Then I learned that they were going to double cross me and risk exposing my entire operation before I was ready." He shook his head. "I couldn't allow that. I just couldn't."

"Mark O'Donnell," I said. "He was my friend."

"You know what they say about curiosity and cats," he taunted.

"You killed them all."

"I was nowhere near any of them when those unfortunate incidents occurred. And anyway, I highly doubt that I'd be prosecuted. Not when the world sees what I have to offer."

"And just what is that?" I asked.

He held my gaze, staring at me with unblinking eyes, and I felt a shiver run through me.

"Survival, Miss Benton," he said, his voice low. "I will be revered for my efforts and lauded as a hero. I will save this pitiful world from destroying itself."

I was stunned because he obviously believed what he was saying. "You're delusional."

He pushed himself away from the wall, startling me. He came right up to me, leaning in close enough that I could smell the pungent richness of his cologne, and I had to turn my head when I felt his breath on my face.

"I'm optimistic," he said, his voice barely above a whisper. "I know how business works, Miss Benton. It doesn't matter how you get to the top. It only matters that you get there first." He stepped back and adjusted his tie and suit jacket, his lips twisting into a smug grin. "Your father taught me that."

My skin tingled and my heart pounded. "My father would have never believed that. He did what was good for business, but he would never hurt anyone."

"You wouldn't think so. At first."

I moved toward him, my anger rising. "Did you know him? Do you know where he is?" I asked. "Did you have something to do with his disappearance?"

He backed away from me, and we circled the room. He didn't say anything, just kept smiling at me. I cornered him up against the wall and grabbed him by the lapels of his expensive suit jacket. He was taller than me and outweighed me by at least fifty pounds, but I was so furious I didn't even care that he could toss me aside without a problem.

"Where is he?" I yelled. "Where is my father?"

The door opened and the guards were on me, pulling me off him and pushing me down. Without another word, Simon Foley walked out. The guards left me on the floor and followed him. I lay there, breathing hard and gritting my teeth to keep from screaming. I rolled onto my side and curled up into a ball facing a corner, my fists pressed to my mouth to muffle my sobbing. I knew he was probably watching me on a monitor somewhere, and I didn't want to give him the satisfaction of listening to me cry. I felt cold all over, even to the tips of my fingers, and I pulled the sleeves of my sweatshirt down to cover my hands.

After several minutes, I calmed myself enough to sit up. I wiped my eyes and stared at my reflection, trying not to feel hopeless.

Above me, the lights dimmed, but they didn't go out completely. I stared at the ceiling, wondering if it was some kind of power surge and what that meant for my sister. It happened again, and then the door to my prison swung open, revealing a male figure in the shadows. I crouched down, ready to pounce if the need arose. When the figure stepped forward, I relaxed for a fraction of a second before tensing up again.

"Come on," Connor said, gesturing toward me. "We have to hurry."

"What are you doing here?" I hissed.

"I'll explain everything later. We have to go now."

I wanted to hit him, to hurl insults and scathing words at him for betraying us, but it looked like that would have to wait. I followed him through the door, wondering if this was some kind of trap, surprised to see my mother and Eric just on the other side. Eric was sporting a black eye and a huge gash on his arm that had been bandaged. Mom was disheveled and bruised as well. They pulled me into a hug, and we all cried.

"This is all very nice, but I'm afraid it's going to have to be cut short," Connor interrupted us. He started running down the long hallway, signaling for us to follow. "I have to get you outside before they realize what I've done."

"What have you done?" I asked as we ran with him.

We came to a corner, and he motioned for us to stay behind him. He pulled the gun from his shoulder holster, and peered around the corner, checking for guards.

"What have you done?" I asked again, this time in a whisper.

"I rewired the power to the surgical room," he said.

"Why didn't you cut it? My daughter is in there!" my mom said.

Connor faced us then, and I saw the tired lines around his eyes, the worry playing at the corners of his mouth.

"If I'd cut it completely, they would have suspected something was up. Power surges every few minutes is annoying enough to have them stop and check it out before proceeding. I bought us time," he said.

I was still confused, and I wanted to grill him more. He shushed us then as a guard walked past. Connor reached out with his free hand and with a hard wrench, grabbed the guard by the neck and shoved him into the wall, knocking him out. Connor lowered him to the ground and began searching his pockets. He came up with a gun, which he handed to Eric, and a walkie-talkie. He handed that to me, and I tucked it in my back pocket.

"All right, let's go," he said.

We stayed close behind him, turning another corner and coming upon a row of doors.

"The last one at the end of the hall is an exit. It'll take you outside the building, but you still have to get through the fence. The guards circle every three minutes. If you time it just right, you can get through. There's a hole behind some oil barrels, underneath the 'No Trespassing' sign. Get through it and go two blocks north. A car is there, key in the ignition. Get to it and get the hell out of here," Connor said.

"What about Alyssa?" Eric asked. "We can't leave her behind."

"And Paul, where is he? Is he still alive?" I asked.

I saw the look on my mother's face when I said Paul's name. She hadn't known he was here with us, and now she was even more alarmed.

"You're going to have to," Connor said. "I can't risk your lives when I'm getting them out as well. There's a cell phone in the glove box. I'll call you when I have Alyssa and Paul and give you a meeting point."

I blinked several times. "You're going after them? Why would you do that? Why would you help us after you betrayed us to Simon Foley? Is this really a way out, or is it some kind of trick?"

Connor grabbed my shoulders and gave me a little shake. "I know what you must think of me right now," he said, almost growling at me. "And I wish I had the time to explain it all to you, but I don't. So for now, just know that my feelings for you were real, and my loyalty to this project used to be. I can't stand by and allow innocent people to be hurt by Simon Foley anymore, even if he is my brother."

The gasp that went around was loud and sharp, and it felt like all of the air had been sucked from the room. My chest hurt when I could breathe normally again. Words were on the tip of my tongue, refusing to be spoken, and then Connor was ushering us to the door that would get us out of there.

He opened the door, and my mom and Eric hurried out. Connor tried to get me to go with them, and I pushed against him.

"You might need my help," I said.

"Aubrey, get moving. There's no time for this," he said, and his tone was pleading. "Go."

"No, I'm staying here. You can't do this alone."

"Aubrey, you're being ridiculous," my mother said. "Come on, right now. I mean it!"

"Aubrey, listen to your mother," Eric said.

If it was any other time, I would have laughed at them. They sounded like they were scolding a disobedient two-year-old. I shook my head and stood my ground. "Go without me. I have to help him. I'll be fine, I promise."

Connor checked his watch and gave an exasperated sigh. "Fine, stay with me. Mr. and Mrs. Vaughn, you know what to do to get out. I'll make sure she's okay. You have my word."

"And he's a man of his word," I added, and Connor glanced at me, remembering our trip to New York City.

My mom's eyes filled with tears. She nodded and grabbed Eric's hand. Together they made their way toward the fence, with Eric leaning on Mom for support. Connor pulled the door shut before I could make sure they were on their way.

"If you really want to do this, then let's go," he said. He tossed me a gun from an ankle holster, and I barely caught it.

The gun was heavy and felt alien in my hands, but if it was my ticket out of here with my sister and Paul, I would deal with it. We doubled back the way we had come, passing the room where I'd been held.

"Paul's alive," Connor told me. "The bullet just grazed him. Head wounds tend to bleed a lot."

"Will he be okay?"

"He'll survive. He's in the surgical room with your sister. Simon wanted him near in case they needed him for something."

I shuddered to think of what.

"Stop," Connor said, and I stumbled into him. He caught me and steadied me, and I felt his strong hands at my waist. I trembled a little. He felt it and quickly released me. "We need to get to the second floor. Can't take the elevator, so that leaves the stairs."

We ran into the stairwell and started up. We were making a lot of noise on the metal steps, and Connor assured me it didn't matter. Reaching the second floor, he crouched by the door and checked his watch again.

"We have to wait five minutes for the guards to get out of the area," he explained.

"Five minutes, perfect. Just enough time for you to answer a few questions."

"Aubrey -"

I pressed a hand to his mouth, silencing him. "You owe me that much."

He nodded, and I moved my hand.

"What would you like to know?" he asked politely.

"Who are you?"

He smiled and scrubbed a hand over his face. "Good question, something I wonder quite often myself."

"Is your name really Connor Davenport?"

"It is. Davenport is my mother's maiden name. I changed it from Foley after she died, to honor her." He made a disgusted sound. "I don't think she'd be too honored by my actions."

"So Simon Foley is your brother?"

"Yes."

"And you work for him?"

"Yes. I've been part of his retrieval section for about three years. Simon seems to think I have excellent tracking skills."

"Tracking other Elementals?"

"Yes. Your sister turned out to be a real challenge though. Your parents had done an exceptional job of keeping her hidden. It wasn't until we learned about you that we were able to establish a real line on her whereabouts. Anemone led us to you."

He must have read the guilt that crossed my face, because he squeezed my shoulder. "It's not your fault. We would have found her eventually, but it's because of you that I began to question my real purpose with my brother's organization."

"Why is that?"

"Because before, I just regarded Elementals as other beings with extraordinary powers. They were objects to be used for science. When I met you, I saw them as children with abilities they didn't understand, and they had families who loved and cared for them. They were also scared for them. You gave them human qualities that I didn't see before." He smiled and added, "You gave me back my human qualities too."

"And your brother? Does he have any human qualities?"

The smile disappeared. "He used to. When my mother was alive. She was a very wealthy woman in her own right, able to pay for the best care and treatment, and she still died. He was furious for not being able to prevent it, so he started on a mission to change the world. It was good at first, and then he came across an Elemental, and his mindset changed completely. He still believes his work is for the good of mankind, and while it may be, the way he goes about it isn't. I can't back his ideals anymore, which is why I'm helping you now."

"What will he do if he finds out you've done this?"

"He'll kill me."

Chapter Twenty-Seven

I couldn't believe it. "He'll kill you? His own brother?"

"Especially his own brother. I'm the one person in the world who knows the ins and outs of his operation. The people that work for him? They're not given the whole picture. I could bring him down, and he knows it."

I chewed on my fingernail. "Did you," I started, then paused and took a deep breath. "Did you kill the Grands? Or my friend Mark?"

He took my hand and I felt the warmth from his touch tingle all the way up my arm. He stared into my eyes and said, "No. I did not. I didn't even know either of those things were going to happen, but I was shocked and disgusted when I found out."

"Do you know why the Grands were killed? They were running away. They wouldn't have said anything. They just wanted to keep Carly safe."

"They were running away, yes, but they were apparently planning to make a big fuss about Carly," Connor said. "They were tired of hiding and decided the best way to keep her safe was to make others aware of her. A great deal of information was found with their belongings."

"What kind of information?"

"Personal journals, medical records-"

"Personal journals?" I interrupted. "Whose?"

He shook his head and shrugged. "I'm not sure, Carly's I assume."

Carly had thought her parents destroyed her journal. If Simon Foley had it and we could get our hands on it, it might be useful to Anemone. I took a deep breath, feeling almost dizzy from fear of the answer to my next question.

"Do you know if my father and your brother were working together?"

Connor's lips went into a thin line. He checked his watch and said, "Time's up. Let's go."

My mouth dropped open to protest, but my question and answer session was clearly over. I hoped I would get the opportunity again.

Connor and I made our way to the surgical room. I peered in through a window and saw Paul and Alyssa, both still alive, and both strapped to operating tables. Alyssa was wearing a pair of her pajamas from home. The pink elephant I'd brought back for her from New York was on the table beside her.

"It's supposed to comfort her," Connor said softly.

"She looks calm," I said.

"She's been sedated to keep her from using her powers right now." He saw the horrified expression cross my face, and he put a comforting arm around my shoulders. "She's fine, just not as alert."

I felt the warmth of his touch through my shirt, and I resisted the urge not to lean into it. Whatever feelings I had for Connor were very confused at the moment, and I needed to focus on getting my sister and Paul out of this building, alive and unharmed. I shifted my position so that Connor's arm fell away from me, and I peeked into the room again. Alyssa was awake and staring at the bright lamp hanging above her. I couldn't tell if she was scared; I just knew that I was. Four people in surgical gowns crowded around her, examining her arms, her legs, her eyes and ears. I wanted to scream at them to stop.

Simon Foley entered the room from another door, and he walked over to Alyssa and smiled down at her. He leaned close and began to speak to her. We couldn't make out the words, but Paul was becoming more agitated by the second. He pulled uselessly at his restraints, making threats. He was ignored. I saw the white bandage that covered the left side of his head.

"So what's the plan?" I asked.

"I'm going to walk in, let them know you've escaped. Security will be sent down to the first floor to check it out. Use the walkie-talkie to listen and make sure they go. Then we'll grab Alyssa and Paul and get to the roof. There's a helicopter up there, fueled and ready to go. We'll force the pilot to take us away."

"And Simon? Won't he come after us?"

"We're taking him with us. I plan to turn him into the feds and get this entire operation stopped."

"Why not just have them come in here in the first place?" I asked. "Wouldn't that have been easier?"

"I needed time," Connor said. "I needed to make sure he wouldn't destroy evidence. He's spent a lot of money and time on making himself invisible, as I'm sure you and your friends have already figured out."

"But won't the employees just destroy everything if we take him with us?"

Connor shook his head and took a black key card from his pocket, holding it out to me. "This card grants access to every locked door in this building. No other employee has this key. There are certain rooms with documents, computer files, equipment and other evidence of his experiments. They'd never be able to get to that to destroy it, but he does have a special security measure built into this warehouse. If anyone not authorized to enter comes in, it's set to self-destruct. The whole building would be gone in a matter of minutes. I need to bring the feds in myself in order to avoid that. Or you do."

He pressed the card into my hand and closed my fingers around it.

"You'll be able to get back in if I'm not around to do it."

I accepted the card, ignoring his last statement. "Won't you go to jail too?"

"I can handle it. It's the right thing to do." He handed me a piece of paper. "It's the number for the cell phone your parents will have. In case I don't make it out, you need to call them."

"We'll all make it out," I said, annoyed that he'd brought it up again. I tucked the paper and the card into my pocket. "We will."

His expression was somewhat doubtful, and I didn't like that at all. If he didn't have any faith in this working out, how was I supposed to?

"Why aren't you convincing me I'm right?" I asked, nudging him.

"I wish I could," he said. "The only thing I can convince you of is that I do care about you, and your family, and I want to see them safe. I greatly admire your sister and her abilities." He smiled and laughed a little. "She'll be pleased to know that it was incredibly difficult to keep my thoughts hidden from her. I was always exhausted after being near her. She's quite adept at picking up on feelings."

"How did you do it?"

"I just had to keep my mind clear and build a wall around anything having to do with my real purpose for being here. It really took a toll on me. There were a few moments where I thought she was on to me." He paused and took a deep breath. "Aubrey, I don't want Alyssa, or others like her, to have to hide in fear anymore. Do you believe me?"

I studied his face and read the truth in his eyes. "I do believe you."

He exhaled in relief. "I hope you can someday forgive me for causing you and your family so much trouble." He checked his gun to count how many bullets he had left. "Are you ready?"

"No, but I don't have a choice," I answered.

"Wait until my signal before you come in."

I couldn't let him go in there, at least not without knowing that I cared for him too. Feeling extremely bold for the second time in my life, I grabbed hold of his shirt collar and pulled him close, pressing my lips against his. He was surprised, but then he let go and kissed me back. When we broke apart, my heart was racing, and I could feel his beating rapidly against my hands.

He stood up and holstered his gun. Then he smoothed his hair, took a deep breath, and burst into the room, leaving the door open. I hid behind it.

"They've broken out, all of them," he said. "It was just a few minutes ago."

Simon moved away from Alyssa, and the surgeons all took a step back as well.

"Have all security check the first level. They couldn't have gotten far," he said. "Hold off on the procedure until we have them."

Connor spoke into his walkie-talkie, giving the order. I listened on mine, heard the okay from Blake, and focused on the situation in the surgical room. "Can I talk to you for a minute?" Connor asked, tilting his head at his brother.

Simon came over to him. "What is it?"

Connor kicked out with his leg, forcing Simon to fall to his knees. Connor grabbed his tie and pulled it around, choking him. He aimed his gun at Simon's head.

"What the hell is this?" Simon demanded.

Connor didn't answer. He turned to the four surgeons. "Everyone put your hands up and face the wall. Do it now."

They just stood there, staring, until Connor raised his gun and fired at the heart monitor behind them. They screamed and did as they were told.

"Aubrey, get in here."

My legs felt like rubber as I scurried into the room. I fumbled with the straps that held Alyssa to the table until she was finally free. She looped her arms around my neck and I set her down on the floor.

"You're making a mistake of enormous proportions," Simon scowled, and Connor pulled harder on the tie.

"No, you've done that already, dear brother," he said through clenched teeth.

"You're beautiful, you know that?" Paul said to me as I released him. "But am I hallucinating? Is that Connor, and did he just call Simon his brother?"

"I'll explain everything once we're out of here," I said. "How do you feel?"

"I'm okay," he said, nodding. "What now?"

I looked to Connor. He jerked on the tie, pulling Simon to his feet. "Aubrey, lock them in the supply closet."

I motioned with my gun at the surgeons. Once they were in the closet, I locked the door and jammed a chair under the handle.

"Now what?" Simon asked. "You know you can't leave through the front door."

"Who said anything about that?" Connor asked.

We all headed for the stairs, walking the short space up to the third floor roof access. Alyssa walked beside me, holding my hand. I glanced down at her and realized she wasn't wearing any shoes.

"Are your feet okay?" I asked.

"I'm all right," she answered. "Where are Mom and Dad?"

"They made it out," I said, and I prayed it was true.

"So, Miss Benton," Simon said, "you must have some serious charm if you were able to make my brother break his own rule."

"Shut up, Simon," Connor said, and Simon smirked.

"Never get involved," he said. "That's how Connor was able to complete his missions successfully. He never got involved with the subjects he was supposed to ingratiate himself with. You must be pretty special."

I could feel the tension rolling off of Connor in waves. He said nothing, just pushed his gun harder into Simon's back.

"You know your friends have never truly been safe," Simon continued. "Anemone. Did you honestly think I didn't know about them before now? Or where all of those families are located?"

My stomach rolled violently at the thought, and my mouth was too dry to speak. Even if I could have, I had no words.

"I've kept tabs on all of them for years," Simon said with a chuckle. "I never knew if perhaps they would have another child with special abilities."

I came to an abrupt stop and whirled around, releasing Alyssa's hand. I felt the rage heat my face, heard a roaring in my ears, and then my fist connected with his nose, hard enough that I felt it snap. He howled as blood spurted, and he pressed his hands to his face. From the corner of my eye, I caught the slight grin on Connor's face.

"You deserved it, you know," he said, giving his brother a final shove through the door and out onto the roof.

The helicopter was sitting on the launch pad, and the pilot was lounging inside, flipping through a magazine. He jumped when we approached, and Connor tapped the glass with his gun.

"Open up," he instructed. He had Alyssa, Paul and I get inside first, and he told the pilot to start the engine.

The man's gaze went to Simon, who gave a curt nod. Wind whipped around us as we buckled ourselves in. Alyssa sat on Paul's lap.

"Get in, Simon," Connor shouted over the noise.

Simon took one step up the metal ladder, then threw himself back, slamming his head into Connor's face. They both fell to the cement in a heap, fighting for control. Connor's gun fell from his grip and skittered away, stopping just at the edge of the roof.

"Go, get out of here!" he shouted at us.

I didn't know what else to do, so I pointed my gun at the pilot and screamed at him to take off. I wanted to get out and help Connor, but I knew I wouldn't be able to do much. Simon threw a punch at Connor's head. He ducked, and Simon kicked out at the same time, catching Connor in the knee. He fell, and Simon was up and running for the door to get back inside, or so I thought. I hadn't noticed the glass box with the green button just beside the door.

Simon shattered the box with his hands, blood pouring from the fresh cuts, and pushed the button. A recorded voice blared out from speakers all over the building for everyone to evacuate, that the entire structure would be going up in flames within two minutes.

"No!" I shouted, just as the helicopter began to lift off the ground. "The evidence, the lab!" The pilot kept the helicopter hovering, unsure if he should go or not.

Connor got to his feet, rubbing his jaw.

"Watch out!" Alyssa screamed. Connor looked up at the sound, then whirled around, just in time to see Simon coming at him with a lead pipe. He avoided taking the blow to his head, but the pipe bounced off his shoulder, and he howled in pain as something cracked.

Simon swung again, and Connor head-butted him in the stomach, sending him dangerously close to the edge of the roof. From below, we could hear explosive charges going off from within the building. The smell of smoke and fire was wafting toward us, and I could hear screams as people were running from the building. The roof shuddered, and Connor had a hard time keeping his balance.

I gave my gun to Paul and leaned out of the helicopter, extending my arms out to Connor.

"Come on, take my hands," I yelled.

He reached out with his good arm and grabbed my hand. His grip was slick with sweat, and he slipped out of my grasp.

"Again!" I encouraged him. "Come on, one more time."

This time, I wrapped both of my hands around his arm and tried to pull him up.

"We've got to go!" the pilot yelled at us. "The building is going to collapse any second!"

The helicopter lifted higher, and I panicked. Connor was hanging on, but I wasn't strong enough to pull him all the way inside by myself. Paul moved Alyssa to a seat and put the gun down on the floor. At this point, the pilot was going to fly us away from there with or without a gun aimed at him. Paul tried to help me, taking hold of Connor's elbow and pulling. It was proving to be difficult. Connor was dangling in the air, and we were struggling to hang onto him.

A shiny flash caught my eye, and I first saw the flames shooting from the door to the roof and heard the crack as the roof started to split open. It was like something out of a stunt show, except it was real, and we were in the middle of it.

The flash again caught my attention, and by the time I realized what it was, it was too late. Simon Foley was standing at the edge of the roof, gripping Connor's gun with both hands. He pointed it straight at us, and even from that distance, I could see the crazy glint in his eyes.

"He's going to shoot us down!" Paul yelled, tugging harder at Connor to get him inside.

Something exploded beneath us, sending a ripple of movement and heat through the helicopter, and loosening our already fragile grip on Connor. Then we felt his body jerk hard, and he gazed up at us, his eyes registering what Paul and I already knew. Simon's bullet had hit its mark.

"Don't let go," I pleaded, tugging at his hands. "Please."

His hold went slack, and I felt him slip an inch. We were rising higher into the air, away from the blazing inferno that had housed a lab of Luminesk Enterprises. I risked a glance at the burning building. I didn't see Simon Foley anymore. The roof had collapsed.

Connor's eyes locked on mine, and I felt tears burning in my own as I looked at him. He wasn't going to make it, and we all knew it.

"I'm sorry, Aubrey," he gasped. Then he opened his hand and pulled away from us.

Paul and I tried to grab him again, but he was already falling. He didn't scream or flail as he tumbled toward the fiery mess, and I threw myself against Paul, burying my face in his shoulder. I couldn't watch Connor fall to his death. Paul held me and when I felt him flinch, I knew Connor had disappeared beneath the flames.

Sobbing, I crawled toward Alyssa. She was crying silently, her hands over her face. As I reached for her, she fell into my arms, and we hugged each other. After a minute, she calmed herself enough to peer out the window. Then she closed her eyes, and a heartbeat later, the cloudless sky began to pour down rain.

Chapter Twenty-Eight

The helicopter pilot landed in a nearby park and let us out, then he disappeared into the night. I doubted we'd be hearing from him again anytime soon. We found a pay phone, and I called Mom and Eric. Mom began crying the second she heard our voices, which caused Alyssa and me to cry again. She asked about Connor, and my silence was her answer. She passed the phone to Eric who asked where we were. They had Connor's car, and they were eager to come and get us.

Paul and I looked around. We had no idea. He ventured off on his own to see if he could find a sign or a park directory. Alyssa and I huddled together by the pay phone. I know Eric was talking, but I wasn't listening. I was too busy trying not to throw up. The thought of Connor sacrificing himself for Alyssa, for all of us, was enough to make my stomach churn.

Paul returned a few minutes later and was able to tell Eric what park we were in and where the nearest entrance was. Eric knew the location and promised they'd be there soon. We must have been quite the sight when Eric pulled up in front of us. He jumped out of the car and grabbed us all in a bone-crushing hug. Paul sat in front, while Mom, Alyssa and I sat in the backseat. Mom refused to let go of either of us until we got home.

To our surprise, Monica and her father were there, waiting for us. We learned from them that Connor had promised them he would keep us safe, and then he'd let them escape. Monica caught my eye, and I just gave a slight shake of my head. She covered her mouth with her hands and squeezed her eyes shut.

Monica and Jonathan stayed over that night, and we regrouped the next morning, piecing together the events as best we could. Physically, everyone was fine. Eric's arm injury had required stitches that Simon Foley's men had graciously provided. We cleaned up the house, and Mom and Eric shared with us how the Luminesk team had broken in, breaking windows on both the first and second floor. Eric had tried to fend them off, dragging Mom upstairs to their room. Two men had been waiting for them, and in the struggle, Eric had been sliced with a piece of broken glass.

Alyssa had wriggled free, climbing out the dining room window and running several blocks away, hiding in someone's backyard bushes. She'd stayed there until she could no longer feel their presence at our house. She returned just after Paul and I arrived. The location of the building we were taken to made the news, but only as an empty warehouse fire. There was no report of any bodies found, and nothing was said about any medical or laboratory equipment left in the facility. The entire structure and everything inside had been destroyed. It pained me that Connor's death would go unnoticed by the rest of the world, especially after all that he had done to help us.

Alyssa didn't want to talk much, and I only shared the details regarding Connor's involvement. I kept our kiss to myself. That wasn't something that I felt like discussing with anyone, and I didn't think that I would for a long time. Connor's death was affecting me hard. I showed them the black key card and told them that if we could find the other labs, we may be able to get in. Jonathan studied it for anything that could help him determine what kind of system was used so he could do some research.

He and Monica were packing up and headed elsewhere. Even though Simon Foley could be presumed dead, they weren't taking any chances. It had spooked them to hear that Simon claimed to know everything about them, so they were going into hiding for a while. They promised they would stay in touch. We were just starting to get somewhere, and we couldn't stop now.

Paul's head injury wasn't noticeable when he brushed his hair down in front of it. He didn't want to tell his mother about being shot. Even though Mom and Eric wanted to share with her everything that had happened, Paul refused. She was angry enough at him for leaving the dance without telling her, and he was grounded again. He feared she'd lock him away for good if he tried to explain that Alyssa was an Elemental.

A couple of days after the fire, I found Alyssa in the backyard. She was planting flowers.

"For Connor," she said, patting the dirt around the bulbs. She watered them, and then a few minutes later, there was a line of blue poppy anemones in full bloom. We stood together and just stared at them.

"He saved us," Alyssa said.

"I know."

"He didn't have to."

I nodded. I knew that too.

Paul was incredibly understanding. He knew that he couldn't help me make sense of my relationship with Connor. He just gave me the space I needed to think. I finally ventured out of the house and drove to the address where Connor's apartment building was located. I realized I didn't know which apartment was his. I scanned the names on the mailboxes, not finding his at all. I knocked on a few doors and asked the people if they knew Connor. The building super informed me no one by that name lived there. I showed him a picture, and he shook his head.

I can't say I was surprised. Connor must have been waiting for me inside the doors when I arrived to pick him up before our trip to New York. Jonathan checked into the Hamilton University records to see if Connor's name showed up anywhere, and there was nothing. He hadn't been registered for any classes, neither past or current, anywhere that Jonathan could find. I had no reason to believe that Connor Davenport wasn't his real name, and he had said his brother spent a small fortune making himself invisible. He must have done the same for Connor.

Later that same evening, we were eating dinner together as a family, each of us lost in our own thoughts, when the doorbell rang. We all jumped, and Eric went to answer it. He came back a minute later with a woman that I thought I recognized.

"Hello, Aubrey," she said.

I stood up, trying to come up with her name.

She smiled. "I'm Samantha, from the dance studio. You and that nice young man Connor came for a lesson awhile back."

The memory of that night hit like a shock, and I actually jolted a little. "Of course," I said. "How are you?"

"Busy," she laughed. "So busy that I didn't realize this package was addressed to you, but sent to my studio."

I hadn't noticed she was holding a box, about the size of a box of file folders. It was wrapped in plain brown paper. She handed it to me, and I gingerly accepted it, expecting it to start shaking or spewing smoke.

"It showed up two days ago. I thought it was the new set of pamphlets I'd ordered, so I set it aside."

There was no return address. Somehow, I knew it was from Connor.

"Thank you," I said. "Thank you very much."

"Will I be seeing you and Connor for another lesson?" she asked, smiling. "You both showed a great talent for dancing."

Alyssa sniffled from her seat at the table, and I shook my head. "No, I don't think so. It...it didn't work out between us," I choked out.

Samantha apologized and quickly made her exit. I was still standing in the same place when Eric returned from showing her out.

"I think I should look at this in private," I said, and took off for my room before I started crying.

Closing the door, I leaned against it and sank to the floor. It was a good ten minutes before I was calm enough to open the package. The box was taped shut, and I used my fingernail to cut through it. Sitting inside was a stack of plain manila folders. Resting on top of them was a handwritten note on a single piece of white paper.

Dear Aubrey,

I've just been given orders to take your sister and bring her in for testing. I want you to know that I will do everything I can to keep her safe and out of harm's way. I am also going to do my best to stop Simon Foley from hurting anyone else.

I'm so sorry for deceiving you and your family. It was never my intention to hurt you. When I joined Simon in his operation, I was full of optimism and hope for the future. As my older brother, I've always looked up to him. He's a brilliant man, and I believed in his promises to save the world from disease and disaster. I never expected it to turn into this. Please know that it was you and Alyssa that made me realize the world can still be saved, just in a different way than my brother has imagined. I believe the power of the Elementals can be used for good, if the right person will guide them. Unfortunately, my brother is not that person.

The files included with this note contain an overview of his operation, and a preliminary report on the abilities of Elementals. Maybe your step-father or Anemone can use it in their own research.

There is so much I want to tell you, but my time is limited. Perhaps we can meet up after this ordeal is over and I can explain everything in person. I would like to apologize to you face to face, although I understand if you never want to see me again. I do care for you, and I am truly sorry for the pain I've caused you.

Take care of yourself, Aubrey. And take care of Alyssa. She is especially unique in her abilities and the most astonishing of the Elementals that I have come across.

Connor

I was in tears when I finished reading. A lot of what was in the note he'd already said to me. He must have written it thinking he wouldn't have the chance, and that saddened me. I had to set the box aside. It was amazing to me how right and wrong I'd been about him, and I wondered how long this pain I felt over losing him would last.

A soft knock on my door made me move. Wiping my eyes, I opened the door to find Alyssa standing in the hall.

"Are you all right?" she asked.

"As good as can be expected."

I stepped aside to let her in and shut the door behind her. I showed her the note, and she read it, wiping tears from her eyes.

"He was a good man," she said.

I moved the box to my desk and began flipping through the files. Jonathan was going to have a coronary when I showed him all of this information. There was even a listing of the other lab facilities across the United States, as well as a few in other countries. But it was the last file that had me gripping the edge of the desk for support. It contained a single photograph and nothing else. I dug around frantically in my desk drawer for a magnifying glass. Finding one, I pressed it to the paper and gasped. I swallowed several times, trying to find my voice.

Alyssa was by my side in an instant, prying the photograph from my grip.

"That's the Tower Bridge in London," she said, confused. "What's so special about that? I mean, I know it's beautiful, and it can raise to let tall ships pass through."

The photograph had been taken from a distance, but I immediately recognized the figure standing by the railing. It was the man I'd seen that day at Mark's funeral, with the same beard covering his face and the same watch on his wrist. He wasn't wearing sunglasses or a hat in the photograph, and he was dressed casually, yet I could clearly see that it was my father. He appeared to be speaking to another man whose back was to the camera. Judging by the height and build, and his stance, I believed it was Simon Foley. It was proof that they'd known each other and had done some kind of business together. It was what my father was holding that rendered me speechless. He had a folded newspaper under his arm, the *Times*, and the date was two weeks ago.

I pointed to the newspaper, and Alyssa took the magnifying glass from me to look for herself. When she saw it, her eyes widened. "This means, it proves-"

I nodded, numb with realization. I was going to London as soon as possible.

My father was alive.

www.ingramcontent.com/pod-product-compliance
Lightning Source LLC
Chambersburg PA
CBHW062007170626
46813CB00001B/59